# A Dog's
## Chance

BOOKS BY CASEY WILSON

*A Dog's Hope*

# A Dog's
# Chance

## CASEY WILSON

**GRAND CENTRAL**
**PUBLISHING**

NEW YORK   BOSTON

Copyright © 2020 by Storyfire Ltd.

Excerpt from *A Dog's Hope* copyright © Tammy L. Grace

Cover design by Ami Smithson/Cabin London. Cover photo by New Africa/ Shutterstock. Cover copyright © 2021 by Hachette Book Group, Inc.

Grand Central Publishing
Hachette Book Group
1290 Avenue of the Americas, New York, NY 10104
grandcentralpublishing.com
twitter.com/grandcentralpub

First published in 2020 by Bookouture, an imprint of StoryFire Ltd.
First Grand Central Publishing edition: November 2021

Grand Central Publishing is a division of Hachette Book Group, Inc. The Grand Central Publishing name and logo is a trademark of Hachette Book Group, Inc.

The publisher is not responsible for websites (or their content) that are not owned by the publisher.

The Hachette Speakers Bureau provides a wide range of authors for speaking events. To find out more, go to www.hachettespeakersbureau.com or call (866) 376-6591.

Library of Congress Cataloging-in-Publication Data has been applied for.

ISBN: 978-1-5387-3793-4 (paperback)

Printed in the United States of America

LSC-C

Printing 1, 2021

*For Izzy, who healed my heart and gave me a second chance at the joy only a dog can bring.*

# CHAPTER 1

## Duke

With a harsh shove I sail through the air and land with a thud on the stained concrete outside the gas station. The man's eyes dart from the building to the driveway, and his dirty boots scrape against the concrete as he hurries to the driver's door. He slams it shut, and the battered old truck's engine roars to life. Bits of dirt fly out of the back of it as it bounces over the curb and rumbles down the street.

A dog's instinct is to wait for his human. We know our place is right by his side: sitting in the front seat of the truck, nose set on the top of the half-open window, wind flapping our ears with rhythmic thuds, finding people to watch when he dashes into the store, guarding him, loving him, snuggling close against him. But this is not my human.

I lift my nose in the air and search for familiar scents. The sharp odor of fuel is overwhelming. I shy away from the commotion of cars driving by on the street in front of the gas station and hurry to explore the area behind it. Gone are the scents of hay that fill the barn where I've spent most of my life so far. My head to the ground, I sniff in all sorts of new and interesting smells: several other dogs have passed this way, there's a hint of some sort of meat, some sugary sweetness in places, and I smell lots of new people while I gobble up a few errant chips along the sidewalk.

I lift my nose higher and let the fresh air waft through it. The sweet smell of pollen is heavy. Across the street, people are walking along the sidewalk in front of a row of buildings. I've never seen so many buildings bunched together in one spot. A young girl holding her mother's hand points at me and smiles. I can't help but wiggle my tail. She tugs on her mother's arm, taking a step in my direction. She wants to pet me, I can tell. The woman gives her a stern look and turns the girl's shoulders away from me. They disappear around the next corner.

There are more buildings along the street in the other direction and I have to decide which way to go. My mother told me I was the runt of the litter and that meant I would be smarter than the others. I had to work harder and burrow under my brothers and sisters to find a spot to nurse. She told me I'd have to be cleverer than the others and that she could tell I was destined for greatness. Since I was the smallest, none of the people who came to pick puppies wanted to take me. Just because I was different and smaller, didn't mean I wasn't powerful. Stature, breed, looks—all are labels that serve only to limit, but they don't determine our strength. Dogs know what's on the outside isn't important; it's what's deep in your heart that defines you. Those qualities that aren't always visible, those are the ones that truly matter.

Being the last of the litter meant I got to cuddle up with my mother, just the two of us, and she told me stories of brave dogs: the difference that rescue dogs and therapy and service dogs make in the world. The heroes she described came in different sizes and breeds, ages, and colors, but they all shared an inner strength, a resolve, and a servant's heart bound by the love they had for their families. I've dreamed of great things in my future.

I would have been perfectly happy to stay with my mother forever, but you have to learn to stand on your own four feet, and one day I was taken to town and left in a box outside the feed store. It didn't take long for someone to pick me up. Or for them to abandon me again. Now I have to be wise, like my mother told me. I sniff the air again, hoping to pick up my mother's scent, but I don't catch even a whiff of her.

I take a few more steps away from the bustle of cars and people, and when I get to the end of the sidewalk, the babble of slow-moving fresh water beckons me. A wooden walkway arches over the water and I hurry across it and down the grassy bank for a refreshing drink, letting it rinse away the taste from the salty chips I found. I take my fill, lapping up the water in a slow rhythm before continuing.

My thoughts drift to my mother and I still miss the comfort of her. The thought flashes through my mind to head back the way we had come, but then I remember her telling me I'd have to live with someone new eventually. She had a way of explaining it that, despite my wanting to stay close to her, made me dream of an owner and a family of my own. It was hard to imagine I could love someone more than my mother, but she assured me I'd have a connection like no other where my human would be my whole world. I would find a best friend forever. I just haven't found them yet.

While I'm walking, I keep an eye out for anyone that looks friendly and give those I pass by a few pleading looks. I hold my head high and act like I know where I'm going. I make sure I don't look too desperate and attract attention from the people my mother warned me about: the ones who snatch up lost dogs and put them in cages.

Despite all my charm and my best behavior, I still don't understand why none of the families who came to the farm were interested in me. Mom said they were foolish and ignored me because I was the smallest. More than anything, I want to feel safe, like I did with her. I want to be part of a pack, to belong. I want to find a family.

The inviting fragrances coming from the flowers in the huge yards of the houses I pass by are hard to resist. I surrender to their pull and rush across a thick lawn to sniff at the moist dirt in the planters filled with colorful rhododendrons. After inspecting several of them and following a honey bee as she went about her work, I spot a shaded park in the distance. The mid-afternoon sun is beating down on me and the idea of taking a nap under a tree entices me. I'm tired and haven't slept for several hours.

The quiet street ends at the entrance to a park. I take the main pathway and meander along the grass in search of the perfect spot. My ears perk at the sound of a man's voice halted by heavy sobs. To my right, sitting on a bench, is a man with white hair. He's hunched over and reading from sheets of paper he's holding. As he looks at the papers, he rubs the space next to him and murmurs, "Oh, Rosie, I'm not sure how I'm going to make it without you." With a gentle touch, he strokes the single pink rose lying on the bench next to him.

Sorrow and grief waft from him and I feel his need for comfort. With slow steps, I approach the bench. He takes a handkerchief from his pocket and wipes his eyes and face. He draws in a long breath that quavers, continuing to read softly to himself.

"'Dearest Arthur, I know my time is short. I've asked Beatrice to write this for me, as I fear I'm too shaky and you wouldn't be able to decipher it. I'm truly not afraid to go, although I know it will break your heart. I'm weary and feel myself fading each day. The only regret I have is leaving you, my love. I will miss your gentle soul, your wisdom, your laugh, your smile, all of you. You've given me a lovely life and made me so very happy. I won't miss what's become of me, this old body failing, but I'll miss you and I'll miss us.'" Tears spill onto his cheeks and he takes another swipe at them.

"'Think of me when you are in the garden and know that I'm there with you. Think of me when you sniff the soft scent of my roses, see the first shoots of the spring bulbs, watch the green leaves change to fiery orange and red, and marvel at the first snow that blankets our little world. Those things and you, my dear, are what I'll miss. Don't grieve me for long; instead find something new to enjoy or someone kind with whom to spend your days. You are so much happier when you have something to do. I know I've become your job now and having you spend your days with me has brought me so much comfort. I can't imagine being here alone like so many are. Don't dwell on these last years; remember the happiness we've enjoyed and be grateful for the wonderful years we were given. Arthur, my dear husband, my best friend, my loyal protector, I will always love you and will be waiting for you until we meet again. With all my love, Rosie.'"

Inching closer to him, I lean against his leg. Startled, he bends forward and his watery eyes meet mine.

"Where did you come from, little guy?" His voice is kind and gentle.

He pets me and a slow smile begins to form between his tear-stained cheeks. He focuses on the sun, low on the horizon, as he strokes me. He doesn't say anything or even look at me, but glides his hands over my fur. His pulse slows and his breathing steadies as he rubs behind my ears. I love the feel of his fingers in my fur. After several minutes, he's calmer, which makes me happy. It's like my mother told me: I would give a sense of great comfort to someone special.

His eyes wander to the pathways and beyond to the grass. After folding the papers in his hand and putting them inside an envelope and tucking it away in his shirt pocket, he stands, retrieves the rose, and places his hat on his head. He begins to walk along the concrete, and I stay close to him.

We traverse the park and I resist the pull of all the wonderful scents drifting from the fragrant grass and trees that summon me, remembering what my mother told me about humans. They like dogs to walk beside them and not wander. Her advice replays in my head, as I do my best to impress this man with my manners. Despite his smile, I recognize his loneliness and fear. They match my own.

His eyes probe each bench and pathway, perhaps in search of my owner. The only people we meet are two women powerwalking and chatting animatedly. They show no interest in me, but smile at the man, who tips his hat to them. He leads the way to another bench and settles onto it with a heavy sigh.

As his fingers massage my head and ears, his sadness eases. He searches my neck for a collar and shakes his head. "Are you lost?"

More like abandoned. Nobody will be missing me. I stare into his eyes with what I hope is a charming look and place my paw on his knee. He chuckles and a warm smile fills his face.

"You're hard to resist," he says, with another shake of his head. "I'm not set up for a dog, but can't very well leave you out here all alone." He rises from the bench and motions me to follow him. "Just for tonight." The authority in his voice surprises me.

We stroll through the park and reach the street near the entrance. As we are leaving, a man passes by us and nods. "Fine-looking dog you have there, Arthur."

Arthur. His name is dignified and formal, much like him. Arthur mumbles something to the man about having a good evening and continues walking. He turns the corner at a mass of rhododendrons in full bloom and leads me to a house on the quiet cul-de-sac and through a gate to his backyard.

"Yard" is an understatement. It's lusher than the park and filled with all sorts of flowers and bushes that tempt my nose. I follow Arthur on the curved stone pathway to the back of the house. He leads me by the area with fluffy cushioned chairs and a big table. I note the potting bench in the corner and sniff at the scent of roses coming from the flowered gardening clogs nestled next to a larger pair of rubber slip-on shoes that smell like Arthur. A pair of pink gardening gloves rest on the counter above, next to an array of gardening tools and pots.

Arthur goes through the door and into the house, and returns with a pile of sheets and blankets. He drapes the sheets over a couch and situates the blanket across the seating area. When he is done, he pats the cushion with his hand and says, "Come on up here, boy."

I take a few tentative steps toward the couch, and he taps his hand on it again. I've never been allowed to sleep inside a house. "I wish I knew your name, little fella." His rheumy blue eyes stare into mine, and his voice is gentle. "You remind me of my grand-dad's dog he had when I was a young boy. His name was Duke."

I like the name Duke. It sounds magnificent—regal and noble, and important, like my mother knew I'd be. I've never had a name before.

After a bit more urging from Arthur, I bound onto the couch.

"Good boy. This is where you'll sleep tonight. You'll be safe here." He strokes my head and back as he talks, and I hope with all my heart that I can live here with him. After a few minutes, his hand stops moving. I turn my head at the soft snoring sound coming from his mouth and notice his eyes are closed. I snuggle closer to him and rest my head on his lap.

# CHAPTER 2

## Madison

## Two Months Later

I turn into Creekside Village and park in one of the visitors' spaces in front of the office. I roll my shoulders and rotate my neck a few times, feeling the soreness in my muscles as I close my eyes to do so. At least the long drive is behind me. With a sigh, I glance at my daughter, slouched in her seat, earbuds inserted. "Abbie, do you want to wait in the car or come in with me?"

Unsurprisingly I get no eye contact. Just a hand held up in front of me as I hear the piano music drifting from my old phone. As a compromise to my refusal to allow her a cell phone, I let her use the inactivated phone for photos and music. I'm not on social media and Abbie doesn't need the difficulties of that often uncaring world added to her teenage years. She takes every opportunity to remind me that she is the only girl in high school who doesn't have a working cell phone.

I grab my purse from the floor and groan as my joints protest the long drive. "I'll be right back." She's old enough to stay on her own and the car is in clear view of the office, but I still glance over my shoulder to look behind me as I take a few steps forward.

As I make my way down the sidewalk, I survey the grassy expanse in the midst of the mobile home park and the large building bearing a wooden sign indicating "Creekside Clubhouse," along with an outdoor pool and tennis courts. The space reminds me of a town square but it's in the middle of the mobile home community, with the well-kept trailers, all with manicured yards and colorful flowers, surrounding it. I take a few minutes and rotate my shoulders, noticing the entryway I drove through and the gate arms in the open position on both sides of the large planter serving as a median. Signage on the office building makes it clear trespassers will be prosecuted and reminds any would-be criminal that security cameras are in use throughout the property. I soak in the quietness, broken only by the rhythmic plops of a tennis ball against the court, as a couple, dressed in tennis whites, volleys.

Creekside is a far cry from the noisy apartment complex in Wyoming. The rusty old swing set atop a dirt area behind it was hardly the playground the manager claimed it to be.

Upon opening the office door, a cheerful woman with wisps of red hair, so thin I can see her pink scalp underneath, greets me with a smile, accented with vivid red lipstick, some of which is smudged on her teeth. The woman looks over her purple reading glasses. "I'm Gladys and you must be Ms. Ward?" she says; her penciled-on eyebrows arch high with the question.

I nod and smile and pull my paperwork from my purse. "It's Madison."

Gladys's dimples deepen and she waves her hand in the air, and I notice the red glitter on the ends of her pearl-colored nails. "I've got your keys ready. Regency Health did all the paperwork. Everything is taken care of; they're covering rent, utilities, and your yard maintenance. It's all paid by them until the end of December. The only thing you need to worry about is your Internet connection, and the company was out yesterday to hook all of that up for you. I just need you to sign for your keys, agree to the park rules, and I'll make a quick copy of your photo ID."

I scan the paperwork while Gladys chats on about how excited they are to have me living at the park. "Most of our residents are on the mature side, so it will be wonderful to have you and your daughter here. Like a breath of fresh air. Not to mention how thrilled we are to have you at the Millbury Life Center." She scoffs and adds, "They don't like to call them senior centers anymore, but that's what it really is, you know? Lillian, she's the nurse who was there for years, retired when they opened the new building. Told us she and the old center could make their exit together. We've been without a nurse for the last month. All of Millbury is buzzing with interest in you."

Why would I be the talk of the town? I'm not looking to be the center of attention and hope Gladys is exaggerating. I pull my Ohio license from my wallet and my eyes linger on the old photo from four years ago. That carefree woman with a hint of a smile doesn't exist anymore. Too much has changed since that day. My license expires in a couple of months and I make a mental note to search out the nearest Oregon DMV office.

Gladys fingers the license and with a spark in her eye says, "You know, your next door neighbor is a nice young man, around forty. He travels for work, so he's not home much and is gone now, but his name is Jeff and he's single." With a wink she turns and walks across the office to the copier.

I don't encourage her. I can tell Gladys has her thumb on the pulse of what's happening in the park. I only hope she isn't a serial matchmaker.

Gladys returns with my license and hands me the keys and two keycards for accessing the clubhouse and park amenities. She also gives me a tag to attach to the inside corner of my vehicle windshield. "We keep the gates closed during the evening and it will automatically open to let you in by reading this tag. If you have visitors coming in the evening, you'll have to meet them and use your keycard to open the gate. We don't have the budget for a security guard. Same goes if you're not in your car: use your keycard at the gate." I nod my understanding and start to thank her, but can't get a word in edgewise.

"The office closes at five o'clock on weekdays, but if you have an emergency, there is an after-hours number." She presents me with a colored calendar and adds, "This is our activities calendar. You'll get one in your mailbox at the beginning of each month. Hope to see you at one of our get-togethers."

I smile without committing and gather my things, thanking her. When I get to the parking area, Abbie is pacing back and forth along the sidewalk. I take a long breath as I watch her quick steps along the length of the visitor parking spots. I remember the first time I saw her pacing, at my first post after we left Ohio. She shuffled her feet, almost dragging them in the dirt and gravel next to that run-down apartment complex we lived in. I couldn't figure out how come her shoes were so filthy and followed her outside to watch her from the parking lot. After twenty minutes of her constant pacing, I dragged her home. That was almost two years ago. The way she went back and forth along an invisible line reminded me of the way relatives paced in a hospital waiting room, anxious about their loved ones.

I wrote it off as her being nervous about a new school, but she did it again a few days later. Nothing I've said or done since has had an impact. I've tried talking to her and reassuring her about starting over in a new town, and I even resorted to bribing her with treats or small gifts, distracting her each time she looked anxious, but she wasn't interested. It was like she *needed* to pace. Punishments haven't seemed appropriate since she seems to be suffering enough. And since then the hurried steps back and forth have become an obsession.

I twist the sapphire ring that always graced my mom's finger and now adorns my right hand. Uprooting Abbie every six months isn't fair to her, and as I watch her travel back and forth along the edge of the grass, on one of her walks, as she and I have taken to describing her pacing, it breaks my heart. After consulting with doctors I've worked with at all my posts, it's clear her behaviors are related to anxiety, and the physical action of pacing seems to calm her. They've all told me not to make too much of it and that when she's better able to deal with her emotions, she may outgrow it. As she's oblivious to the world around her, I give her a gentle tap on the shoulder and jingle our keys in front of her. "Ready to go?"

She gets in the car, without a word, and I slide behind the wheel and steer us to our new home, until December anyway—space number seven. I park under the carport and turn off the ignition, taking in the gray double-wide with white trim and decking to match. The bright green patch of lawn gives it a charming and cheerful look.

After grabbing a couple of bags from the backseat, I nudge Abbie in the shoulder. "Come on, grab your bags."

With a sullen look mastered by fourteen-year-old girls the world over, she trudges behind me, up the stairs to the backdoor. That musty, not-lived-in smell wafts from the open door. After plopping my stuff in the master bedroom, I pluck an earbud from Abbie's ear. "You can either open all the windows or get the stuff out of the back of the SUV."

Without a response, she shuffles to the backdoor and clomps down the wooden stairs. After opening the windows in our bedrooms, I tackle the rest of the rooms and inspect what will be our home for the next six months while I'm assigned to Millbury. I never imagined I'd be a traveling nurse, but for the last almost two years, it's been my life.

My last post was in a tiny town in Wyoming over winter. I was happy to leave. The fresh summer breeze outside the living room windows begins to fill the air and dispel the stale odor. I give the kitchen a once-over and watch Abbie, laden down with our clothes, make another trip.

All the furnishings look new, including the set of pots and pans and the rest of the kitchenware. My eyes scan the countertop and

I breathe a sigh of relief when I see the coffeemaker, somewhat basic, but with a programmable brewing timer so I can be sure to get my jolt of caffeine in the morning. The sheet with the router password and connection information is on the counter next to the sink and I pull my phone from my pocket and test the connection. While Abbie deposits the rest of our personal items, I make a quick shopping list and turn on the television to connect it to the router.

Along with information on the park and clubhouse amenities, I look through a newsprint community guide. It's filled with a directory and ads for local businesses and organizations, along with a map. I thumb through it and find one chain grocery store I've heard of and two local markets.

Abbie is lounging next to the clothes piled on her bed.

"Let's take a walk through the park, so you can get the lay of the land. Then we can make a run to the store and drive by the center."

I motion for her to leave her earbuds at home, and she rolls her eyes, but removes the tether and follows me outside. We meander along the quiet streets, fortified with thick speed bumps, lest anyone should dare to accelerate through the park. Abbie stops every few minutes to capture photos of flowers. They are her latest obsession, and researching native plants in Oregon provided a measure of excitement for our latest move. The last few years haven't been easy for her.

She stops in front of a beautiful blooming white tree. "Mom, Mom, it's a Japanese snowbell. A small tree with slightly fragrant, white, bell-shaped flowers that drip from horizontal side branches. The foliage turns red or yellow in the fall."

"It's beautiful," I say, taking a sniff of the flowers.

She rushes to another yard and holds her phone over a mound of vibrant purple blooms. "This is alstroemeria," she says, all smiles when she shows me the screen, "also known as the Peruvian lily or princess lily and comes in dozens of varieties, all native to South America. They grow from a tuberous root."

She has such a joyful smile when she's involved in something that interests her. I only wish there was a happy medium between her sulking and this exuberance. It's easy to get frustrated with her—that is, until I remember it's my fault she's like this.

When we get to the furthest point from the entrance, I point out the other exit onto a street that runs behind the mobile home park. "Abbie, if you feel the need to take one of your walks, I want you to stay along our street or near the clubhouse. Under no circumstances can you walk this far or leave the park, understand?"

She's busy looking at another plant and rattling off what she has learned about it. I grip her shoulder and force her to look at me. "Abbie, did you hear what I said?"

The blank look on her face betrays what I suspect. Her sole focus is on the flowers, and when she gets like this, she shuts out the whole world around her. I hate snapping at her, but I don't want to have to worry about her leaving the park or venturing too far away from our trailer. I take a breath and soften my voice to remind her again about the rules for walking and guide us away from the yards and distractions to the clubhouse.

The keycard for the clubhouse door works like a charm and I lead the way on a quick tour of the space: it's outfitted with a commercial kitchen, dining area, and a large open area for meetings and gatherings. We pass by a billiards room and lending library, a cubby with a couple of public computers, and several other rooms for classes or private functions. Past the gym, we follow the signs to the pool and outdoor tennis courts, accessed via the locker rooms.

Everything is a bit dated, but well-maintained. We meander along the edge of the pool that smells of chlorine. My eye wanders to the hot tub tucked into the corner nearest the building. Maybe

I can talk Abbie into swimming while I try to soak away the aches in my back and neck.

As we leave the grounds, Abbie's stride is picking up steam. She's anxious to get home and add the plants she found to her notebook. When she's honed in on her obsessions, it's difficult to get her attention or tear her away from them without a fight. I'm too tired to battle with her right now and let her record her findings, but hurry her along so we can get to the store.

The mobile home park is only half a mile from work and the market is between the two. We pass by Nelson's Market and turn in to the parking lot, still smelling of fresh asphalt, of the Millbury Life Center. I consult the oversized dial of the vintage Hamilton watch I wear—the one that was always on my dad's wrist—and realize we need to hurry.

The immaculate building surrounded by staked trees and new plants closes in a few minutes, but I slide into a parking spot. "Let's run inside and take a quick look, just so I know what I'm up against tomorrow when I have my orientation."

Abbie doesn't hide her lack of enthusiasm, but follows me through the automatic glass doors.

Behind the reception counter, a woman with stylish gray hair smiles at us. I extend my hand and say, "I'm Madison Ward, the new nurse practitioner. This is my daughter, Abigail."

Her smile widens. "Wonderful to meet both of you," she replies. "I'm Barb, the volunteer receptionist. Everyone has been eager for your arrival." She glances across the lobby. "I'm afraid Mr. Cox, our director, has already gone and we're just getting ready to close."

"Oh, this isn't official. I just got to town and my daughter and I are running to the store, but I wanted to stop in and just take a look at the place and peek at the office."

Barb smiles. "I can spare a few minutes." She reaches for a keyring and motions me to follow her down the hallway. Barb points out the rooms we pass by—arts and crafts, computers, classrooms, game rooms, and a music room. She slips the key into the lock of the door labeled "Health and Wellness Center" and holds the door for us.

The smell of fresh paint hangs in the air. I notice the new carpet and still-wrapped-in-plastic furnishings. I flip on the light and take in the purple and lilac accents with hints of green, all of which match the scrubs Regency Health provides. The small waiting area and desk give way to two examination rooms, a restroom, an open cubicle area for quick vital sign checks, and my office.

While I delight in the modern space, notes from a piano drift from the hallway. I recognize one of Abbie's favorite pieces and cringe as I shrug at Barb. "I'm sure that's Abbie. She loves to play the piano and we don't have one. I'm sorry."

"A few of our regulars are skilled pianists. It's open to anyone who has the gumption to play it." She stops to listen and adds, "She plays beautifully."

"I need to find her something to do this summer. I hate to leave her on her own all day. Mr. Cox told me she was welcome to spend some time here at the center, as it's open to everyone, which is wonderful, but I know she can be a handful, and she plays pretty loudly."

In truth, I know Abbie won't want to hang out at the center. She'd rather spend the day alone at home, listening to music or researching flowers, but since I'm working Saturdays, she agreed to spend one day a week here. When school is in session it will be easier—she can stop by and spend an hour or so with me before I get off work at four o'clock—but summer is another story.

I take a deep breath, thank Barb again, and hurry after my daughter.

# CHAPTER 3

## Duke

Arthur and I have settled into a routine. On Mondays, after tending to the garden, we always spend the morning walking the path along the creek to the reservoir. The first time we drove there was right after leaving the vet where he took me to get checked. I was a bit anxious at the vet, but everyone was nice and talked to me with kind voices. They examined my ears and mouth and then used a plastic device and ran it over my neck and shoulders. It didn't hurt, but I wasn't sure what they were doing. They explained to Arthur they were scanning me for a chip, but I didn't have one. The vet promised to keep searching for my owner, and the idea filled me with dread. But on the way home, Arthur stopped at the feed store and loaded his trunk with enough dog food to feed a dozen dogs. Or one dog, for quite some time.

I had never been in the water until that sunny day, but now, the reservoir is one of my favorite places to go. I run with abandon along the shore of coarse sand and throw myself into the cool liquid with all my might, sending splashes of blue water into the sky. The cool water feels wonderful as it filters through my fur. Arthur lets me play while he sits on a bench and watches. I love hearing him laugh and encouraging me to play. He always brings my floatie toys with us, and I wiggle with excitement waiting for him to toss them into the water so I can rush to retrieve them.

I know he can't wade in himself, so I always bring them right back to his feet.

Most of the time, we stop at Creekside Coffee on the way home. Arthur always jokes with the owners, Lori and Lisa, that he has a hard time telling them apart. Twins with shiny brunette hair they wear in ponytails, they are always friendly. Their aprons always smell of coffee, sugar, and cinnamon, along with chocolate. I have an easy time telling them apart, since Lori always bends down to greet me first and runs her fingers through the hair on my back that's growing thicker every day.

They fuss over Arthur, and Lori makes sure I get a crunchy dog treat they keep in a canister behind the counter for me. Sometimes she adds a dab of whipped cream to it and it makes me lick my lips to get every drop.

We usually don't get back to the house until after lunchtime. Arthur has something to eat, fixes me a snack, and we both take a nap. There's a sun-filled square that appears on the wooden floor right after lunch and it's my favorite afternoon napping spot.

Tuesdays are laundry and housekeeping days, but Arthur is always cleaning and picking up around the house, no matter the day of the week. He seems quite particular about keeping my toys corralled and wiping the floor where my food and water bowls sit. He has a long wand with a fluffy pad he runs across the floor, and I love to try and chase it and pounce on it. Once we're done outside, Arthur tunes the television to the classic movie channel and gathers up clothes and towels. He uses the scary vacuum I don't like and lets me sit atop a blanket in his recliner while he runs it over the floor. Once the house is shipshape, he's taken to letting me rest on his lap while he watches a movie and waits for the washer and dryer to do their work. As I had hoped, his initial offer of a one-night stay has turned into much more.

Arthur has installed a dog door for me, so I go to and from the backyard whenever I like. In addition to the couch on the back porch, I also have a bed indoors and sleep next to Arthur in his room, where last night he told a framed portrait of Rosie goodnight before he shut off the light.

At least he didn't fall asleep in his recliner again.

Several times over these last weeks, in the middle of the night, I've felt Arthur's hand stroke my back. I sometimes dream about my mother and miss having her and all my brothers and sisters to cuddle with at night. Perhaps Arthur senses this.

Each morning, we get up early, and Arthur lets me out the front door to retrieve the newspaper. I love to fetch things, and the first time I saw the paper on the sidewalk, I picked it up with my mouth. Arthur liked the idea of me getting the paper for him and, although it took several days for me to stop ripping at it, I mastered how to grab it and hold it softly in my mouth, hurrying to bring it to him. He tells me it will save him from bending over first thing in the morning, and I'm happy to help. When I deliver it to him, he rewards me with a happy smile and a tiny soft treat that tastes like chicken.

On Wednesdays, we have to put the trash out by the curb and always do that first thing in the morning. I love the fresh smells that fill the air and the feel of the dew on my paws as I wander through the grass. My coat is changing; it's no longer the light and fluffy puppy fur I had when I found Arthur. It's getting thicker, coarser, and heavier. The cool morning air provides the perfect temperature for romping without overheating.

Wednesdays are busy. It's Arthur's day to play cards and, since I've arrived, he's invited his card group to the house so he doesn't have to leave me on my own. It's so exciting when they come over. All of them are dog lovers, but only Pete has a dog at home. He tells me it is a Yorkie named Corky. Henry and Karl pet me and smile whenever they see me. I tend to get over-excited when they arrive and it takes me a few minutes to calm down. I love seeing them so much, I jump and put my paws on their legs.

When Arthur says my name, he sounds so annoyed, but I'm not sure why. Maybe he's excited to see them too and doesn't like me monopolizing them. Karl, who loves old cars and on whose hands the faint smell of grease lingers, has the softest heart, and removes my paws from his pants with a kind whisper. He's my favorite of Arthur's friends.

Sometimes they play at the table on the patio, and I run around the yard until I get tired and take a nap under the tree. They snack on crackers and cheese, or Arthur's favorite, pistachios, while they play and there's always a few crumbs that find their way to the ground. I sit on the cool stone and watch for those tiny morsels, nabbing them as soon as they fall. I like to sit close to Karl since he seems to be the clumsiest eater of the bunch.

Each morning, Arthur brews coffee and fixes my breakfast and then selects a rose to cut, puts it in a vase and carries it to the table on the stone patio and places it in front of Rosie's chair, before working on the crossword puzzle in the paper.

"Duke, what do you think about fourteen across, desk drawer items?" He has an expectant look on his face, as if I might answer, but he stares with longing at the empty chair in front of him. And I know I'm not the person he'd normally ask.

I've gotten accustomed to the tinkling sounds from Rosie's collection of windchimes that decorate the backyard space. Arthur smiles when he hears the melodic chimes and tells me he likes to think of them as Rosie chattering to him.

"Rosie had an eye for flowers and I was just the workhorse," he says, recounting her laying out the design and making sure he dug the holes just so. "What I wouldn't give for just one more season here with her." A tear leaks from his eye and he retrieves his ever-present handkerchief, embroidered with his initial, and wipes it across his eyes.

Life with Arthur is a dream come true. Despite me chewing the side out of his favorite slippers while he took a nap last week and the holes I've dug in the flowerbeds, Arthur never threatens me. The look in his eyes and the tone of his voice conveys his disappointment, but after he cleans up the mess and tells me not to do it, he pets me with a gentle hand. I'm not sure why I do those things, but it seems to always start, at least in the yard, with the scent of a chipmunk or squirrel. I know they're under that dirt and I have to keep excavating until I find them. Arthur's slippers smell so good, like him, and though it's fun and feels good at the time, I hate upsetting Arthur. He's so kind to me, I've got to try harder.

The last few nights, Arthur has been closing up the house earlier and going to bed when it's still light outside. He always spritzes the pillows on the bed with a frosted bottle of perfume from Rosie's dresser, and smiles and holds the pillow close to him when he gets into bed. I imagine Rosie was like the scent she wore—soft and clean, yet warm and cozy, with the notes of rose and honey.

I've noticed Arthur losing his balance a bit and holding his head after working in the yard. I thought maybe he was getting overheated, but it happens in the coolness of the morning. When he's unsteady and grasping for something to hold, I rush to him, but he always assures me he's fine and makes excuses that he's just tired or hot or got up too fast.

I'm baffled as to why humans can't be more like dogs. If we need help, we'll hold up a paw and get our owner's attention, or lead them to the door, letting them know something is wrong. We make our needs known and don't try to hide them out of fear of being weak. We can't do everything for ourselves and I've never considered it a failing. Humans, though, they look at needing help as a vulnerability. It seems the kind ones, like Arthur, who are always willing to help others, are the last ones to ask for help themselves.

Arthur puts the phone on speaker, while he pets me and urges me, with a firm hand, to stay off of his lap. Sonny calls first thing every Saturday. Arthur is mindful to be in the house near the phone so he doesn't miss the weekly call from his brother's son. Arthur's voice is always stronger and happier when he talks to Sonny. I know Sonny asks how he's feeling and today is no different than the other times. No matter what, Arthur always says he's fine.

"Are you planning your yearly trip this summer?" Arthur asks.

Sonny clears his throat. "I'm not sure, Uncle Arthur. Work is crazy, but I'm trying to schedule a break. I'll let you know when I get it figured out. I'm sorry I couldn't stay more than the one day when I came out for Aunt Rosie's service."

"I know you're busy, Sonny. It was a real comfort to have someone else there."

"How are you managing without her? Are you keeping busy?"

Arthur smiles down at me. "Well, I've got a new roommate." He chuckles and rubs my ear between his fingers.

Concern fills Sonny's voice. "A roommate? If you need money, I can help you out. I don't want you resorting to having strangers living with you."

Arthur doesn't miss a beat. "I'm not charging him anything. His name is Duke and he's about four months old, twenty-five pounds of energy, with dark golden fur and the softest ears you've ever felt."

Sonny's laughter fills the air. "You had me worried there for a minute. I thought you'd fallen prey to some scam artist that you let move in with you." He laughs again. "So, you've got yourself a puppy. I seem to remember old photos of my great-grandpa and a dog named Duke."

"That's right. Grandpa George always had several dogs, most of them hunting dogs, but this pup reminded me of the dog that I remember as a young boy, a beautiful golden dog that went everywhere with him." Arthur gives me a scratch under my chin. "This guy is a sweet one. The vet told me his dark ears mean he'll be a darker caramel color when he's full grown. I found him in the park. I need to spend some time training him or find a class or something."

"I think it's terrific that you have a dog. I'm sure he's great company for you."

Arthur's smile deepens. "I've become quite attached to him. He makes the house feel so much less lonely."

"That's wonderful. I'm happy you found each other. Look, I'm going to have to go, Uncle. I'll talk with you next week, okay? Love you."

"Have a good weekend. Love you, Sonny." Arthur disconnects the call and gazes at me.

Since my siblings left and then I had to leave my mother, I've longed for a connection, a family. I'll always be here for Arthur. We're family now.

Arthur has promised me a walk this morning and as soon as he rises from his chair, I'm at the door, ready to go, tugging on the leash he leaves hanging there. Today, we're going to the new Millbury Life Center. Henry attended the grand opening and told Arthur he needed to visit. Henry thinks they should move the weekly card group meeting to the center.

Arthur dons his town hat, a soft charcoal-colored fedora, and snaps my leash onto my collar. I scratch at my neck, but Arthur isn't falling for it and insists I have my leash on when we leave the house. He says he can't trust me yet.

We set out walking in the opposite direction of the park and at the corner turn onto Main Street. It's a warm day and despite Arthur's hat shading him, I notice the sheen of sweat on his face. We stop at the bench under the canopy of trees near the market we've visited before and Arthur slumps into the seat. His hands are shaky and his face is pale.

Not sure what to do, I stick close to him, licking his hand. He's breathing heavily.

A police SUV stops in the driveway of the market and the driver's door opens. The man who steps out is dressed in a dark uniform with a shiny badge. He puts his hand on Arthur's shoulder.

"Judge Patterson, are you okay?" Admiration and concern fill the man's eyes.

"Fine, Bill, just needed to take a break on our walk to the center."

"I'm heading that way, how about a lift?"

"Oh, I don't want to bother you. We'll be fine." A hint of pink appears on Arthur's ashen cheeks.

Bill wraps an arm around Arthur and supports his elbow. "I insist. It's warm this morning and it looks like you could use some cool air and water."

Arthur doesn't protest. I'm so glad Bill is here.

I trail behind Arthur as Bill leads him to the passenger seat. Bill retrieves a bottle of cold water from a cooler in the back and removes the lid, handing it to Arthur. After he gets Arthur settled, I stare at the seat towering high above me, but before I even think about jumping, Bill tucks his arms under me and helps me into the backseat. The air inside is cool and Bill increases the flow of cold air coming from the vents. Arthur takes a long drink from the bottle and puts his hand against the dash and nods.

"That's better. I don't think I've been drinking enough water. How's your family, Bill?"

"Summer vacation, so the kids are driving Sally nuts. We're going to squeeze in a trip over to the coast next weekend." He turns onto the street and glances in the rearview mirror at me. "I don't remember you and Rosie having a dog."

Arthur grins. "We didn't."

Bill turns into a parking lot in a matter of minutes and stops under the shaded portico outside the main entrance. He turns to me and pats me on the head. "You've made a great choice.

Goldens are some of the best dogs. Perfect companions, loyal, and smart."

I like this guy. I take in the large building with young plantings surrounding it. The odor of oil wafts from the black asphalt parking lot, overpowering the soft scent of the young flowers. Arthur takes hold of my leash, and Bill walks next to him, his arm positioned at Arthur's elbow, should he need to steady him. Arthur's shoulders relax with Bill by his side. Bill is careful not to take hold of Arthur, but his hand is never less than an inch away.

We walk through the sliding glass doors and all sorts of new and exciting scents greet me. The aroma of sweet apples and beef with gravy fill the air. I spot a large dining room filled with tables and chairs and lift my nose to the source of the enticing smells wafting from it.

While Arthur is checking in at the counter and talking to Bill, I turn and spot a woman. Her blondish hair is pulled back in a ponytail and I can smell the coffee in her hands. There's something about her that beckons me to her. It's like when I see a squirrel in the yard: I just have to hurry to investigate. That same instinct is driving me forward now.

Is Arthur telling me no? I can hardly hear him, my brain focused only on the woman.

I forget the delicious aroma from the dining room, don't give the potted plants a second glance, and dash past the shelf of used books full of scents that would normally tempt me.

There's something about her, a natural warmth, a scent maybe? I think she needs to meet me and I know I need to meet her. I slide across the smooth floor and can't stop before slamming into her legs.

# CHAPTER 4

## Madison

I feel the weight of something firm but flexible strike against my calf. I steady my coffee and look down at a young puppy looking up at me with soulful eyes. From his size, I'd say he's four months old, at that crazy puppy stage when they're all wiggles and teeth. I run my fingers over his furry head and linger at the softness of his ears—like velvet. I look into his eyes and they remind me of my favorite dog I had growing up, Sparky.

"Aww, aren't you a cutie pie." I take the end of the leash and add, "Looks like you made a run for it, huh?" I scan the entry area and spot a well-dressed older man, a smart hat atop his white hair, his face flush with embarrassment.

I walk the dog over to the reception counter and recognize the concern in the man's eyes. "Looks like this one got away from you."

The man shakes his head at the dog. "I'm so sorry. Duke and I aren't trained yet."

Bill nods at me and says, "Madison, I'd like you to meet one of our most esteemed residents. This is Judge Arthur Patterson. Madison is the new nurse practitioner that came on board a couple of weeks ago."

Arthur clicks his tongue and shakes his head. "That's 'retired judge.' Pleased to meet you, Madison, and sorry for Duke's exuberance. I wasn't sure he'd even be allowed in here."

I give Arthur a reassuring smile as I stare into his sky blue eyes that remind me of my dad's. "With the exception of the

dining room, we welcome all dogs, as long as they're on a leash."
I move closer to Arthur and whisper, "And, you're supposed to
hold on to the other end of it." I laugh and scratch the top of
Duke's head.

Duke's ears perk at the squeal and chatter coming from Bill's
radio. Bill speaks into a microphone attached to the shoulder
of his shirt. "I've got to run. I'll leave Judge Patterson in your
capable hands, Madison. He and Duke were walking here and
he was feeling a bit shaky and tired."

I nod my understanding. "How about we go in my office and
see what we can figure out?"

Arthur takes a step back and I recognize the beginning of a
protest. I link my arm in his and take hold of Duke's leash with
a firm grip, shortening it and keeping the dog close to me as I
lead the way down the hall, giving them no choice but to follow
alongside my steps. Arthur hesitates, but accepts my nudging and
we make it to my office door.

Arthur takes a chair in front of my desk, and I look at the
dog. "Duke, sit," I say, moving my hand up toward my shoulder.
Duke's nose twitches as he detects the treat I have in my hand.
He can't help but plop his rump on the floor as I raise my hand
and bring it closer to me high above him. He sits and raises his
nose. "Good sit, Duke," I say and produce a tiny ball of cheese,
which he gobbles from my hand.

I move my hand closer to the floor and say, "Duke, down."
He follows the scent of the enticing cheese, drooling, and sliding
down, letting his elbows and chin touch the floor. I wink at
Arthur and give Duke a smile while I deliver another bite to him
and ruffle the top of his head. "Good down, Duke."

"You're amazing," says Arthur. "You must have a dog?"

I shake my head. "Not for a long time. I grew up with dogs
and always trained them." I move the string cheese I was snacking
on to the side of my desk.

Arthur glances at Duke and sighs. "I'm afraid I'm not very good at training Duke. I haven't had him for very long. He's a wonderful companion, don't get me wrong...but he's a bit unruly."

I can see the spark of love in Arthur's eyes. "He's just a puppy, but he's a smart one. I can tell." I smile at Duke and turn my attention to Arthur, retrieving a blood pressure cuff.

"So, Bill says you were shaky. Have you been light-headed?" I strap on the cuff and squeeze the bulb, bending to listen with my stethoscope.

Arthur divulges that he's been light-headed, especially when he's bent over in the flowerbeds and then stands up or if he sits up too fast when he wakes, but he's hesitant to tell me much more. I nod as I scribble on a notepad and ask him about the medications he takes.

Arthur rattles off several names, and I note each one inquiring about the dosages. "Tell me more about your homelife. Are you married? Do you have children? How long were you a judge and how long have you been retired?"

"I was a lawyer and judge in Salem and then when my wife's mother's health declined, we moved here and I took a position as Millbury Municipal Judge. I served there until I retired about fifteen years ago."

The words flutter in his throat and he clears it. I notice Duke inching closer to him.

"I was married for fifty-two years, but Rosie and I were never blessed with children."

I reassure him with a pat on his arm and notice the gold band on his finger that he's twirling with his other hand.

"So, when is the last time you saw your doctor?"

A hint of irritation creeps into his voice. "Dr. Stewart retired about two years ago. Since then, I haven't seen the same doctor twice. It's now a satellite office and urgent care affiliated with one of the big hospitals in Salem. I only go to get my prescriptions renewed, but it's coming up on a year."

I keep my hand on his, feeling his pulse, and offer a gentle smile. "Well, good news for you. Since I'm a nurse practitioner, I can handle your prescriptions. I suspect your blood pressure medication might be the culprit. It's a fairly high dosage. Do you remember if you've always taken the same strength?"

Arthur shakes his head. "No, Dr. Stewart increased it the last time I saw him. My numbers kept creeping up. Probably because I was under some stress." He touches his wedding ring again.

I scribble a note and nod. "That makes sense. I think we'll lower it a bit and see if that helps you feel less light-headed. Your blood pressure is on the low side and that can cause you to feel weak or dizzy; sometimes it can lead to fainting, along with blurred vision and fatigue."

Arthur's jaw relaxes and he smiles with relief. "So, all I need to do is adjust my medication?"

I bob my head while I write out the prescription. "That's right. We'll start there and see if that solves your issues. Be sure and stay hydrated, especially when you're outside working. That doesn't mean coffee or tea. Water, okay?" I open a box from a stack in the corner and hand him a tall insulated water bottle. "Here's one you can use that will keep your water cool for hours. Compliments of Regency Health."

Arthur nods and looks down at Duke. The puppy raises his eyes to Arthur and thumps his tail on the floor, eliciting another grin from his master.

"I'd like to see you back here soon to check your blood pressure and see how the new dosage is working. Will that work for you?"

He puts the prescription in his shirt pocket and nods. "That sounds fine. I haven't been here before, so wanted to come and check out the place."

"How about a tour of the center? I've got a few things to do and then I was going to grab some lunch. I could drop you home on my way. You should take it easy and not exert yourself much until we get your medication regulated." I offer him a hand and grab Duke's leash.

"Oh, I don't want to trouble you. I can get a ride." Arthur plucks his hat from the chair.

"It's no trouble. If you walked here, you can't be too far away, right?"

I make Duke sit two more times and reward him with bites from my string cheese.

Arthur stands and heads for the door. "We're not far, but I'm feeling much better. We'll be fine."

I imagine a gavel banging with the sound of his last word. He has a voice and air about him that command respect.

I show him the classrooms and activity rooms, point out the large open area with the piano, fireplace, books, and games. "They serve lunch each weekday right here. The menus are on the reception counter and they post them online and in the newspaper."

I lead them back to the reception counter and spy Bill's SUV parked in front. He comes from around the corner and says, "Hey, Judge, I finished my call and wondered if I might bend your ear for a little advice."

Arthur stands a little taller and smiles. "Of course, Bill, always happy to help."

Bill motions him outside. "Come on, we can chat on the way to your house."

As he ushers Arthur and Duke to the door, he turns and gives me a quick wink. Clearly, Bill has been in this situation before.

Arthur is such a polite gentleman and his reluctance to accept help concerns me. I'm sure there's something going on with him. Like a few of my other patients, he's not ready to trust me quite yet.

# CHAPTER 5

The following Saturday morning, Abbie is up early, working on her notebook of flowers. These last weeks have been hectic with the start of my new job and it being summer vacation. I haven't found much for Abbie to do while I'm at work. There are plenty of summer activities for kids, but they're all expensive and none of them are a great fit for her. I looked for a music camp, but they were all too far away in Portland or Eugene. She's been content to hang out at the house, looking at flowers each day and watching movies. I finally convinced her to spend Saturdays with me at the center, although it did take luring her with the possibility of ice cream.

I bring my coffee to the table and sit down across from her. "Are you ready? You can bring your project and work on it there."

She keeps writing, but then lifts her head, her big, brown eyes full of excitement. "Are there any new flowers blooming at the center?"

"I don't know, but you could check them out. You could play the piano and I can bring you home at lunch if you get bored."

She nods her approval, and I hurry her along to collect her backpack and anything she wants to bring.

The center is a bit quieter on Saturdays, without the dining room serving meals, and fewer scheduled activities. Still, Abbie elects to camp at the empty front desk in my area.

Within an hour, I've got several clients waiting for blood pressure checks or to chat about something, but when I wander out to the waiting area to get Mrs. Baker, I notice Abbie isn't in her chair at the reception desk. I get Mrs. Baker settled in one of the cubicles and hurry down the hall to find Abbie.

My heart begins to race as I contemplate leaving work to find her. I can't let down my patients, but I have to find her. She wandered off before at the apartment in Wyoming. She gets lost in her own thoughts and doesn't have any idea where she is or that she's traveled so far. It took me hours to find her, and she had walked more than two miles from the complex. Luckily, she was fine and never seemed to understand the worry she caused me. But anything could happen to her.

I breathe a sigh of relief when I spot her in front of the building pacing along the sidewalk. As I turn to go back to my office, I catch sight of Arthur and Duke headed to the entrance. Duke lunges to get to Abbie and drags Arthur slightly.

Abbie stops walking and bends down, plants herself on the grass and gives Duke a thorough head rub, while beaming with delight. Duke rolls on his back and she runs her hands over his belly.

I dash back to my office to the line of waiting patients, and it's close to the lunch hour when I send the last one on his way. I finish updating my patient files and glance at the sticky note bearing Arthur's name. Bill had stopped by earlier to follow up on Arthur and let me know he saw him home safely the other day. He knew Arthur would be too stubborn to ask for a ride home, so he made sure he created an opportunity to be nearby and ask him about a case. It's clear Bill admires him as a person and as a judge. When he explained Arthur lost his beloved wife, Rosie, three months ago, Bill's voice filled with emotion. He reminded me what a strong person Arthur was, but wanted me to know about his profound loss.

Abbie has not yet returned to her chair when I'm finished with my patients and I lock the door and put the sign in the window stating I'll return after lunch. I search the area and find her sitting on the couch nearest the piano, with Duke wedged between her and Arthur's feet.

She's petting the top of Duke's head, talking to him in a low voice. Arthur's eyes move from the book he's reading to me and he gestures to Abbie and gives me a conspiratorial wink.

"I see you've met my daughter, Abigail," I say to Arthur. I bend down to pet Duke, who is full of wiggles as he gets to his feet to greet me. "What are you three up to?"

"Mom," she says, her eyes narrowed. "It's Abbie, remember."

"Sorry, right, she likes to be called Abbie."

Arthur smiles and says, "Yes, Duke and I met her outside when we arrived. She played a few songs on the piano for us." Duke keeps raising his front paws trying to jump on me, and I turn and ignore him each time until he stops.

Arthur's mouth gapes open. "How did you do that? I've been trying to get him to quit jumping on people and, for the life of me, can't make him stop."

"It's important not to reward bad behavior, so I won't give him any attention while he's jumping. Turning your back is the easiest way to get the message across. Puppies especially crave your attention, so denying them sends a strong message." I retrieve the warm and limp package of string cheese I never had time to eat from my purse and tear off a small piece. When I raise my hand, Duke sits. "Good sit," I say and reward him with the cheese. I keep my eye on Abbie and notice her smiling at Duke.

"I haven't seen you for a few days. Remember, I need to keep an eye on your blood pressure with the change we made in your medication. I really need to take your blood pressure today and then get you on a regular schedule," I say to Arthur. "Abbie, could you please take Duke's leash and bring him on back to my office and watch him while I talk to Arthur?"

She nods and follows us down the hallway. I take Arthur into a cubicle and check his vitals. "How have you been feeling this week?"

"A bit better," he says. "To be on the safe side, I drove here today, but for the last three days or so, I haven't been light-headed."

"Your blood pressure isn't as low as it was. We'll leave your dosage where it is for now and keep checking you. It's best not to change it too quickly, but we may have to decrease it a bit more."

He nods his understanding. "Your daughter is quite taken with Duke."

I scribble on Arthur's chart and say, "I know. I spied her outside when you arrived. She has some problems with anxiety and some obsessive behaviors, pacing being one of them. Has she been inside with you and Duke since you arrived?"

He nods, "Yes, except the times we took Duke outside, but she didn't linger and came right back with us. They've been glued to each other all morning." He sighs and says, "Those training techniques you're using, I'd never even thought of them." He pauses and he seems reluctant to go on. "I don't know what I was thinking keeping a puppy at my age. I'm having a hard time getting him to stay off of visitors. Like you saw, he likes to jump on people when they come to the house. He's also nipping at my hands and arms. Do you know how to stop him from doing that?" He turns his arms toward me and I see the scratches on both forearms.

"Those puppy teeth are like razors, aren't they?" I say.

Arthur has been on my mind since the first day I met him. It might be his resemblance to my dad, but I'm drawn to him. I've never gotten close to any of my patients at my other posts. Granted, it wasn't the same type of interaction. I was driving so much of the day to get to my patient visits, I had very little spare time to chat with them or learn much about them. But it's not just that. When Abbie sees Duke, she lights up and she's content when she's near him. It's the first time in two years I've been confident she's safe, that she's not pacing, that she won't wander off. "If you'd like, I could help you train Duke?" I ask him. It would also give me the perfect excuse to keep a closer eye on Arthur without him suspecting. "He's going to be a great dog, but needs a little guidance."

"Really?" Arthur asks with surprise. "I've been going to investigate some type of obedience class, but truth be told, I've been too tired to think about it."

"I'd love it and I think it would be great for Abbie. She seems much calmer around him." I glance over at Duke, sitting next to Abbie. He's looking at her with his gentle eyes, full of understanding, and she's whispering to him, smiling, as she strokes his soft ears. The tenseness that has surrounded her for so long seems to have melted away. It's amazing how dogs have the uncanny ability, with their mere presence, to soothe fears and ease worries. "As long as you don't mind her coming with me?"

He waves his hand in the air. "Not at all, dear. It would be wonderful."

"I'm off Sundays. Shall we plan on something for tomorrow?"

"Perfect." Arthur's eyes light up. This is the most upbeat I've seen him and the eagerness in his smile tells me he's longing for visitors. Maybe that's something that he's been missing since Rosie passed. "What do you girls like to eat? I could grill something tomorrow."

And suddenly the sparkle in his eye and his enthusiasm make me hesitate. I should have thought this through better. The only thing worse than having nobody, is having somebody you could lose. And we're not here permanently. "That's very kind of you, but I don't want you to go to any trouble or wear yourself out."

Arthur's smile widens and I spot the gleam in his eyes. "Nonsense, it would be wonderful to have the company."

I gather my things and lead Arthur back to Abbie and Duke. Abbie is giggling as she moves to touch her hand to Duke's paw and he pulls it away just before she gets there, like he's teasing her. I love hearing Abbie laugh and seeing her enjoying herself. I can't deprive her or Arthur of something that means so much. I sigh, resigned to the idea, reminding myself it's just one barbecue. "We'll eat anything, so whatever you like. I'm happy to bring something, but I'm not much of a cook."

"How about you handle dessert? You can pick up something you and Abbie would enjoy."

Duke is sitting at Abbie's feet as she rambles on about the flowers she added to her notebook. It's almost like he's listening.

"Abbie," I say in a loud voice, to get her attention, "I'm going to help Arthur train Duke tomorrow and he's invited us to a barbecue. Doesn't that sound like fun?"

"I think you'll enjoy looking at my flower garden," adds Arthur.

Abbie's eyes go wide. "You have a flower garden? How many types of flowers do you have?"

Arthur chuckles, placing his hat atop his head. "Oh, I have no idea. It seems like my wife, Rosie, had me plant hundreds of them."

Abbie darts off to retrieve a notebook, and Arthur turns to me.

"I lost Rosie in April," he says, tears clouding his eyes. "She was ill for just over two years, in and out of the hospital and the care center." Arthur takes a long breath. "After I did the gardening and chores around the house, I'd go and sit with her there each day. I hated that she had to be there." Tears dot his cheeks and he takes out his handkerchief and glances down at Duke, who has moved toward him. "It's just me and Duke now, my new buddy."

Two years clicks in my mind with what Arthur said about his blood pressure medication. His stress had been Rosie's declining health. I step closer to Arthur and place my hand on his shoulder. "I'm so sorry, Arthur. I know how difficult it is to lose someone you love, and I'm sure having you by her side eased Rosie's worries."

Arthur dabs at his eyes and bobs his head. "Needless to say, I'm sick of doctors, hospitals, all of it, so I do apologize for being a bit reluctant to come here this week."

I smile and squeeze his shoulder. "I'll take it as a compliment that you did then, Arthur. Maybe Duke was onto something when he introduced us."

Abbie makes her way back to us, and Arthur turns to her with a smile. "We *have* to go tomorrow, Mom. I have to record all the new species," she says, tapping her finger on her notebook.

"We'll be there," I reply, reassuring her with a smile. Seeing Abbie and Arthur like this warms my heart, as Abbie throws her stuff in her backpack and Arthur retrieves Duke's leash from her.

We walk to the parking lot together. He explains his house is near Washington Park, just on the other side of Main Street and gives me his address. Arthur tips his hat and says, "It was a pleasure to meet you, Abbie. We look forward to tomorrow."

Abbie's head bobs with enthusiasm, as she leans down to pet Duke. "I can't wait."

# CHAPTER 6

Early Sunday morning, the floor creaks with Abbie's footsteps. So much for sleeping in on my day off. I close my eyes in an attempt to rest a bit longer, but the thump of her feet up and down the hallway is impossible to ignore. I drag myself out of bed and to the shower and by the time I'm in the kitchen to pour my coffee, Abbie is outside.

After tossing in a load of laundry, I make my way outside and stand in Abbie's path. She sees me and plucks an earbud from one ear and blurts out, "Are you ready to go?" The excited gleam in her eyes tells me she can't wait.

"We're still too early. I need to finish the laundry, so how about some breakfast and then we'll run up to the bakery and pick up some dessert?"

Her shoulders slump, but she follows me back to the front door. While I'm putting together some scrambled eggs and toast, she packs and rechecks her backpack a few times, making sure she has plenty of pens and notebooks.

With our chores done, we head downtown and discover most of the charming little shops are closed on Sunday. It's probably best that I haven't had much spare time to explore them; with the state of my finances I'd rather not tempt myself. Many of the buildings are early brick structures, a few with the original faded lettering still on the side of them advertising long-closed merchants and many more decorated with colorful murals depicting the history of Millbury. Agriculture and timber, two staples of the area, are showcased in several, along with local attractions and landscapes.

Hanging baskets of flowers and benches with potted plants invite shoppers to stroll through the two square blocks that make up the downtown area. Restaurants, shops, and a few offices, along with a bookstore and café dominate the side of Center Street that runs parallel to Mill Creek. With their location, they offer coveted views of the creek for those who wish to dine alfresco on their patios. I make a mental note to visit Village Books & Café on the next Monday I have free.

Our destination, Sinful Sweets, is on Main Street and before we even get there, the aroma of baked sugar and sweet fruit drift from the bakery's open door and down the sidewalk. Charlotte, the owner, outfitted in a purple apron stretched across her plump midsection, introduces herself and greets us from behind the counter.

The woman with smiling brown eyes and permed gray hair hands us each a baking paper filled with a warm thumbprint cookie. "Those are made with my own marionberry jam." She smiles and leans on the display case. "You must be the new nurse at the center, Madison, right? I've heard so many good things about you from my regular customers, and Gladys, of course. We're delighted to have you in Millbury."

My eyes widen as I realize just how small Millbury really is. "It's a lovely town and we're happy to be here." I turn to Abbie, who's chewing her cookie, and say, "This is my daughter, Abbie."

Charlotte smiles at her and plucks another cookie from the tray. "Looks like you could use another. Lovely to meet you, dear."

Abbie thanks her, and we pick out a selection of cake squares, cupcakes, and cookies to take to Arthur's. Charlotte boxes them up and adds another box with a fresh marionberry pie. "On the house. My little way of welcoming you to our town."

"That's very kind of you. Good thing we're sharing with a friend. I don't think we could handle all of these treats ourselves." Abbie and I thank her again as we make our way back to the car.

Abbie finishes off the second cookie and turns to me with a smile. "This is the best place we've lived, Mom. Everyone is so nice here." I nod and smile, not wanting to discourage her, but at the same time not wanting her to get too attached.

\*\*\*

We take the bridge over Mill Creek and turn onto Arthur's quiet street. I scan the house numbers and pull into the driveway of the beautiful house with a huge porch and colorful blooms gracing the walkway. I don't know what I expected, but it certainly wasn't the grand home that stands before me. So many people, especially men, when they lose their spouses, begin to neglect not only their health but the maintenance and chores of everyday life. The loss can be so overwhelming and they're not able to cope with it. With Arthur's reluctance to see a doctor, I had thought he might be so overcome with grief that he'd be living in a run-down house that needed some attention. That was part of the reason I rationalized the visit and offered to help with Duke.

Abbie rushes from the car, slinging her backpack over her shoulder and darting to the front door. I follow with the bakery boxes and a stash of string cheese in my purse, admiring the pristine plants that line the walkway and pots of flowers decorating the steps leading up to the house.

Arthur welcomes us with a cheerful smile and ushers us inside. "Duke's in the backyard." He takes the bakery boxes from me and adds, "Feel free to leave your things here," pointing to a built-in cubby in the entry with hooks and a storage bench.

Abbie tightens her grip on her backpack, while I hang my purse on a peg and retrieve the cheese I had stashed in the front pocket for Duke. I give her my serious look and lower my voice. "Leave your pack here for now and you can come and get it when it's time to look at the garden."

She huffs and narrows her eyes, but relinquishes the heavy bag and follows me across the living area and into the light-filled kitchen, where Arthur is busy at the huge island counter. "Your home is beautiful, Arthur," I say, marveling at the gorgeous dark wooden floors and white cabinets.

As I turn to take in more of the kitchen, the sound of something crashing to the floor startles me. A flash of golden fur tells me the likely source of the commotion.

Arthur raises his voice. "Duke, sit." The dog pays him no attention and makes a beeline for me. "His tail is getting so long, I don't think he can control it, but I really wish he'd listen to me." Arthur moves to pick up the stack of plastic glasses and utensils Duke sent flying across the room.

With my eyes, I motion Abbie to help Arthur while palming my stick of string cheese. I hold my hand up high and move it toward my shoulder and say, "Duke, sit." His nose moves high and his backside hits the floor. "Good sit." I reward him with a nibble of cheese.

Abbie and Arthur situate the plasticware and join us, watching as Duke obeys my commands to sit and lie down.

Arthur smiles and says, "That's progress already."

"Dogs take their cues from our hand movements, so this is a great one to use for sit." I demonstrate again by holding the treat out and then bending my elbow and moving my hand to my shoulder. "Keep working with him on it with a treat and then when he's mastered it, don't always have a treat, keep him guessing. Always remember to use his name and reinforce the word for the command you are teaching."

Arthur nods his understanding. "I'm going to put him in the backyard for a few minutes while we get situated." He takes a bit of cheese, and Duke follows him out the porch door.

When he returns, I'm still in the kitchen admiring the workspace. "I love your home, Arthur."

"It was my mother-in-law's home and we remodeled it after she passed away. It's all Rosie's doing. She had an eye for beauty and design." He places a bowl in the refrigerator. "She was also a much better cook and entertainer than I will ever be, but I made her famous potato salad. Hoping I did it justice."

"I'm sure it will be terrific," I say, looking across to the open living space, not common in most Craftsman style homes, taking in the evidence of Rosie's touches in the subtle color palettes and floral influences. "I think Rosie missed her calling as a designer."

Arthur chuckles. "She loved to decorate and often did help others, but not as a business, just for fun. She drew up all the remodel plans and handled the whole thing herself. I was always busy at work, so left it all in her capable hands. She was an amazing woman."

"She did a marvelous job. I love the open design, it's perfect."

"We basically bulldozed this level and made a master suite down here, modernized everything, and took down as many walls as the engineer said we could. Rosie was planning for our old age and designing it so all our essentials were downstairs, and I'm sure glad we did. I don't relish the thought of trudging up those stairs and, truth be told, haven't been up there for months."

He gazes out to the back porch and patio. "We better get out there and check on the busy boy and make sure he's not digging."

I raise my hand and say, "I brought several pieces of my magic cheese."

Arthur turns to Abbie and says, "Maybe you could help me pour the drinks and let your mom get started with Duke. While he's occupied, you can start your flower research on the plants nearest the patio, so we don't distract the student." He gives Abbie a wink and she's all smiles.

Armed with my treats, I step outside into Arthur's stunning backyard. Duke spots me and comes bounding across the grass, rushing to greet me. I brace myself and when I see his paws leave the ground, turn my back to him. I keep doing this until he keeps his four feet on the ground and then reward him with a bite of cheese.

I walk to the furthest end of the yard around the corner, so the patio is out of our view, and begin using the cheese to teach Duke to sit. After dozens of times getting it right, I'm confident in his abilities and move to giving him the command for down. It takes a bit of doing, but he masters it. Duke's tongue hangs out of his mouth and it looks like he's smiling. It takes all his effort to sit still and not pop his rear off the ground, but he understands there is no reward unless he does it correctly. When he does well and gets a treat, he's so happy and his eyes lock with mine. When I see the love in them, I feel so connected to him. It reminds me of when I was a kid and spent hours with Sparky, teaching him to do tricks.

Remembering Sparky makes me think of my parents. The three of us had such fun with that dog. Dad had grown up with dogs, so he taught me how to train Sparky and make him focus on me. He wanted Sparky to be my dog, my best friend. Mom sometimes even let me slide on doing my homework when I first got home, so I could spend time with Sparky, playing in the yard. He made us laugh all the time and was such an important part of our little family. Those were the best of days.

After working in the sun for an hour, I feel sweat form at the back of my neck and forehead, and I guide Duke back to the patio area. We demonstrate for Arthur, and Duke doesn't disappoint, delighting in the praise he receives.

Abbie is focused on the flowerbed along the fence and pays us no attention as she takes photos and records each new find in her notebook.

"Let's work on making sure Duke will come to you when you call him," I say and hand Arthur several small bites of cheese to hold.

Arthur watches while I show him how to get Duke excited about coming to him and caution him not to call Duke if he's angry or if Duke is going to get in trouble, since that ruins the dog's willingness to come when called. Arthur decides to use the simplest of commands, and I watch as he shouts, "Duke, come." They go back and forth across the yard, the puppy enjoying all of the attention and bite after bite of the cheese he adores as a reward when he does as he's asked.

I leave the two of them to keep practicing and wander over to the clump of flowers Abbie is recording. "How's it going?"

Her flushed cheeks bulge with a huge grin between them. "He's got tons of flowers I need to add to my list. It's going to take me forever to record all of them." The sun highlights the gold flecks in her dark brown eyes.

"I think you should take a break and cool off. Have something to drink and we'll see if Arthur has some sunscreen. I didn't bring any."

She rolls her eyes and keeps scribbling. A few minutes later, Arthur and Duke come from around the corner, Duke panting and Arthur's cheeks rosy. "I'm ready for a cold drink. Anyone care to join me?"

I drag Abbie over to the patio, where the iced tea, lemonade, and water await us. Arthur tells me he thinks there is some sunscreen in the guest bathroom upstairs and gives me directions.

As I go through the porch door, Abbie is telling Arthur the names of all the flowers she has recorded and showing him her photos. Duke is tuckered out and resting at Abbie's feet in the shade of the table. Duke's proximity to her warms my heart. They're never far apart and seem to calm each other. His attention diverts her need for constant movement and he has endless patience when it comes to listening to her.

I take the wooden staircase and wander past the bedrooms upstairs, noticing the furnishings covered with a layer of dust. Rosie used more of the soft barely-there pastels in the paint and color schemes. The effect is simple, yet elegant. I find the stylish and modern guest bathroom and open the cabinets. Tufts of lint and dust fly through the air at my disturbance.

I dig through a few bins and unearth a handful of suncare products, many of which are old and expired. I put them all in one of the organizer baskets in the cupboard and take them downstairs.

Arthur and Abbie are chatting, sipping lemonade. I pour an iced tea and take a chair at the table, handing Abbie a tube of cream. "Put this on and make sure you get your face."

"There's a powder room right off the porch by the mudroom," offers Arthur, gesturing at the house. With my head, I gesture toward the door and with exaggerated slow movements full of reluctance, Abbie takes the sunscreen and slogs to the porch.

"If it's okay with you, I'm going to toss these expired ones. You should really wear sunscreen, too, you know? Especially all the time you spend gardening."

"I wear my trusty hat. I don't like all those chemicals."

"I'll find you one that's zinc based without all the chemicals. Deal?" I ask, raising my brows. "They have hats made from fabric that has UV protection. That would help."

He grins and says, "You sound like Rosie, looking out for me."

"I know you don't like going to the doctor, but there's a great dermatologist that comes to Millbury each Monday. He uses my space at the center since I'm off on Mondays. You should go see him and get a skin cancer screening."

He shrugs, but doesn't say he won't go. "You can set that up for me next time I'm in to see you?"

"I'm happy to," I say, refilling both of our glasses.

Moments later, we hear the beautiful melody of "A Thousand Years," one of Abbie's favorite instrumentals. I gasp and start to get up from my chair. Arthur puts his hand over mine. "Let her play. It's good to have the house filled with music again."

"She should have asked permission, I'm sorry." I shake my head, embarrassed by Abbie's lack of manners. "Did Rosie play?"

He nods and shuts his eyes, soaking in the lovely music. He leans his head back against the tall chair and smiles. I take a long breath and let the song calm me. Abbie is gifted and, despite not practicing for months, sounds terrific. The last notes of the song echo outside and she begins another. She is obsessed with Yurima, a Korean pianist, and begins to play "Kiss the Rain," which I recognize from his album.

The soothing music and sunshine in the gorgeous park-like setting make for a perfect day. It's been a long time since I've spent a day like this, just relaxing and not worrying about Abbie, stressing about money, or thinking about work. I like Millbury and working with the seniors at the center. My last post consisted of home visits to patients and having my own clinical setting is much better. As I listen to Abbie play, I remember I need to see if she can get into the music program when I visit the high school to get her registered. She missed out on that in Wyoming and I'd like her to be able to be part of it here, even if it's just for a time.

# CHAPTER 7

I promised myself, once I was settled, I'd get into an exercise routine and, with it being Monday, it's the perfect day to start. I get up early and leave Abbie sleeping, placing a note by her bedside to let her know I'm on a walk. I slip on my ratty old tennis shoes, their soles worn smooth, and head toward town. There's a fresh smell in the air thanks to a sprinkling of rain last night.

As I approach the main road, I meet Gladys and another woman walking in the opposite direction. "Morning, Madison. How are you settling in?" she asks.

"Hi, Gladys. It's a gorgeous morning and we're doing just fine, thanks."

She turns to the woman with her and says, "This is the new nurse practitioner I was telling you about. Madison, meet my walking buddy, Lois."

"Nice to meet you, Lois," I say, taking a few steps forward. "I've got to run, ladies, enjoy your day."

"Oh, I meant to tell you, Jeff will be home this week. So, don't be alarmed if you see activity next door," Gladys shouts as I keep walking. I wave my hand in understanding and hurry to make the turn out of the park, expecting she'll be telling Jeff I'm single and anxious to meet him.

I chuckle as I head to the center of town and Millbury Creek, where I learned there is a paved walking path that runs alongside of it. I follow it in the direction of the reservoir and breathe in the sweet smell of flowers growing among the leafy foliage near the creek. The pleasant sound of the water trickling over rocks is my steady companion and muffles the soft sound of my footfalls on the pathway. The all but non-existent cushioning in my shoes does little to protect my feet against the errant gravel and rocks scattered across the walkway.

As I follow the curve of the creek, I spot a man running toward me and move to the side. Sweat streaming down his face and collecting in a dark V-shape at his neckline, he smiles and nods. A serious runner, with toned and muscular legs and the wrinkled, bony, almost skeletal face that comes from loss of fat under the skin due to intense exercise. I return his silent greeting and continue my pace, confident I'll never suffer from such a problem.

The colorful flowers and varieties of plants I encounter remind me of Abbie. If she knew about them, she'd probably want to come with me, but I relish having a sliver of time all to myself. Millbury is quite idyllic, with the clean light of morning glinting off the moving water and the surrounding greenery and blooms. I love this time of morning, when the town is quiet, preparing for the day.

None of the three places I've been posted thus far have felt like they could be home. This is the first town that's given me a hint of a connection, a real community. It's welcoming and friendly, although a little small; it reminds me of an old pair of comfy slippers. Nothing fancy, but warm and snuggly and cozy. I could get used to a place like this. I fantasize about the idea of finding somewhere like Millbury to call home until I come to the next curve in the trail.

I check my watch and realize I won't be able to make it all the way to the reservoir at this speed. Reality settles over me and extinguishes the tiny spark of excitement at the thought of a permanent home.

But I can't stay here. I can't stay anywhere.

I turn around and vow to work on increasing my pace each day with the goal of getting to and from the reservoir in less than ninety minutes.

On the way back I take a quick detour at the bridge and stop by Creekside Coffee and reward myself with a large breve and take the free muffin they offer home for Abbie. I swallow a sip of the warm coffee and the rich frothed cream. The first taste of the day is always delicious, but this is heavenly.

I turn and look down Arthur's street as I pass by it, but don't see any sign of him or Duke. They're probably in the backyard working in the flower garden. The balls of my feet are burning by the time I reach my door. I slip the key in the lock and give it a slow turn, listening for signs of life, but it's still quiet.

I leave the bag with the muffin and tiptoe down the hallway to the shower. By the time I emerge ready for the day, Abbie is up and has eaten her muffin. She doesn't require my usual prodding to get dressed this morning, since she's anxious to go to Arthur's and continue cataloging flowers and see Duke. By the time she got around to asking me last night, Arthur had already indulged her request to spend the day at his house. I couldn't bring myself to wipe the happiness from either of their faces.

This is the first place I've worked where I've had a weekday off and it's convenient to be able to take care of errands. It feels a bit like the thrill of playing hooky. Working Saturdays, with it being a shorter shift and quieter, isn't as bad as I envisioned when I agreed to take the position, especially when I get Mondays to myself.

Arthur gave me a local's tip yesterday and instead of driving to Salem for my driver's license, I'm heading to a small town in the other direction. Arthur tells me it's where everyone goes to avoid the traffic and lines associated with a visit to the capital city. First, though, I've got an appointment at the high school to get Abbie set for the new year.

I find the office with three minutes to spare for my eight o'clock appointment. A middle-aged woman with a cheerful smile introduces herself as Ms. Lucas, Abbie's guidance counselor. She leads the way to her office and produces a stack of forms for me to fill out and sign.

She reviews the core classes Abbie will be in and highlights the electives available for freshmen. I point to the music classes. "Abbie has some struggles with anxiety, which manifest as obsessions and usually pacing if she's upset. She loves music and is a talented pianist, so it's important to me that she have some opportunities to play and be involved in the music program."

Ms. Lucas nods her head and taps her keyboard. "It looks like we can slot her into band class, and I'll send the teacher, Mr. Freeman, a message to let him know she's a pianist. We also have a school musical in the fall and spring, and she could volunteer to play the piano for it. It's after school and they usually start working on it in late September."

"I'll talk to her about it. Because of some of her behaviors and interests, she doesn't always fit in. She keeps to herself for the most part, so I'm not sure she'd be willing, but I'll encourage her."

I finish filling out the paperwork and we discuss Abbie's grades, which are a bit above average, but nothing stellar. Ms. Lucas reviews the forms and her eyebrows arch. "You don't have an emergency contact listed or anyone who can pick Abbie up if we can't contact you?"

I shrug. "We're new to town. I don't really know very many people."

"We really need someone." She runs her finger across the line where I marked her father as deceased, but doesn't say anything. Her serious look tells me I'm not leaving until I put something on the form.

I scribble down the center's name and main phone number. "There you go," I say, sliding the paper back to her.

She bobs her head in approval, satisfied that the line is no longer blank, and places all the forms in a folder. Before I leave, she gives me a student handbook and new student information package, along with Abbie's tentative schedule. "There's a freshman orientation for students and parents in August, right before school starts."

I thank her and make my way to the exit, toting the load of information in my arms. The high school is only a few minutes from the mobile home park, and after dumping the paperwork on the kitchen counter and filling my water bottle, I hurry back to my car.

As soon as I get to the end of the driveway, a voice I recognize bursts from the shrubbery in front of the office. "Yoo-hoo, Madison," says Gladys. I turn and see her pointing at the trailer next to mine. "Jeff's home now. You ought to go over and introduce yourself."

"I'm in a bit of a hurry right now, but I'll make sure and say hello, soon." I wave and step on the gas before she has time to respond.

The drive takes twenty minutes, and after a pleasant experience at the registration counter, filling out paperwork and obtaining my Oregon license, along with registering my car, I can't resist an inviting little café for a coffee and a homemade scone.

Like Millbury, everyone here is friendly and the coffee is superb. I check my watch and decide to take some time to stop at the outlet mall I saw when I came into town. I'm in desperate need of a new pair of shoes.

I stroll through the outdoor mall, noting some stores that carry clothes Abbie might like for school. At one of several shoe stores, I find a pair of shoes on sale I like that are comfortable enough for work but I could wear all the time, and a pair of tennis shoes for walking that are on clearance. I hand the clerk my credit card, while I cringe at the thought of adding to my financial woes, but can't deal with sore feet, especially with as much time as I spend on them at work.

I toss the bag in the back of my SUV and turn the key, only to hear a clicking sound, but the engine doesn't start. "No, no, no," I whisper. "Please start." I try it again with the same result. I grit my teeth and groan, resisting the urge to scream. "I should have never stopped to get my shoes."

I use my phone to search for tow services and repairs shops. After spending a few minutes reading reviews and comparing a few, I call Abbie. The phone rings and rings, and I hope she isn't so engrossed in the garden she'll ignore it. I close my eyes and will her to answer.

"Mom," she says, with her most peeved tone.

"Abbie, my car broke down. Could you put Arthur on for me?"

I hear all sorts of muffled sounds, and a few minutes later, Arthur's kind voice. "Madison, are you okay?"

"I'm fine. I took care of my license and registration and am stuck at the outlet mall right by the highway. My car won't start. I'm sorry to bother you, but I was hoping you might be able to recommend the best auto repair place. I don't want to get ripped off and I'm not sure what to do."

"Not to worry. We'll pop over and pick you up. I've got a great mechanic and will give him a call and see what he can do for you."

"You don't need to do that. I've got tow service coverage on my insurance. I'm just not sure where to have it towed."

"Oh, that's terrific. They can take it to Mitch." He gives me the address and name of the shop, along with a phone number to a local tow service. "I'll call Mitch and let him know your car will be arriving. Abbie and I will load up Duke and be on our way in a few minutes."

"I can ride with the tow truck or find a ride share. I hate being a bother."

He reassures me and I disconnect, letting out a breath. Tears sting my eyes, but I blink them back, hating to feel weak. When I was home and had my parents around to rely on for advice or help, it never felt like I was fragile. They were just there, always on hand. Ever since we left Ohio and without them, I've felt unsure. I no longer have anyone to ask and want to handle things myself, but don't always have the knowledge or the confidence to do so. I tap in the number for the tow service and, after grabbing what I need from the car, proceed to wait. A few deep breaths later, my hands quit shaking.

Tow insurance was a necessity at my last posts. I had to drive to patients' houses all over the county, and if I couldn't get there, I didn't get paid. Luckily, I forgot to cancel it when we moved here.

Arthur and the tow truck arrive within a few minutes of each other. I climb into the leather passenger seat of Arthur's immaculate sedan and notice Duke in the back with Abbie. For once, her earbuds are missing, and Duke's head is in her lap. Soft classical music emanates from the radio as Arthur steers us out of the parking lot.

Abbie doesn't handle a change to her routine well. Seeing her content and relaxed, stroking Duke's ears, is an unexpected relief. She and Duke have bonded in such a short period of time. It's odd to see her without earbuds. I make note of the station Arthur is tuned to, hoping if we listen to it in the car, we might enjoy a few outings without Abbie in her own world, shut off from me.

"I gave Mitch your cell phone number and he promised to call you as soon as he knows what's wrong with the car," Arthur says, making the turn to the highway that takes us to Millbury.

"I appreciate that. I hope it's something simple." I lean back against the comfortable seat and let out a breath, bringing my wrist to eye-level to check the time.

Arthur turns toward me. "That's quite a handsome watch you have there. A bit large, but a nice one."

"It was my dad's. I treasure it." I run my fingers across the face of it.

"We've got plenty of leftovers, so I'll just drive you back to my house and we'll have dinner. Then, I can drive you both home."

I smile at his offer. "We can walk, it's not that far. I'm thankful our place is so close to work. I can get by without a car for a bit."

"I've got two cars; you're certainly welcome to borrow one while yours is in the shop."

I shake my head. "I'll be fine, Arthur. If I get in a jam, I'll take you up on it, but I could use the exercise."

When we get back to Arthur's I take Duke and Abbie into the backyard. Before I know it, she's got her notebook open and scribbling, while Duke is lounging in the shade, watching. I take a deep breath and let the beauty of the trees and flowers calm my mind. The last thing I need is a car repair bill. I scrape the bottom of the chair when I move to sit down at the table, and Duke's ears prick. In seconds, he's up and running across the yard.

I turn in the nick of time before he can plant both of his front feet on me and keep turning away so he doesn't get my attention until he's calmer. Abbie takes no notice of either of us. After making Duke sit for me, without any rewards, I lead him to the lawn.

I give Duke a few more commands, but need some treats for the training to be effective.

I wander through the backdoor and spy Arthur sleeping in his recliner. It's getting close to the dinner hour and guilt washes over me that Abbie was here all day. Duke's training will have to wait. I tiptoe into the kitchen and go about getting the leftovers from the refrigerator and making a semblance of dinner for the three of us.

As I'm finishing cutting up the rest of the watermelon, my cell phone rings. Mitch from the garage tells me I need a new starter and we agree on a price just as Arthur steps into the kitchen.

"Oh, my, I must have slept longer than I thought," he says, apologetic. "You've got dinner all set for us."

"It's the least I can do after sticking you with Abbie all day. Sorry, I bet my phone woke you."

He puts a gentle hand on my shoulder. "Having Abbie around has been wonderful, so don't fret about it. Take a breath. It's all going to be okay."

I nod, reluctant to say anything for fear my voice will break. It's been a long time since someone has reassured me that things will be okay. Arthur has a calmness and wisdom about him that reminds me of my dad. I finish the watermelon, regain my composure and say, "I can't tell you how much I appreciate you, Arthur. I don't know what I would have done without you today. Some days being on my own is hard, and today you came to my rescue."

He chuckles as he walks to the backdoor. "I have no doubt you would have figured everything out, my dear." He opens the door and gazes from the porch, watching Abbie chat with Duke, lying in the grass. "Dinner's almost ready, come on in, you two."

Duke springs into action and rushes to the house, where Arthur grabs him to wipe his paws on a towel before permitting him past the porch. Abbie follows, lugging her backpack, her face shiny with sweat.

I slip my arm around her shoulders. "You look like you've put in a long day. How about you use the powder room and wash your hands and face. I'll fix you something cold to drink."

She dumps her bag in a corner of the porch and says, "That sounds good. I'm starving."

Arthur fixes Duke his dinner, which he eats with gusto, while I get everything on the table and pour lemonade over ice. Abbie digs into her plate and in between bites tells us she only has two more flowerbeds to catalog.

Arthur wipes his mouth and clears his throat. "Have you two been to the Oregon Garden? It's a few miles down the road."

I shake my head, and Abbie's eyes sparkle with interest.

"I've read about it online and want to go. It's huge, Mom. Remember I told you about it while we were driving here?"

To be honest, she talked so much about plants on our way here, I tuned her out and don't remember anything about the Oregon Garden, but I nod my head regardless.

"Rosie and I are members and our membership includes guest passes, so if you are interested, I'd love to take you there. Maybe next weekend or next Monday, when you're off, Madison?"

A huge smile fills Abbie's face and she nods her head with excitement.

Arthur's smile expands and he adds, "It's pet friendly, so Duke can come with us."

I wish Arthur hadn't brought up the idea in front of Abbie, but I try to hide my disappointment. There's no way to refuse her the opportunity. I know Arthur is just being kind, but it feels like things are moving too fast. I should have thought through my offer to visit and help with Duke. It's too late now. "Well," I say, glancing at the dog, full from his dinner, sprawled on the floor, "that's very generous of you, Arthur, thank you."

With dinner finished, Arthur persuades Abbie to play the piano, and I help him tidy the kitchen. As we work side by side, he leans close and says, "If Abbie enjoys the garden, she might be able to volunteer there. She has such enthusiasm for plants and flowers, she could put it to good use there. I know the board members and staff and could connect her with them, if you think it's a good idea."

The thought of Abbie having a safe place to explore her latest passion and spend her summer days relieves the angst I've been feeling about finding her something to do. Something I can afford, which, with the latest addition of a car repair, isn't much. "That sounds like an incredible idea. I'll talk to her about it and see if she thinks she could do it. She can be, uh . . . I'm sure you've observed her tendency to fixate on something and it's hard to budge her from it. I've noticed when she's with Duke, she's more relaxed, not pacing or anxious, which is a relief."

Arthur nods as he folds a dishtowel. "As you say, she's consumed with her endeavor. It's hard to get her attention or get her to take a break, but I can think of no better place or environment for her to indulge her zest for all things floral. Rosie was instrumental in the creation of their rose garden. It's quite lovely. I know they are always looking for volunteers."

"I'll talk to her tonight and, if she wants to do it, I'll let you know and you can arrange a meeting." I move my head in the direction of the piano. "Shall we work on a couple more exercises with Duke while Abbie finishes her performance?"

He chuckles and grabs a stick of string cheese from the refrigerator.

It's been a long and chaotic day, but Arthur coming to my rescue made it less so. I know Arthur's trying to help, and appreciate his kindness, but I hate relying on someone. Truth is, there's a part of me that loves the idea of having a shoulder to lean on, but I don't want to get too dependent on someone else, especially when I know we won't be here long. I also don't want Arthur to become too attached to us. He's already suffered a devastating loss and he doesn't need another one.

# CHAPTER 8

## Duke

Families are interesting and, like my mother explained so long ago, you don't have to be born into one to be part of one. Families care about each other, sacrifice for one another, and are always there in good times and bad.

As I witness the interactions between Arthur and Madison, it's easy to see they both long for what they've lost—a family. I know that feeling all too well. There's no reason all of us can't be a family. Arthur's my family now and we have room for Madison and Abbie. That's the beautiful thing about sharing the love in your heart—it doesn't mean you have less of it. Love is the only thing that grows the more you give away.

Arthur and Madison are so good for each other and so much stronger together. That's what family is all about. The phone rings and I know it's Arthur's nephew. I recognize Sonny's deep voice on the other end of the phone and settle in at Arthur's feet.

Arthur's voice is infused with enthusiasm as he chats and brings Sonny up to date on the week's happenings. "We've had a marvelous week and even squeezed in an outing to the gardens with Madison and Abbie."

Concern tinges Sonny's tone as he asks Arthur a bunch of questions about Madison and what he knows about her. The cheerful smile on Arthur's face fades, replaced by the furrowing of his brow and a tensing in his jaw. He listens to Sonny drone on and then takes a deep breath. "I'm not easily bamboozled. Being a judge for all those years, I can spot a con artist six ways from Sunday and I know Madison is a good person."

In all the weekends I've listened to Arthur's calls with Sonny, I'd never heard that bite in his voice that's evident today. His shoulders sag as he adds, "I know you're trying to protect me, but really, it's unnecessary. I'm still quite capable."

He hangs up the phone and shakes his head. "Sometimes he treats me like a feeble old man," he says to himself.

I wonder why Sonny is so suspicious about Madison or for that matter why he doubts Arthur's perception of her. From what I've seen, Arthur is more than competent. Compared to Pete and Henry, who sometimes forget it's their turn and have a hard time keeping score, he's much more aware, much quicker. Henry and Pete struggle to go up and down the stairs, and Arthur's in good shape now, always active, and takes excellent care of the garden. I know people want to protect their families, but sometimes you have to let them make their own choices. Arthur is certainly old enough to be trusted.

Our mother taught us about the importance of keeping ourselves clean, how our whiskers above our eyes could detect the tiniest movement in the air and signal our brains to react to protect ourselves, and to be wary of food that we find, always using our noses to investigate and sniff for danger. She explained these and other important things we would need to know and told us it was then up to us make our own choices and our own way in life. Arthur has much more experience than I had when my mom trusted me to find my own family. If humans used all the time they wasted worrying and, instead, enjoyed what was right in front of them, they'd be much happier. They're far more capable than they think.

Dogs never worry and that's why we're always ready to play and have fun. I'm teaching Arthur to do more fun things and love seeing his eyes sparkle with cheer and hearing him laugh when we play. I think he's had too much weighing on him these last years and has forgotten how to enjoy himself.

Normally, Saturdays are when Arthur is happiest. His phone call with Sonny brightens his mood and never fails to widen his smile. It's unlike Arthur to be upset and the slouch of his shoulders matches his state of mind today.

It seems to me that Sonny's doubts and questions today have wounded Arthur's pride. The loss of Rosie left Arthur vulnerable and, despite his outward bravado, fragile. He's a man who has spent his entire life solving problems, resolving disputes, and dispensing justice. His sound judgment and intelligence run through every fiber of his being and to have them questioned shakes him to the core. His hands tremble as he brings his coffee cup to his lips.

I inch even closer to him and rest my head on his knee, reminding him how much I love him and need him. If Sonny could only see how much happiness Madison and Abbie bring to Arthur, he'd understand. They make Arthur's smile light up just like Sonny's calls do on Saturday mornings.

And Abbie is relaxing too.

The first time I saw her outside of the center, she was pacing back and forth, and I picked up on the waves of anxiety surrounding her. Sometimes, something comes over me and I get so excited I have to zoom around the yard, running in a big circle a few times. Then, I'm calmer. Maybe that's what it's like for Abbie, and when she paces, she settles down.

But I still feel worried about Madison. I thought she'd relax once Abbie did, but there's a tension in her. She's always distracted, always rushing. She hasn't accepted this family yet.

When we went to the Oregon Garden, so that Abbie could enjoy the flowers, and see about volunteering, Arthur asked Madison about herself, but at first, she didn't say much. The variety of fragrances I detected in the gardens was overwhelming and I was concentrating on separating them. The delicate florals and the rich earth mingled with the scents of people and food. Abbie was already nose deep in the rose garden, and Madison said she felt overwhelmed, that it was in moments like this that she missed having a family around to help.

"Where is your family?" Arthur asked.

Madison's smile faded. "I lost my parents a few years ago," she said. "My husband, Jeremy, Abbie's dad, died when she was just a baby. She doesn't even have a memory of him." Tears clouded her eyes and she took a sip of the coffee in her hands.

Arthur patted Madison's arm. "I'm so very sorry, that had to be horrible losing him at such a young age," he said, and shook his head. "I can't imagine it. I'm struggling and Rosie and I had a lifetime together. Not to mention, you with a baby to care for."

In that moment, while I was tucked under her chair, Madison's scent reminded me of Arthur's in the evenings when he's going to bed. That musty, heavy smell of emptiness surrounded her. She'd suffered the loss of her family, much like Arthur.

"My parents died in a car crash almost three years ago. That's when I felt like my life began to unravel," she admitted.

Arthur nodded and looked across at the stunning roses. The breeze carried their sweet aroma and it softened the melancholy emanating from both of them. They both reached to pet my head at the same time, and I felt their grief. It made me happy to see them look at me and smile.

"That's the perfect way to describe what I've been feeling since Rosie left. Even before that when she had to move to the care center. Everything was beyond my control." Arthur's fingers pushed deeper into my neck.

Some of the tension they both carry eased as they opened up to each other. I thought, *Maybe they're starting to trust each other a bit more. Can't they see they both need each other?*

There was a happy tone in their voices from then on, and Madison even found the courage to ask Arthur if he'd be an emergency contact for Abbie's school.

We're not meant to be alone. Dogs and humans are alike in that aspect. Like our masters, we're happiest when we feel needed and loved. That's why Arthur and I get along so well: we both need each other. Nothing makes me happier than helping Arthur by easing his worries and making him feel less alone. I knew he was kind and gentle the first time I gazed into his eyes, and he's done nothing but reinforce my belief.

He was so heartbroken that day we met and being able to elicit a smile from him was the best feeling. Sharing my joy with Arthur, greeting him with boundless excitement, making him laugh, and comforting him when I know he's not feeling well or missing his beloved wife, gives me immense satisfaction. Arthur takes excellent care of me, making sure I always have plenty to eat, fresh water to drink, outings and toys, a warm place to sleep, and most of all the love and care I crave. Ours is a relationship of pure and mutual adoration.

I think back to the two months I spent with Arthur before we met Madison that morning I jumped on her at the center. I knew, even that first day, that they would be good for each other. He's been more cheerful and upbeat since they've been coming to the house and he's been opening up to her. He talks to me all the time, but she can tell him things I can't. When Abbie's anxious, I can focus her attention on me, and it calms her. Madison's happier and more relaxed when Arthur's around, and I can't get enough of that cheese she always has with her.

But I do sense she's still holding something back. There's a part of herself she hides from the rest of the world. Maybe she just needs more time to trust us. I think we all met for a reason—we need each other.

# CHAPTER 9

## Madison

Today is Abbie's first day volunteering at the garden. With Arthur's help it's all coming together, and I couldn't be more grateful. Since there's no local bus service, he's even agreed to transport Abbie and pick her up each day. She's scheduled for Tuesdays, Thursdays, and Fridays. That means she's only on her own on Wednesdays, which eases my guilt a bit. I've let Gladys know that Abbie will be home on her own and she assured me she'll keep an eye on her.

Not only is Arthur her personal taxi driver, but he's invited her to stay at his house for the two hours before I get home from work when she might have been alone. Despite my doubts about the idea of letting Abbie get too attached, his kindness and calm wisdom are good for both of us. I know I don't have to worry about her. I don't want to take advantage of Arthur's generosity, but it's also good for him to have some company.

I've never gotten close to any of my patients and most of them were homebound and not living a full life. My interactions with them were limited to my visits. Arthur is different. His mere presence reassures me, as Duke does for Abigail. Knowing he served as a judge and seeing the way people like Bill admire him, gives me even more comfort. I have absolute trust in him, as I think he does in me. I haven't had someone I could rely on to help me with Abbie since I lost my parents, and knowing he's there, I've felt some of the worry lift from me.

Being off on Mondays, and the clinic used for specialty doctor visits, my Tuesday is booked solid with patients. Regency Health still hasn't assigned a receptionist to the clinic, so we make do with a clipboard where everyone signs in with the time they arrive and note if they are a walk-in patient or one with an appointment. Despite a couple of misunderstandings, it's been working well, but today it's been more of a challenge. In spite of explaining the schedule is full, the walk-in patients don't understand there are no time slots and choose to wait, counting on no-shows.

I don't have time to keep explaining it or I'll get further behind. To top it off, a handful of patients with appointments show up late because they couldn't get a ride. My heart breaks for them, as I know it's not easy for them to get here and rescheduling them to another day means they may not return at all. I forgo lunch and squeeze in two of the latecomers.

When I dart out to fill my coffee cup in the early afternoon, I find Maxine, who I saw first thing this morning, still waiting for her ride to collect her. She's holding a book, but barely keeping her eyes open, slouched in her seat. She hasn't been feeling well, getting over a bout of pneumonia, and needs her rest.

I shake my head and dart back to my office, hoping to pack in the rest of the people in the waiting room before the end of the day. I hate rushing anyone, but a few of the patients only need their blood pressure checked and recorded, so I hurry them out the door without our usual chats. At four o'clock, when I should be on my way to Arthur's, I still have two people to see.

Thankfully, one is only a recheck of a wound I stitched and is uneventful. The last patient is Lena, who suffers from horrible arthritis and has a terrible time walking. She cuts holes in the cheap tennis shoes she buys so her gnarled toe joints poke through the tops.

She's a sweetheart of a woman and I can't bear the thought of turning her away. Before I bring her into the exam room, I make a quick call to Arthur and explain I'm running late, but will pick up dinner on my way to his house, as a peace offering for the inconvenience. Lena's here to discuss one of the new biologic medications that is given by injection.

I offer her a chair, rather than the exam table. "So, did you decide to try it?" I ask, pointing at the dog-eared brochure she is holding with a shaky hand.

With a tentative voice she says, "It sounds promising, but I'm not sure I can give myself the injection."

"The new style pens they use are quite easy, but I'll do the first one for you and then we'll have you come in for the next and practice. You can come as often as you need to until you're comfortable. How's that sound?"

Relief floods her face as tears spill onto her cheeks. "That would be wonderful, Madison. I've been working myself into knots worrying about it."

I verify her supplemental insurance information and give her information on getting assistance from the pharmaceutical company to help defray the costs. "Call them to sign up for their program and then I'll contact your insurance company to get this approved. I'll be in touch with you and once you get the medication, we'll set up a time for your first injection."

"I can't believe this is so easy. I've been a wreck all day, dreading this. Thanks again for your help."

I usher Lena to the lobby to wait for her ride and accept her hug of thanks.

I organize my desk while I put in a call to Moon Pie and order two of their take-n-bake pizzas and a garden salad, thankful for their ten dollar Tuesday special. I gather my things and lock the office, surprised to see Lena sitting on a bench in the entryway, waiting.

With a shy wave, she says, "My friend who is picking me up is delayed. How long can I wait here?"

I spot the apprehension in her face and say, "I'm happy to give you a ride."

I offer her a hand up and she says, "What would I do without you? You're an angel." Listening to her reminds me of my grandma. She always called me an angel when I was a little girl. Lena has her same sweet disposition and is a bit hunched over, like Grandma Gertie.

I help her into my small SUV, which starts right up after its brief stay with Mitch. Lena's place isn't too far out of my way. Once I see her to her door, I hurry to collect the pizzas and make it to Arthur's just before five thirty.

Piano music and Duke greet me at the front door. I hang my purse on the hook and proceed to the kitchen to preheat the oven. I slip into one of the comfortable leather chairs in the great room, and Arthur gives me a smile, tilting his head in the direction of Abbie at the piano. After the hectic day I've had, it feels wonderful to sit and the peaceful music acts like a sedative. In this comfortable room, my pulse slows and my shoulders loosen as I do nothing but enjoy the sound.

I notice several adhesive bandage strips on Arthur's arms and one on his cheek and remember he had an appointment with the dermatologist yesterday. I point at my cheek and raise my brows to him. He gives me an okay sign and smiles.

Abbie finishes her repertoire. "That was beautiful, Abbie," I say. "I needed that after the day I've had. How was your first day at the garden?"

She chatters nonstop as she follows me into the kitchen, perching against the counter as I set the table and transfer the salad into a glass bowl. "I was assigned to the Pet-Friendly Garden today and learned about a ton of plants that are nontoxic to dogs and cats. Olivia, the master gardener, told me how much dogs love the smell of alyssum, and I remembered Duke always putting his nose in it here in the backyard."

She sighs and adds, "I don't know how I'm going to have time to catalog all the plants I'm finding, but Olivia gave me a ton of information and said I could take any of the materials from the education center I wanted."

I haven't seen her this excited and full of smiles in over two years. Ever since she's been spending time with Arthur and Duke, she's been so much happier and her pacing episodes have diminished. I know having more of a routine and not spending so much of her time alone has to be partly responsible. I haven't been able to alleviate much of the stress we've been living with until now. She has access to a piano, which is another key to her well-being. I had begun to doubt all the doctors who assured me she'd grow out of it or the episodes would decrease if she found a way to deal with her anxiety.

Seeing her progress, I'm not sure how I'm going to be able to take her away from all of this. It makes me worry what will happen to her when we leave. She won't have the security of Arthur and Duke forever and I can't bear the thought of having her struggle again. Will all this progress she's made be for naught?

My heart flutters with happiness as I listen to her describe more of the plants she worked with today. "I had never seen catnip until today. A lady brought her cat with her, on a leash, and the cat loved it. She couldn't make it stay away from the foliage." Abbie giggles like she used to when she was younger.

Arthur steps into the kitchen and says, "Do I have time to get in a bit of watering before dinner?"

"You've got about twenty minutes," I say, sliding the pizzas into the oven. He plucks his new wide-brimmed fabric hat, which I suggested he buy, from the hook near the door and scuttles out to the porch.

"Have you heard from Cody lately? I wanted to tell him about my new job." Abbie's eyes sparkle with enthusiasm.

I turn my attention to the oven. "Not lately. Remember, he's not always able to send emails. His location could be quite remote."

Abbie frowns. "When do you think he'll be home? How will he know where to find us?"

"It will probably be sometime next year before he's done with his assignment. He's working hard and can't be distracted. Remember, we talked about this before."

She sticks out her lip, like she did when she was little. "I know, it's just, well, sometimes I miss him."

"I know, sweetie, but he's doing important work and, don't forget, it's top-secret and we can't discuss it."

Her bangs flutter with the heavy breath she expels. "It's already been a long time. I thought he'd be done by now."

The porch door thumps closed, and I see Arthur stepping from it and down to the patio. He must have forgotten something and came back inside without me noticing.

"Dinner's almost ready. Go wash up and then run outside and tell Arthur to come in." I turn my back on her to check the pizzas, hearing Abbie clomp across the floor to the powder room.

Turning, I look over my shoulder out the windows of the porch and exhale. I see Arthur trying to keep Duke out of the spray from the hose. I wonder how much of our conversation he overheard.

# CHAPTER 10

Yesterday was another busy day at work and I only managed to check on Abbie a few times by phone. She spent the entire day working on her plant notebook, eating leftover pizza for lunch, and her irritated tone each time I called conveyed her annoyance with me for interrupting her work. It made me chuckle and also made me realize she's growing up and adjusting to our life in Millbury.

With the card group moving their Wednesday pastime to the center, Arthur stopped in my office for his blood pressure readings, which were normal. I checked his wounds from the dermatologist and applied ointment and new bandages for him. He suggested that I stay for dinner when I collect Abbie later. As much as I know I should distance myself, I didn't hesitate to accept his invitation. Spending time with him and Duke is the highlight of my week and I know Abbie enjoys it there.

This morning, I make it to the reservoir on my morning walk and treat myself to a coffee before hurrying back home. I stop at the mailboxes and, as I'm turning, scanning the envelopes, I run smack into the middle of a man I don't recognize.

"You must be my neighbor, Madison, right?" he asks, with a kind smile.

"Yes, and you must be Jeff."

He laughs and shakes my hand. "Gladys considers herself a bit of a matchmaker, I'm afraid." Jeff rolls his eyes.

"She's not so subtle, is she?"

"I'm hoping I squelched her enthusiasm. I saw her last night and told her I met someone and am off the market. I'm a catastrophic insurance adjuster, so I'm always on the road and never home, but I met Wendy a couple of months ago and I think it's serious."

"That's a relief," I say and then laugh. His brows rise and his eyes narrow to a squint. "Uh, that came out wrong, sorry. I'm not looking for a relationship, serious or otherwise, so it'll be nice not to have to contend with dodging Gladys."

He grins. "She means well and is a sweetheart, but can be a busybody."

"I don't think anything happens here without her knowledge. I bet she keeps the crime rate down in the park." I laugh and step toward the street. "I need to get going, but nice to meet you."

"You, too. Take care," Jeff says, jogging off toward the other side of the street.

My chat with Jeff puts me behind schedule and I hurry inside, happy to see Abbie ready to go. Jeff has a nice smile and seems like a nice guy. He reminds me how much I miss having that closeness, that companionship. At the end of a long day, I crave having someone to talk to, a shoulder to lean on, someone to tell me things will be okay. Being a mom is hard; being a single mom is tough, and moving away from any form of support has made it exhausting. Sometimes I think it would be nice to have someone to come home to, someone to help with Abbie, but it's too complicated to even consider. I'm certain any man I meet, once he gets to know me, would see the flashing yellow caution lights signaling danger ahead, and run the other way.

I speed through my shower routine and drop Abbie off at Arthur's and get to work with a few minutes to spare. I have time for a trip to the dining room to fill my cup with coffee before my first patient arrives.

Today isn't as hectic as it has been and I use my spare time to investigate an idea Arthur mentioned yesterday. I spend a couple of hours online and compile a list of resources. Before I know it, it's time to close the office. When Arthur asked us to dinner, I insisted on bringing something, so I make a quick stop at the market for some ice cream on my way to his house.

I find Arthur in the kitchen. "How'd Abbie do today?" I ask, slipping the ice cream into the freezer.

In a low voice, he says, "She's calmed down now, but she was in a state when I picked her up."

I crane my neck and look through the porch windows. I see her sitting in the grass, talking a mile a minute to Duke, resting beside her.

"From what I gather, she was in the Children's Garden today and a group came through. A couple of older girls started making fun of her and that set her off. Olivia was there and diverted Abbie to work in the Rose Garden, so there wouldn't be any chance of her meeting up with the group again."

A lump hardens in my throat. If Abbie couldn't volunteer, it would devastate her. "Was Olivia upset with Abbie?"

Arthur shakes his head. "No, she felt bad for her and was sorry Abbie was so distraught. She had a hard time convincing Abbie to stay, but got her refocused on the roses and that seemed to do the trick."

I slide into a chair at the island counter. "She's different and kids can be mean. This happens. Often. If someone is unkind or rude to her, she shuts down and runs off to pace, which usually only results in more drama and impolite comments. She's come a long way, but I should probably find a therapist for her here." I press on my temples. "I was hoping we could just deal with it ourselves."

"I know a woman who works with adolescents, from my time on the bench, who I could recommend," offers Arthur, as he wraps a bowl with plastic and puts it in the fridge.

I tilt my head and say, "Thanks, I'll call her." With a sigh, I turn to check on Abbie again. She and Duke have moved to the patio and she's got her earbuds installed. "It's amazing how quickly Duke can calm her. She's taken to him so much. She has a hard time making friends, but he accepts her just how she is and makes no judgments. He's gotten her to remove her earbuds and play and even partake in his training sessions. She struggles with new things or anything that disrupts her norm, so having him around has been good for her confidence. I think Duke does more for her than any of the therapists we've seen. To be fair, moving all the time doesn't give her much of a chance to make much progress with them."

"Maybe you could consider staying in Millbury?"

"Uh, I'm not sure I can. The post was only advertised as a temporary one until the end of the year."

"I see," says Arthur, pouring us each a glass of iced tea. "Maybe it's worth checking into. You like it here, don't you?"

"I do. It's the nicest town I've been assigned to yet. When school starts, I'll have a better idea of how Abbie will do here. She's bound to encounter more of the same type of girls she ran into today."

"Sometimes struggles make one stronger and more prepared for life." He grips his glass and adds, "I don't want to pry, but I overheard Abbie ask you about someone named Cody and when he was coming back. Will he be joining you here?"

I snort on my mouthful of tea and cough. "Sorry," I say. "Uh, no, he will *not* be joining us. He was my boyfriend. Actually, I thought he was much more than that, but it ended about two years ago. Abbie thinks of him as a father figure, since he's been in our lives since she was about six years old. I didn't want to upset her when we split, so I made up a story to put him in a good light and told her he got a new job with the government and had to leave for a secret assignment."

Arthur's brows rise above his intelligent eyes, but he doesn't say anything.

The heat of embarrassment travels from my neck to my cheeks. "I know," I say, unable to meet Arthur's eyes. "It sounds ridiculous, but I just couldn't deal with her thinking he abandoned her. It was all I could come up with at the moment and she believes it. Every so often I send an email from a phony account I set up that's from him." My heart is racing as I tell him.

Arthur holds up his hands. "I'm not judging. I'm sure you did what you thought best. I won't divulge your secret." He moves toward the hallway. "I'll run to the office and get you that name and number of the therapist."

I take a deep breath and drum my fingers on the granite counter, willing my pulse to slow. I ponder what Arthur said about staying in Millbury. It would be wonderful to stay in one place and quit uprooting Abbie. This is the first place that feels like it could be home. I shake my head. If only it were that easy.

Arthur returns and slides a heavy notecard across the counter. In perfect penmanship, he's written the contact information for Dr. Tessa Ernst. I finger the card and slip it into my purse. On my way back to the kitchen, I step to the porch and spy Abbie resting on one of the chaise lounges with Duke sprawled across her, both napping.

I chuckle and tiptoe back to the kitchen. "They're both sacked out on the patio. She probably wore herself out pacing."

Arthur grins and says, "Yes, she and Duke went back and forth across the yard when we got home. She didn't say much, just went from the car to the backyard. I did get her to drink some lemonade, but that's it."

"I'll call Dr. Ernst tomorrow and see if Abbie can get on her schedule soon. I'd like her to have a good semester at school."

"I agree with what you said about Duke being such a good friend for her." He pauses and adds, "I had an idea I wanted to propose. What do you think about making this dinner arrangement permanent? In that you two could plan to eat here on the nights you pick her up and you could work with Duke a bit more."

Arthur's expectant look makes me smile. He reminds me of a teenager asking to borrow the car for a date. I know I should probably limit our interactions, but my heart overrides my brain. He and Duke bring a stability to our lives and I can't resist the pull of it. "You don't have to twist my arm. That sounds terrific, but we share the cooking duties. If you liked the pizza, I could do that on Tuesdays and then we can each take one of the other days."

His eyes crinkle as he smiles and says, "Deal, but remember you're helping me train Duke, so I owe you."

I roll my eyes at him and take a long swallow of iced tea. "I meant to tell you I looked into that idea you told me about last night."

"Wonderful, do tell," he says, gathering a cutting board and selecting fruit for the salad he's making.

"Like you mentioned, I've noticed several of my patients and clients at the center have to rely on others for rides. It impacts their ability to get to their appointments and leaves some of them waiting longer than they should to get home. When Abbie got the opportunity to volunteer, I looked for some type of bus service and there isn't any. That got me to thinking about transportation services in other communities I've been in and I know they were able to secure grants to fund large vans. I've done a bunch of research and found some sources, but they all require some hefty matching funds. There aren't any straightforward grants."

"Ah, yes. That's the barrier the city ran into years ago. They didn't have anyone to spearhead the fundraising arm to secure the required matching funds." He raises his brows at me.

"It's definitely needed. There aren't many options for transportation in a town this size. I hate to see my patients suffer because of it and it could be utilized by so many others. Kids like Abbie."

"Sounds like a wonderful idea. You strike me as someone who makes things happen when you set your mind to it." He turns and winks. "I think you'd do a great job heading up an effort to get the community involved in fundraising. Talk to Mr. Cox, I'm sure he'd be delighted to have you take charge of it. It would be a real boon for the center. The whole community, really. What do you think? I could help."

"Wow, I don't know if I'm up for leading the charge, but I agree with the importance," I say, making my way to the counter to slice a bunch of grapes for the salad.

"Nobody ever changed the world by sitting on the sidelines. I think you're exactly the right person to do this. There's no one better than you to champion it. You've seen what it meant to those other communities you've been in. You've got energy and ideas and all the help you can handle from this old man."

I didn't sleep well, so am up earlier than usual on a Saturday. On my walk, my mind is occupied. The grant project I spoke about with Arthur would be a huge undertaking and I can already feel that there is so much riding on it. If we don't get the funding, I'll be the one responsible for getting everyone's hopes up and then dashing them. I contemplate the workload and run through the logical steps we'll have to take to raise enough funds to qualify. It's going to be difficult, at best. The timeframe is tight and I need another thing to do like I need another bill on my credit card, but when I think of my patients and all the seniors at the center, I shuffle those worries to the back of my mind.

I chuckle as I think of Arthur. I'm not sure how he convinced me to be the ringleader of this project, but he's persuasive and clever. Before I knew it, I had agreed and we were brainstorming ideas into the night. His eyes shimmered with enthusiasm as we plotted out strategies.

Yesterday, I talked to Mr. Cox about the idea. We'd call it the Jump Around Millbury (JAM) Bus, the catchy name Arthur and

I came up with, and outlined the idea of getting buy-in from the community to help fundraise for the project. The grant application deadline is at the end of September, which doesn't leave us much time to raise the required funds, but he promised his support.

After we got home from Arthur's last night, I talked to Abbie about the idea of seeing a therapist again. She lacked enthusiasm, but agreed to go to the first appointment and meet the therapist. I reminded her how much she grew to like Dr. Linda when we were in Colorado last year and how she looked forward to talking with her. At least she's willing to try it. And I have my fingers crossed that she hits it off with Dr. Ernst.

As I make my way back to the trailer park, my thoughts focus on the depressing balance in my checking account. After paying my bills this morning, there isn't much left until my next payday. By dropping Arthur's name, I was able to get Abbie scheduled with Dr. Ernst next week and hope she makes progress with the visits my insurance will cover, since her normal hourly rate is beyond my means. Rather than sink into despair about my finances, I focus on my steps forward, the beauty surrounding me, and the new grant project. Mr. Cox offered to accompany me to the Chamber of Commerce meeting next week, where I could address all the business owners and explain the process and elicit their help, but I need to have the materials ready by then.

The only way I get Abbie to come to the center with me this morning is by reminding her Duke will be there with Arthur. Since the incident at the garden on Thursday, she's been more subdued and withdrawn, focusing on her ever-growing list of plant facts. When she's upset, her behaviors intensify.

I'm beginning to love working on quiet Saturdays. I only have two appointments today, both for blood pressure checks, with Arthur being one of them. I give Abbie the task of critiquing my flyers I designed for the fundraiser between patients yesterday. She has a creative eye that I lack. When I worked at the hospital back in Ohio, we raised a ton of money with a golf tournament. I am hoping for the same results, and Arthur offered to connect me with the local golf course owners and set up a meeting with them on Monday. Penny drives and bake sales aren't going to cut it; we need some serious cash.

This morning, I made egg salad sandwiches using the croissants I picked up from the bakery yesterday and called Arthur to see if he wanted to meet us for lunch in my office. He and Abbie join me at the conference table, with Duke keeping watch for any crumbs that might hit the floor, while we talk about the fundraiser. Arthur suggests some of the larger businesses in Millbury for possible sponsorships of the golf tournament and tells me to be sure and mention his name.

By the time the day is over, I have a list of likely sponsors for all eighteen holes on the course and an encouraging reply to the email I sent to Regency Health seeking a premium sponsorship. Arthur assured me the business owners I want to target never miss a Chamber of Commerce meeting, where I hope to persuade them to write some sizable checks. In addition to brainstorming with Arthur, I set up an online donation site for the project and publicize it, using the Millbury Life Center's social media accounts.

I always feel better helping people. Being in the medical field all these years has taught me that my problems seem smaller when I can ease someone else's struggles. This new project keeps my mind occupied and gives me less time to think. It's exciting to have a new undertaking and one that I know will make a huge difference in the lives of my patients and the entire community.

But then I remember that if we do get the grant award in October, I won't be here to celebrate when the van arrives next year.

# CHAPTER 11

## Duke

This morning when Sonny called, Arthur told him we are attending a movie night in the park with Madison and Abbie. I'm not sure what's involved, but I'm always eager to go to the park and know I'll have more fun with Abbie and Madison there. With Abbie holding my leash, I can go faster than when I walk with Arthur, and Madison usually brings cheese with her.

On this morning's call, Arthur makes a point of telling Sonny about Madison's work to secure a grant to fund the bus project in Millbury. Like the past few Saturdays, he mentions how much she helps everyone at the center and what she does for him. Sonny still has questions, but his tone is gentler and Arthur is more patient in his responses.

The days Abbie stays with us after her shift at the garden and Madison comes for dinner are our best days of the week. Arthur's too busy to mix his customary cocktail and instead of grief surrounding him, he visits with Madison and laughs as I romp around the yard with Abbie. She continues to read me the names of the plants she adds to her notebook each time she visits the garden and, while I have no idea what she's talking about most of the time, I enjoy listening to the happiness in her words. She has a need to explain things in detail and I don't mind listening.

Madison has been teaching me to heel over the past week, and Arthur and I have been practicing several times during the day. It's not easy and I have a hard time focusing when there are squirrels and butterflies to chase. Madison suggested we practice in the house with fewer distractions and I'm earning more treats inside than I was in the yard.

Over this last week, whenever the topic of school comes up, I've noticed a nervousness in Abbie. She's been pacing and more withdrawn than usual, and so I poke my nose against her leg and urge her to follow me outside.

I sniff at a few blooms and she plants herself in the cool grass next to my favorite flowerbed. She looks so serious and I can feel anxiety coursing through her. She worries too much, and I wonder if Madison knows how much her daughter watches her. Is affected by the tension she still holds. She needs to adopt my way of thinking and concentrate on what's happening right now.

I wiggle closer to Abbie and rest my snout on her leg, hoping to distract her from the thoughts weighing on her shoulders. I stretch and touch my nose to her fingers, and she smiles at me. I know she'll feel better if I can get her to play with me.

Her fingers ruffle the fur on my neck and her hand glides down my back. Apprehension quivers in her fingers. She sighs and continues to pet me, her hands steadier. She leans closer to me and rests her head against mine. I concentrate as hard as I can and with my thoughts signal my affection for her. I feel her eyelashes brush against my face, and when she pulls back, I stare into her eyes. Her eyes meet mine and her smile is my reward. Beneath all that energy and anxiety is a kind and gentle soul.

I'll miss having her around the house when school starts next week, but she's been lobbying Madison to let her walk to Arthur's after school each day and, from what I've overheard, Madison is agreeable but worried about taking advantage of Arthur's hospitality. Arthur has promised to make sure Abbie spends her time on her homework and only when she's done will she be permitted to play with me. That seems to have satisfied Madison, though I'm not so happy about it.

Abbie gives me a quick kiss on the head and pushes herself into a standing position. I follow her as she makes one more loop around the perimeter of the garden, admiring the plants.

We wander back inside and find Arthur whistling as he gathers a large basket and fills it with plates, napkins, and disposable cutlery. We stopped by the market on our way home today and picked up some fruit. As Arthur washes it and slices it into a bowl, he slips me a few bites of apple, and after crunching through them, I sit and stare at him, willing him to part with more.

Seeing Arthur happy brings me so much joy. Having me around, making him get up to take me outside, and urging him to play has made such a difference in his mood, but Madison and Abbie are responsible for his renewed interest in getting out of the house and socializing. I've come to care for them, almost as much as I do for Arthur.

Abbie amuses herself playing the piano while Arthur continues prepping the food. I'm able to snag a few more bites of apple before they finish loading the basket. "Did you know a local group is providing some music before the movie starts?" Arthur asks, gesturing toward Abbie.

Abbie stops playing and joins us in the kitchen. "What kind of music?"

"They play all sorts, a few oldies, some country, a mixture, really."

Her face falls. "No classical?"

"Ah, I'm afraid not. You'll have to wait for the symphony at the garden. That will be in September." He turns to her. "I've already reserved three seats."

Abbie rushes toward him, her eyes twinkling with excitement. She wraps her arms around a startled Arthur. "Really? That's the best surprise. I love you."

Abbie's smile transforms to wonder as Arthur pats her on the back. "I'm delighted you're so happy, dear."

As Abbie releases her grip on him, I notice Arthur turn his back on her and rummage in a drawer. He sneaks his handkerchief from his pocket and runs it across his eyes, moving to another cupboard as he feigns looking for something. My heart swells at Arthur's happy tears and the smile filling Abbie's face.

I show Arthur I love him as best I can and I know he loves me, but hearing Abbie say it and watching the impact on Arthur is magical. Arthur longs to be needed, to be relevant. He's the most important person in my world, but I know humans are social animals and he requires more than just me in his life. With Rosie and their life together, Arthur had experienced happiness and fulfillment, and with her illness, his focus and purpose had been her. Now, with Rosie gone, Arthur fears being alone and, worse, useless. That's where I came into the picture. I gave him someone to care about again, someone who relies on him, and in turn I'm happy to offer him comfort and joy. I opened his heart, and Abbie, in her innocence, with three small words, filled it.

I stretch out on the floor, feeling fortunate to have a home with such a fine man. I trust him completely and only wish Madison would do the same. She's concealing something from him and while I'm not sure what it is, I know it's at the root of her angst.

When I see Abbie struggle to deal with her emotions and anxiety, I know it's not just from moving to a new town or a new school. Like me, I think Abbie senses her mother has a secret and it's something that causes both of them pain.

Sometimes when Madison is talking with Arthur, I can tell she longs to say more and unburden herself, but she restrains herself. As much as her heart wants to impart her deepest truths, her brain stops her. She seems almost afraid to get too close, despite her deep affection for him. I'm hopeful the longer she knows Arthur, her feelings will change. Her trust will grow and she will know she can tell him anything without fear. When he told her she could lean on him and think of him as someone who could fill in for her parents, it touched her more than she revealed.

I know that feeling of being alone, without my mother, and how scary it is. I never knew my father, but would have enjoyed meeting him. Humans spend so much longer with their mothers; I can't imagine the pain and loneliness Madison feels without her parents. A hint of what she felt for them shines through her eyes when she runs her hand over her dad's watch or twirls her mother's ring around her finger. Those small reminders bring her a measure of comfort. If she would only realize the man in front of her could provide so much more.

I wish I understood why humans, whose brains are so advanced, can't seem to figure out the simplest things. Why is it that they are so afraid to appear weak or in need of help? Madison constantly gives of herself to help others and goes above and beyond to make sure her patients at the center are cared for and happy. She cares deeply for Abbie and I feel and see the affection she has for Arthur, always happy to help him. Maybe she only sees herself as a giver and never the recipient of help. Maybe she's afraid she won't be independent if she accepts Arthur's offers of assistance.

Arthur's life has been one of service to others. He, like Madison, is stuck in this pattern, unable to accept help.

I'm hopeful Madison will eventually disclose whatever she keeps locked inside her, whatever she thinks she has to hide from everyone, even Abbie and Arthur. He's such a kind and caring person, I know he would help her and never judge her, whatever her secret is.

I just hope she knows she can lean on us. That she doesn't have to leave. I'm not sure Arthur and I will be able to handle life without Madison and Abbie.

# CHAPTER 12

## Madison

While I chop tomatoes, I'm listening to an online continuing education class, hoping I'm absorbing enough of the information to pass the test at the end. The topic is one I know well, so the refresher is easy to follow. I cover the tomatoes and slide them into the fridge next to the avocado, shredded lettuce, cheese, and olives. I grab an onion and get to work on it. I promised Abbie tacos tonight to commemorate her first day of school. Dr. Ernst usually sees Abbie on Mondays, but has to see her tomorrow this week.

I've spent most of the day working on the golf tournament idea for raising money for JAM, instead of completing my coursework. We've been getting lots of traffic on the donation site, and my office is filled with raffle prizes for the tournament. Millbury has gone all out to come together and support the fundraiser. The bus is important to so many and the local businesses are promoting it. I think we'll hit our goal, which will be a huge accomplishment for the center. Mr. Cox even promised an ice cream social celebration if we raise the money needed for the grant.

I haven't really been involved in the community since I lost Mom and Dad. Before that, I was always up for helping raise funds for causes at the hospital or helping the fire department with their events. I've missed that feeling of belonging and spearheading this grant project has reminded me of the joy that comes from contributing to something bigger, something that will outlast me. While it's tiring, with all my other work and Abbie, the gratification and community spirit I've discovered while involved in it feels terrific.

I glance at my phone, as I've done a hundred times today, anticipating a call from Abbie or the school, but with only an hour left in the school day, I'm beginning to relax. Arthur and Duke are joining us for dinner at our house tonight, which will brighten Abbie's day.

I hope Abbie can make a friend or two here, but in my heart, I know she's a lot of work for most kids her age. When I think back to my high school years, as much as I'd like to say I would have befriended Abbie, if I'm honest, I wouldn't have. When you're young and in high school, it's not easy to understand kids that are different. It's more convenient to ignore them and let them be alone, since so many times you're judged by the friends you keep. When you're fourteen, you don't have the confidence, patience, or wisdom to comprehend what a profound difference a friend would make to someone like Abbie. I hope there's someone at school, someone who is wiser than I was at fourteen, who will take a chance and reach out to her.

Tears run down my face and I tell myself it's the onions.

Arthur and Duke are Abbie's best friends. They're my best friends too. Arthur has a way of reassuring me and calming me without saying a word. He's kind and so very patient, not peppering me with a bunch of questions about where I'm from or why I've moved so much. After hoping to befriend a few people in the other towns we've lived in, I gave up on that idea. They'd ask questions and when I dodged them, they'd get suspicious and probe more, not understanding I didn't want to talk about it. It made me avoid getting close to anyone. It was easier just to focus on work and not get involved on a personal level. There's a comfort and steadiness about Arthur that makes me feel safe here.

For Abbie, who has such a hard time fitting in and making friends, Duke has been the companion she has needed. She spends so much time alone and sometimes even when I'm with her, she's not really there, withdrawn into her own little inner world. With Duke, she's different because he accepts her just how she is. I owe him a debt of gratitude for bringing us together that day at the center. He and Arthur have filled our time in Millbury with fun and happiness. It's been so long since I've felt connected to anyone or felt part of a real community. On days we don't see Arthur and Duke, I always feel like something is missing.

Finished chopping, I add the dirty dishes to the stack from breakfast that is still soaking in the sink. I give the ground beef mixture on the stove a stir and adjust the heat to let it simmer before turning to face the pile of dishes. I made Abbie pancakes this morning, forgoing my early morning exercise until she left for school. I walked with her part of the way today, but knowing that being seen with her mom would makes things worse for her, I stopped at the bridge and watched her walk away toward the building, until I couldn't see her any longer. I swiped at a tear running down my cheek and took off on my walk to the reservoir, glad for the distraction of the physical activity. I never stop worrying about her.

As I wash the dishes, I listen to the end of the webinar and yawn, weariness creeping over me. Abbie had begun pacing the hallway long before the sun was up this morning. I got up and tried to distract her with conversation, but she waved me away, intent on her ritual. Duke is the only distraction more powerful than her obsession with pacing.

I dry a few dishes and let the rest sit in the rack. Despite my tired and wandering mind, I plunk down at the counter and poke the button on my tablet to advance to the exam. I zip through the questions, knowing most of the answers and am proud of myself when I recall a few items mentioned in the video. I'm unsure of only two questions, take my final stab at it, close my eyes, and submit the test. I get an instant response telling me I passed the exam and breathe out a sigh of relief. One task handled.

Now, if only I had time for a nap, but Abbie will be home in a few minutes. As the minutes tick by, I'm getting nervous. A new experience is always stressful and I never know how she'll respond. Days like these make me wish we still had her piano. Duke is such a calming influence and good companion for her, but there's no way I could get a dog for just us. It's terrible enough that I force Abbie to move with me wherever we need to go; it's not fair of me to drag someone else along.

I brew a cup of tea while I add grapes, cheese, and apple slices to a plate. Remembering I haven't eaten since my latte this morning, I eat a piece of cheese and pop a few grapes into my mouth. Thank goodness for the ladies at Creekside Coffee. Ever since I started championing the funding for the bus, the sisters have insisted on giving me free lattes. I've been too anxious to eat a proper meal today, but the calories from this morning's drink are long gone and the aroma of dinner cooking makes my stomach growl.

The back door squeaks open and I brace myself in preparation for the mood I dread will greet me when she turns the corner. Her cheeks are flush, but I don't sense any agitation when she flings her backpack into the chair.

"How was your first day?"

She shrugs. "Okay." She reaches for an apple slice. "The music teacher, Mr. Freeman, is my favorite. He was excited to know I could play. I had his class right before lunch and spent much of it playing. I barely had time to eat."

I let out a breath. "That's terrific. Did you like any of your other classes or meet any nice kids?"

She wrinkles her nose. "Not really." She unzips her bag and plucks a bundle of paper from it. It smacks against the counter and she says, "You've got to fill all these out by tomorrow."

I eye the stack and begin to sign my name to the pile of classroom behavior agreements and the school rules as Abbie munches on her snack.

"What time are they going to be here?"

I look at the time and say, "About thirty minutes." A smile fills her face. "Do you have any homework?"

She rolls her eyes. "No, not on the first day."

Apparently, I'm the only one with homework tonight. I lick my finger and turn to the next page in the stack. After separating all the school supply lists and picture day information, I return the signed papers to Abbie's backpack and gather her insulated lunch bag from the bottom of it.

Taking a peek inside, I smile, relieved to see she ate most of her lunch. "You've got time for a snack before they get here."

As she pops another apple slice in her mouth, the dryer buzzes. "You can handle the laundry or wipe out your lunch bag and get it packed for tomorrow."

She frowns and, with a heavy sigh, plods into the utility room. I check on the simmering meat before wiping out her bag and reloading it with Abbie's favorites. Her soft footfalls down the hallway and the squeak of dresser drawers tell me she's done folding.

She joins me in the kitchen and I toss her a towel so she can dry the dishes still in the rack, while I arrange plates and utensils for the taco bar. I check the time and hurry to my room to change out of the ratty exercise clothes I'm still wearing.

As I come down the hallway, the front door slams, and Abbie rushes down the steps to greet Arthur and Duke. Her gentle manner with Arthur and the way she offers to help with Duke, so he can navigate the steps warms my heart. That softer and more loving approach has been absent for so long, really since she lost her grandparents; it's a relief to see it resurface.

I open the front door and Abbie hollers, "I'm going to take Duke for a quick walk, okay?"

I nod and wave. "Just be quick and don't go far."

Despite her back being turned, I know she's rolling her eyes.

Arthur greets me with a warm smile and a tip of his hat. "Seems Abbie had a good first day?" He raises his brows.

"I think so, thank goodness. I've been a nervous wreck all day."

Arthur retrieves a bright orange flyer from his shirt pocket. "I wanted to show you this and see what you think before Abbie returns."

I give it a quick scan and smile, noting the information related to the Annual Pet Palooza and Parade taking place in the garden the weekend after the golf tournament. "Abbie will be thrilled. I won't be able to come until I get off work, but if you're up for having her, I'm sure she'd love to go."

His shoulders relax and a smile fills his face. "I was hoping you'd say that. It's always a popular event and I've never had a dog so this will be my first year participating. I could use Abbie's help with Duke."

I glance out the window and see the two of them rounding the corner, approaching our trailer. "I'll let you share the good news. I just hope you know what you're in for, since you know how she can get fixated on something she enjoys."

"I was hoping it would give her something to look forward to, especially knowing how she wasn't looking forward to school starting." Arthur sits at the counter and smooths the crease down the middle of the flyer.

"That will be two weekends in a row. I don't want you to get Abbied-out. She takes an enormous amount of energy."

He chuckles and turns at the sound of feet and paws on the front deck. "So does Duke. I think we're even."

The two come through the front door, and Duke begins sniffing the place, like a police dog looking for drugs. He's ruthless and runs his nose over every surface and corner. He has been going through a growth spurt lately and is getting longer and taller. At just over seven months old, he's losing some of his puppy look and is at the awkward stage where his back legs look longer than the front ones, making him a bit clumsy. I've been working with Arthur on walking him on a leash and reinforcing Duke's leash manners. He's still quite excitable and distracted by anything we happen to encounter, so it can be challenging. I notice he's not on a leash tonight. I know Arthur struggles with getting him to behave, but having him off-leash is dangerous. I shudder to think how Arthur would feel if anything happened to the sweet pup. If we have time, we can try walking him around the mobile home park tonight.

"Go wash up for dinner. It's ready to go," I tell Abbie. Duke, of course, follows her down the hallway and into the bathroom.

I add the meat and toppings to the counter, while Arthur pours our drinks. I let Arthur and Abbie load their plates while I distract Duke with some commands and a few bites of cheese when he performs well. Arthur's done a good job of not feeding him food from the table, so he doesn't linger and beg and I'm able to get Duke to lie down in a corner where he can see all of us, but not be underfoot.

As I'm settling him, Arthur slides the orange flyer over to Abbie. Arthur asks her if she would like to go and help him with Duke and walk him in the parade. She lets out a squeal of excitement, which makes Duke raise his head and start to leave his spot. "Mom, did you see this? We'll have to get Duke a costume. This is going to be lit."

As I stroke Duke's ears to reassure him that he can stay where he is, I chuckle. She's obviously picked up on the latest teenage slang. From the confused look on Arthur's face, I can tell he hasn't heard the phrase.

I catch Abbie's eye. "What she means is thank you, Arthur, for the invitation and that she'd be happy to help you with Duke and the Pet Palooza sounds amazing."

She bobs her head. "Yes, that's what I mean, Arthur. I can't wait." She slips an arm around his shoulders and leans her head into him.

Watching their tender exchange, I'm reminded I need to start laying the groundwork with Abbie to prepare her for the fact that we'll have to move again in just a few months. She's never attached herself to anyone where we've lived these last couple of years. I'm not sure I can deal with the fallout and tell myself to let her enjoy this while she can and wait until after the Pet Palooza to mention it.

# CHAPTER 13

The early morning sunlight peeking into my bedroom announces the big day has arrived and despite my body being tired, I'm so pleased with what we've accomplished and excited to see our grand total after today's event. The fundraiser has really brought the community together and created such a buzz not only at the center, but all around Millbury.

I've been staying late at work, which has worked out since, thankfully, Abbie agreed to play the piano for the school musical and they've started practicing this week. Arthur has been picking her up after practice and letting her stay with him and Duke, making sure she does her homework and eats dinner. I've been ending my days working on the fundraiser late at night and can't seem to shut my brain off to sleep, constantly thinking of things I need to do or check.

Between Arthur's connections with the folks at City Hall and Mr. Cox, we have a small crew of helpers who will be at the golf course early to set things up before the tournament starts. Arthur has helped me recruit volunteers to station at each of the eighteen holes to observe and provide any assistance to the golfers.

The Foothills Golf Course is a gorgeous venue that sits between Millbury and Salem. They've gone above and beyond to keep our costs low, donating some prizes, and giving us a great deal on the luncheon they're catering for everyone after the tournament.

Abbie is excited to wear one of the purple T-shirts Charlotte at Sinful Sweets sponsored. She embraced the whole JAM theme and loved the idea of mentioning her homemade jam and pies with her bakery logo on our official shirts. Each golfer gets one and they are also for sale at our registration table. Abbie and Arthur, along with Duke, are teaming up in a golf cart and will be my official gophers, helping out wherever they are needed today.

Between the school musical, the golf tournament, and the upcoming Pet Palooza next weekend, Abbie has been excited. She and Arthur picked out costumes for Duke and they're not telling me what they are. They want me to be surprised when I see him.

I have a feeling Duke will be more surprised than anyone. I'm not sure he's going to be too happy about wearing a costume. Having Abbie help me today, and Arthur asking her to walk Duke in the parade, has been a huge boost to her confidence. I still haven't heard much about school, other than her love of her music class and the musical, but she is thriving and her spirits are soaring, which is something I've been missing these last two years.

After a hot shower to ease my aching neck and shoulders, I emerge in my stretchy exercise pants and JAM T-shirt to find Abbie at the stove scrambling eggs. "Wow, you're up early and those look yummy."

She's wearing a pair of black yoga pants with a purple design I found for her at a thrift store. They still had the tags on them and the purple matches our T-shirts. She was thrilled and has been waiting to wear them until today. Routine is something Abbie craves, which makes me feel less guilty for not being able to afford to outfit her in new clothes all the time. She gravitates to the comfort of her favorite shirts and jeans or shorts, but when we were at the thrift store, she got really excited about the yoga pants. It's another subtle little change I've noticed in her since we've been in Millbury and makes my heart happy.

After our quick breakfast, we head to Arthur's. Abbie hurries to the door and takes charge of Duke's leash while Arthur follows, wearing his new sun hat and toting a bag with his and Duke's supplies.

Duke hops into the back with Abbie and proceeds to lie down with his head in her lap. Arthur greets me with a smile. Rebecca, the event coordinator at The Foothills, has made a special exception to allow Duke to attend the event. She always refers to Arthur as Judge Patterson, and approved Duke as long as he stays on his leash and is in a cart or the registration tent at all times.

It's a beautiful morning, with just a touch of crispness in the air, and a gorgeous blue sky. All my fretting about rain and wind was put to rest when I checked the forecast last night. I take another sip of my latte and sigh.

"You couldn't have ordered a more perfect day," says Arthur, pointing out the window at the sun-streaked horizon.

"I was thinking the same thing. So glad we don't have to contend with a weather problem." A glance in the rearview mirror assures me my two passengers in the backseat are calm.

Arthur raises his cup. "Here's to you, for excellent work. You should be proud of all you've done."

I sit taller in my seat and wink at Arthur. "I couldn't have done it without you and the help of everyone in Millbury. I'm thrilled with our numbers. We'll announce it today, but we've met our goal as of this morning. Anything we bring in today will just be a cushion."

Arthur beams with pride. "Well done, my dear."

I turn off the highway where the early morning crew has placed a sign directing JAM participants to the event. The winding road, amid the manicured greens and beautiful trees, leads to the parking area and clubhouse, where purple banners and flags advertise the JAM fundraiser. I pull close to the large white tent that is set up for our event. Between the volunteers and the staff at the golf course, all the tables and chairs have been placed.

The staff is busy setting up a continental breakfast, and we concentrate on getting the registration tables organized. Arthur and Abbie take one of the golf carts designated for volunteers, and head out to the course with a cash box and a roll of raffle tickets, hoping to drum up some last-minute sales. Duke is big enough now that his presence in the front makes it a bit crowded, so Abbie rides with him on the backseat.

After I attach our fundraising poster, which is a thermometer that I've been filling in with a red marker each time we hit a milestone, to the wall of the tent, I pour myself a cup of coffee and take measure of the space. I hadn't filled in the last section on the thermometer, hoping to elicit more donations and raffle sales today and give us a bit of a buffer. I breathe a sigh of relief, noting everything is in place and ready for the tournament.

I check my watch, which makes me think of Dad. He would have loved a day like today. He was always one for volunteering and serving the community, having been a firefighter and a man who enjoyed spending time golfing. Millbury would have been a place where he and Mom would have been at home. Seeing all the happy faces and excitement of the golfers as they register, enjoying the easy banter back and forth with Barb and Mr. Cox as they check people off the list and try to sell more raffle tickets, brings back memories of similar events back home, where friends gathered and felt more like family.

I'm greeted with more hugs today than I can remember and it makes me feel so loved. I haven't felt at home in the other towns where I've worked, but this sense of belonging pulls at me. Tears sting my eyes and I make a beeline to refill my cup so nobody sees them. When I think of losing all this, leaving it all behind, I can't face it.

The idea of starting over makes my heart sink. Lena kisses my cheek and tells me she thinks the medication is helping her arthritis, as she settles into a table to visit with some other spectators. There's a hum of electricity in the air, as the excitement and chatter builds surrounding the prospect of getting a JAM bus. My heart fills knowing I've played a part in easing their burden and only wish I could be here to see their faces when the van actually gets delivered.

Leaving these people is going to break my heart. Leaving Duke and Arthur is going to crush me and I fear it will shatter Abbie. What if it plunges her into such despair she's actually worse than when we arrived? How can I keep doing this to her? I take a long breath and try to shake off the dread that keeps building inside me, while I focus on registrations.

When all the golfers are on the greens and the tournament underway, I visit with a few more of the seniors who've come out to enjoy the day and the luncheon. After tallying the cash box and adding another two thousand dollars to our total, I take a break with a muffin and another cup of coffee.

As I'm finishing the last bite, my phone pings with a text. It's Abbie using Arthur's phone telling me he needs a break and they're on their way from hole number sixteen. I wait for them by the cart parking and offer to take over the wheel, while Arthur gets a snack. Abbie is in the back of the cart, holding on to Duke's leash.

"How's he doing with all this excitement?"

She sighs and says, "He's better when we're moving."

"Do you want to drive and I'll hold him?"

Her eyes go wide. "I don't know how. Will they let me?"

"If you're with an adult, you can drive on the course. It's easy, I'll show you and drive us out and you can drive us back." I'm not sure she'll agree, since new things are always challenging for her, more so than for others. Many times, if I suggest something new, she shies away or shakes her head and I can see the fear creep over her, but today, there's a spark of interest.

A smile fills her face and she scoots across the seat so she's behind me to watch how it's done. After showing her how to turn the key on, where the reverse switch is, and the gas and brake pedals, I ease out to the paved pathway. "Just go slowly and don't slam on the brake, be gentle."

I steer us along the beautiful pathway, lined with lush greens, ponds, and sand traps, as we watch the teams golfing and wave hello to several people I know from the center and from all the begging for prizes I did downtown. Mel, one of the regulars at the center, and his teammates each buy twenty dollars in tickets and then we're off again. Duke likes the motion and has quit straining on the leash, sitting calmly next to Abbie.

One of the beverage carts is coming toward us. I scoot over as far as possible. "See how I steered us over to the edge. If a cart comes, just pull over as much as you can and don't panic. If you get nervous just pull over and step on the brake, but don't slam on it, just use gentle pressure."

Her serious eyes get bigger. "I'm not sure I can do it."

"You can, I'll be right here." I guide us to the fourth hole and wave hello to the volunteer who's watching over it. "Okay, let's switch places. I'll see if I can get Duke to sit on the floor and I'll sit next to you in the front."

I realize how much Duke has grown when I judge my ability to squeeze his sixty-pound body into the space. I reflect on that first day I met him, when he was just a little bundle of fur, and now he's so much bigger and is losing some of his puppy features. It's not lost on me how much Abbie has grown, not physically, but emotionally. She's so content and her smiles, that were so rare before, brighten my days.

Reluctance clouds her eyes, but she nods and hands me Duke's leash. While she's getting settled behind the wheel, I make Duke sit while I pour a bottle of water into his bowl. He laps it up, and I guide him to sit at my feet in the front of the cart, giving him a bite of cheese I had stashed in my pocket. It makes for cramped quarters, but I know Abbie will feel better if I'm right next to her.

Abbie looks at me for assurance as she places her fingers on the key. I check that she has her foot on the brake and nod. She takes my warnings about light pressure seriously and I have to keep telling her to press a bit harder until we're moving. As we crawl along the pathway, I soak in the perfect day, with just the slightest breeze and the sun still shining. I glance over at Abbie, both hands on the wheel, concentration and determination written all over her face.

These last few months have been so good for Abbie. For both of us. I run my hands over Duke's silky ears. He's settled down and is sleeping in the footwell. We pass by the sixth hole and Mel hollers out a hello and waves to us. I wave back, and Abbie stares straight ahead, not daring to take her eyes off the road, but she grins.

Abbie hasn't been this happy or willing to step outside of her little bubble since we left Ohio. It makes me sick to my stomach thinking about making her move again in December and leaving Millbury and all of this behind. It's going to be next to impossible to find a place like this one, where I finally feel like I belong.

With a glance at my dad's watch, I encourage Abbie to increase our speed. "I need to get back before lunch. Are you okay to keep driving?"

"Yeah, I like driving," she says with an impish grin, as her grip loosens on the wheel. She's not hesitating as much on the gas pedal and her shoulders drop as her bangs flutter in the breeze. I like seeing her confident instead of worried or locked in her own tiny world.

"Maybe you can drive again and help Arthur check the greens when we're done and make sure all the signs and flags are collected."

She beams and takes Duke's leash, leading him to the tent and his master.

The luncheon buffet is already set up and I recognize several ladies from the center, who, just like always, have shown up early for lunch. I spot Gladys and Lois at one of the tables. Gladys greets me with her signature smile and a warm clasp of her hand.

"We're so excited. This all just looks wonderful. You've done a remarkable job, dear."

I pat her hand and smile at Lois. "It was a team effort. Everyone in Millbury has been so supportive and helpful. You ladies enjoy lunch."

In between bites from the lovely buffet luncheon, I do a final tabulation on the raffle tickets. We've got almost four thousand dollars from all the sales today to add to the total. I can't wait to fill in the thermometer and make the announcement after lunch.

Duke is tired from all the activity and on his best behavior, dozing behind our chairs until I tickle his ears and make him do a few tricks for bites of cheese from my plate. After he does all the things I ask, I pass Arthur the rest of the cheese and head up to the prize table with Mr. Cox. He's got a microphone, doing his best to urge last-minute purchases of raffle tickets, touting the selection of offerings.

As the golfers and guests enjoy cookies and brownies, Mr. Cox announces the raffle sales are closed. He scans the crowd and points to Arthur. "I was looking for the most honest man I can think of. How about it, Judge Patterson? Will you do us the honor of choosing the winning tickets today?"

The crowd erupts in applause, urging Arthur from his chair. Abbie takes charge of Duke, who is sleeping through all the commotion, and helps herself to another cookie. While Arthur is drawing tickets and prizes are claimed, I add the last of the sales to our total and color in the thermometer, making sure I go above the top line. As Mr. Cox announces the grand prize winners, I add the total dollar figure in thick black marker and circle it. Brett, from the *Millbury Gazette*, is on hand to take photos of the winners, surrounded by their prizes. I give Mr. Cox a nod and he directs the crowd's attention to the poster.

I steer clear of Brett and his camera and direct him to talk to Mr. Cox. With Millbury being such a small town, I doubt their local news goes further than the county line, but after all I've done to stay under the radar, I don't need any publicity. I probably should have thought of that before I agreed to champion this cause. I underestimated the importance of the grant to the community and the celebration that was bound to follow once we hit our goal. It was definitely newsworthy; I just hope it doesn't have far-reaching consequences.

Amid all the whooping and applause, Mr. Cox's voice booms in the tent. "This is extraordinary. I want to acknowledge Madison Ward, without whom our bus would still be on a wish list, instead of close to a reality. The people at the state office told me if we get the matching funds, it's almost a sure thing we'll be awarded the grant. Madison has helped us do that and more. Just think, in a few months we could have our very own ADA-compliant fourteen-passenger purple JAM bus."

Cheers and whistles fill the tent, and Mr. Cox steps closer to me, with Arthur on the other side. "We thank you for your hard work in spearheading this project. Not only are you a terrific nurse practitioner, but you show how much you care for everyone who comes to the center. You may be new to Millbury, but you've found a place in our hearts. You've gone above and beyond and as a small token of our appreciation, we have a little gift for you."

Fiona, the local florist who donated all the centerpieces, carries a huge bouquet of lavender roses, purple stock, and button mums amid shiny greenery. She hands it to me, and I breathe in the lovely scent. My eyes begin to water and I feel Arthur's hand on my back. I murmur my thanks, overcome with emotion at the standing ovation. As we're standing, Barb comes forward with a huge gift bag and presents it to me. While I'm opening it, Mr. Cox announces that while the Silver Threads Quilters, a group of women that meet each week at the center, is responsible for the handiwork, the gift is from everyone at the center. I unwrap a gorgeous quilt and Arthur helps me unfold it, to reveal what

I recognize as the landscape of Millbury. The beautiful creek flowing through the trees and buildings of downtown, the mountains above, and the sun shining at the top of the quilt, all of it trimmed in the signature purple color of our fundraiser.

A lump forms in my throat and I'm speechless. My knees weaken when Arthur turns it around and I see the back of it is made up of fabric photo squares. Through my tears, I see all the smiling faces of the people at the center, interspersed with purple squares of our JAM T-shirts. They don't understand what this means to me. They don't know how much I'll treasure this, these memories. They don't know I'm leaving soon. I manage to croak out a quick thank you, but am overcome with emotion.

I can feel the love surrounding me and realize the only thing worse than being alone is knowing this closeness and friendship from this loving community is something I'll soon be without. I've clung to the memories of my happy life before I lost my parents, before everything changed and came undone, and finally, here in this charming little town, feel like I don't have to be content with only memories. I could live here, nestled in this tiny pocket, supported and cared for, where these people comfort me like a warm blanket on a cold night. It's what I long for, but I know it's not realistic.

I stand between the two men, watching so many of the people I've come to know and care for smiling at me. A tear sliding down my cheek threatens to unravel what little composure I have left. How am I ever going to be able to walk away from Millbury and all of this? I wish there was a way I could stay.

# CHAPTER 14

Having Monday off, after a full day of work and more on Saturday, is heavenly. After I get Abbie off to school, I take my customary walk along the creek and to the reservoir, treat myself to breakfast, and stroll through the shelves at Village Books & Café. I buy a couple of fiction books on sale and spend the rest of the day catching up on housework.

I manage to sneak in some reading and a nap before I have to pick Abbie up from practice.

My days are filled with patients Tuesday and Wednesday and I don't get time to finalize the grant application until Thursday. After adding the final total of our fundraising efforts to the grant application, I take it to the post office myself after work to make sure it gets postmarked. It's such a relief to have it done, and the center has been buzzing with excitement since the weekend event, knowing we exceeded our goal.

I wait in the high school parking lot for Abbie, thankful Arthur is cooking dinner tonight. I lean my head against the headrest and shut my eyes. The long days I've been putting in and the strain I've been under to make sure we raised the money are catching up with me. I shiver with a chill and am weak with fatigue.

A few minutes later, Abbie opens the door and tosses her bookbag in the backseat, startling me from any hope of a cat nap. I start to ask about practice, but before I can, she's chattering about the Pet Palooza coming up on Saturday. "I think we should go early, that way I can help Olivia with anything she needs at the garden."

The dull ache behind my eyes begins to pound. "I think you should call Olivia and see if she needs you before just showing up. Remember, Arthur is in charge Saturday, while I'm at work, so you'll need to do what's convenient for him."

That earns me a huffy look and an eyeroll, followed by an exaggerated sigh. I ignore her and steer us toward Arthur's. It's a short ride and as soon as I pull to the curb, Abbie pops out of the car, grabs her backpack, and runs to the front door. I don't have the energy to correct her. By the time I get to the door, Abbie is already inside, petting Duke, while Arthur is at the stove.

The air is infused with a mouth-watering aroma. It reminds me of my mom's chicken soup. Arthur, wearing his "Trust me, I'm a lawyer" apron, turns and greets me with a smile. His cheerfulness turns into concern as he steps closer to me. "Are you feeling unwell?"

Along with the headache I felt in the car, my throat is sore. "I'm not feeling great, but it could just be I'm exhausted. I hate to eat and run tonight. I know we planned to watch a movie, but I think I need to get home and get to bed."

"Of course, dear. As luck would have it, I made Rosie's favorite soup tonight. That will make you feel better. Let me put it in a container for you and you can get home. I'll bring Abbie home later." He turns to open a cupboard door. "She can get her homework done and we'll watch the movie."

His kind offer overwhelms me and tears burn my eyes and irritate my scratchy throat. I nod and whisper, "Thanks, Arthur."

I tell Abbie I'm going and Arthur will bring her home later. Her only concern is if she'll be able to watch the movie, not that I'm feeling ill. I carry the cloth shopping bag Arthur packed with two tubs of soup and fresh baked bread from the bakery to the car. By the time I get home, the middle of my back, between my shoulder blades, is aching. That's a telltale sign that this is more than just being tired.

I eat a bowl of soup, take some over-the-counter medicine with three glasses of water, make sure to leave the door unlocked, and snuggle under the blankets in my bed.


The next thing I know, Abbie's tapping me on the shoulder and it's morning. I can't believe I didn't hear her come in last night and start to lift my head off the pillow and realize it's still pounding. I can barely swallow and point to my throat.

Abbie frowns. "You're going to be late for work."

I shake my head and whisper, "I can't go, I'm sick. I'll call Arthur and see if he can pick you up tonight, okay?"

She has that same look on her face she had when we left Ohio without her piano. Her disappointment is unmistakable. "You were going to help with Duke's costume tonight, remember?"

"I might feel better by then," I croak out before getting up to take some more medicine.

She huffs out the door and says, "I sure hope so."

If only she meant it for my sake. Her tendency to become hyper-focused overrides her ability to empathize, and I know she doesn't mean it, but it makes me feel worse. The Pet Palooza has usurped her interest in flowers for the moment. She's been obsessing over the costumes Arthur ordered and wants my help to select the best one. I had put her off until tonight and now, the way I feel, I don't have much hope I'll be able to make it to Arthur's. It's my night to cook, but that's not going to happen either.

Arthur is not the best texter, but I've been encouraging him to do it more and tap in a message to him, hoping he'll check his phone. Despite my efforts to show him the wonders of his cell phone, including video chatting, he's told me he prefers using a landline. My voice is barely a whisper and talking right now isn't an option. While I'm waiting for him, I text Mr. Cox and let him know I'm under the weather and am unsure about tomorrow. I suspect I have more than a cold and the achiness I'm feeling points to the flu. The last thing I want to do is expose anyone to it.

I get an immediate reply from Mr. Cox telling me not to worry and he won't plan on seeing me until Tuesday. I mix up my concoction of lemon juice, apple cider vinegar, honey, and a touch of cayenne pepper that is always a sure cure for a sore throat, while I wait for my cup of hot tea to brew. I find some cough drops in a plastic bin in the bathroom and shuffle back to bed. I feel miserable and despite being in the medical profession and knowing I just need to rest and drink fluids, whenever I'm sick, I miss my mom even more.

I let myself get run-down over these last weeks and I know better. I've been rushing around and trying to do too many things. Thank goodness Arthur helped, especially with Abbie, or I probably would have been sick during the tournament. I close my eyes, hearing nothing but the occasional brush of a shrub against the window. Being on my own is hard enough, but when I'm not feeling well it only adds to the vulnerability that is always lurking under the surface.

As I remember the days Mom would fix me cinnamon toast and spiced tea and bring it on a tray to my room, a tear slides onto my pillow. She'd sit on the edge of my bed and make me take bites and sips, sometimes stroking my hair, encouraging me to rest and assuring me I'd feel better. She did that even when I was grown and no longer living at home. She would come over and fix tea and toast and put together a batch of her chicken soup. How I long for those days now.

I know if Mom and Dad were still here, our life would be so much different. They'd be there for Abbie and give her the stability I know she needs. We wouldn't be here; we'd still be back in Ohio, where everything was familiar, instead of living like nomads, wandering across the country.

That low-level anxiety that's always there when you're on your own buzzes louder in my head. I'm sure it's part of the reason I'm drawn to the population I serve. Most of my patients are older and alone, many of them without family nearby. Medical issues spark a special panic in those patients who lack support. Being able to treat them in their homes or now at the center, where the atmosphere isn't intimidating, eases some of their concerns.

I've come to care for them and, just as Arthur didn't want to go visit a new doctor each time he made an appointment, which happens far too often, especially in rural areas, my patients like being able to have a relationship with me and chat, not just about their medical issues, but about things happening in their life and in Millbury. I enjoy having my own little clinic and have come to love this welcoming community.

As I drift off, I dream of being able to stay in Millbury, where Abbie could finish high school and not have to change and go through all that drama of being the new girl twice a year. Where we'd have Arthur and Duke in our lives, and they'd have us. It's strange, but knowing he's here soothes my soul.

As the idea of making Millbury our home takes hold in my muddled brain, I'm sure I feel my mom's fingers brushing the hair from my forehead.

When I wake, it's after four o'clock in the afternoon. I could swear I just shut my eyes, but my throat is dry and sore. I reach for my phone and see I have a reply from Arthur that I missed. He tells me he'll handle Abbie and not to worry. He offers to pick up anything I need and will bring Abbie home after they go out for tacos.

And suddenly I can't help but burst into tears. Arthur is such a sweet and kind man and I don't know what I would do without him. I remember that day at the garden when he told me he was no replacement for my parents, but I could lean on him when I needed help. I have a hard time asking for help and, truth is, this is the first time since losing my parents that I've felt like I have someone I can ask. Someone reliable, someone trustworthy, someone who accepts Abbie, someone I care about and I know cares about us.

I carry my phone into the kitchen and tap in a response while I brew another cup of tea and guzzle down more water. After thanking him, I request he pick up the spicy chicken tortilla soup from Mario's, where he and Abbie will be eating tacos. If that doesn't clear out my sinuses, nothing will.

My phone beeps with another text from Arthur. He's getting good at this. Abbie wants to bring Duke by tonight so I can see his costumes. Arthur wants to know if I'm up for it.

I take a long swallow of my tea laced with plenty of honey and lemon. I know how much Abbie is looking forward to the parade tomorrow and she'll be so disappointed if I'm not involved, but I don't want to take a chance on Arthur catching this. I suggest they take photos of Duke for me and I can offer my suggestions and remind Arthur not to come inside, just to send the soup with Abbie tonight.

While I don't want Abbie to get sick, her immune system is more robust than Arthur's and my other patients' at the center. I can hole up in my room and steer clear of her until I'm feeling better, which is hopefully soon. I fix myself some cinnamon toast, knowing it will never be as good as Mom's, and wipe down the counters with an antibacterial wipe before going back to bed.

As soon as I rest my back against the pillows, fatigue sets in again. I finish off the tea and toast and scroll through my tablet to start an episode of a series I've been meaning to watch. I don't get five minutes into it before my eyes close again.

\*

A faint beep wakes me and I notice the flashing light on my phone. Photos of Duke dressed as a pumpkin and a lion are among the messages from Arthur. Abbie's kneeling next to him, with a firm hold on him in all the photos. Duke doesn't appear to be pleased with either of the costumes and the frustration on Abbie's face makes me think getting him dressed was a challenge.

The little lion mane is cute and I text back and vote for it as my choice. Arthur lets me know Abbie will be home before eight o'clock and that he'll pick her up in the morning and deliver her after dinner tomorrow night. He is my hero.

I'm not sure how I'm going to pay him back for this, but I need to think of something special.

# CHAPTER 15

## Duke

It's raining today, so that means we're stuck indoors. Arthur started a fire and is snoozing in his recliner. He's making something in the slow cooker he calls beef bourguignon. I'm not sure what it is, but the rich aroma of simmering meat fills the air and makes me drool. Abbie and Madison are coming for dinner tonight. I haven't seen Madison for several days, but Arthur said she's finally feeling better and almost back to her old self.

I'm anxious for Madison to visit and hope she notices what I've been observing in Arthur. This week, he has seemed more sluggish than usual. He's not himself and as I watched him gather things from the pantry and cut up the vegetables for dinner, I noticed he had to stop and sit down several times. With Madison being sick, she missed the Pet Palooza, which was a fun day, especially for Abbie. If Madison had been there, she would have noticed Arthur's fatigue. I'm worried that he just keeps ignoring his symptoms, brushing them off, and thinking they're nothing.

The three of us started out on the mile walk that was organized for the pets and people at the event, separate from the longer competitive run that many people entered to help raise money for the local animal shelter. Arthur walked with us only a short distance and then sat on a bench shaded by a gorgeous tree and told us to keep going and he would meet us when we finished, back where we started.

I was reluctant to leave him, but he insisted I go with Abbie and that he was fine, just a bit tired from all the excitement. It was a warm day and his pale look reminded me of the day we were walking to the center and Bill gave us a ride because Arthur wasn't feeling well. The same day I met Madison and introduced her to Arthur.

Abbie brought Arthur a cold bottle of water from the big trough filled with ice and he assured us he just needed to rest for a bit. I snuggled closer to Arthur, feeling the weariness radiating from him. He took several swallows from the bottle and sighed, smiling down at me, reassuring me that he would be fine.

Abbie and I were expert walkers since we had paced many miles back and forth together. Normally, I would have liked to dawdle along the garden pathway and linger over the flowers and shrubs, but I quickened my pace, surrendering to the urgency I felt to get back to Arthur and check on him.

Rather than walk, I trotted for most of the mile, dragging Abbie behind me, anxious to finish and get out of my ridiculous and itchy costume. We completed the mile loop in record time, crossing the finish line first. We both received gold medals with paw prints on them and a goodie bag full of human and dog treats. I had no interest in prizes or treats, only Arthur. While Abbie thanked the organizers at the table, I scanned the crowd searching for him.

Fear washed over me when I didn't see him. I tugged on the leash, pulling Abbie with me. I put my nose to the ground, seeking his scent. I followed the path we had taken at the start of the race and rushed forward, forcing Abbie to run to keep up with me. Arthur's scent was strong and I followed it to the bench where he had taken refuge in the shadow of the large tree. He was still there, looking peaked and tired.

I rushed to his side and startled him. He couldn't believe we were already finished, so hadn't made his way back to the starting area. Abbie had picked up more water at the prize table and handed Arthur another one to replace the empty bottle he held.

He thanked her and blamed his little episode on being dehydrated, asking her not to mention it to her mother, since he knew he hadn't been drinking enough water. I hope she forgets and tells her mom. He rose from the bench and let Abbie continue to hold my leash while we set out at a leisurely pace to the face-painting booth. Abbie had been eyeing it from the moment the woman set up her table. He was doing his best to carry on as if nothing was wrong.

Abbie sat on a high stool while Arthur and I watched from the tables and chairs set up in front of the food vendors. It only took a few minutes before the artist had completed her work. Abbie beamed with pride when she returned with glittery pink roses across her forehead and the elegant design circling around the edges of her eyes. She was giddy with excitement and skipped over to show us.

Despite how tired he was, Arthur fawned over her and after she showed him again how to take a photo, he used his phone to capture several of her smiling face, so she could share them with her mom. Arthur treated Abbie to tacos from the food truck and joined her in an ice cream cone, but ended up throwing most of it in the trash. He also bought me a bowl of dog treats and the lady at the ice cream truck gave me a tiny cup of whipped cream that was delicious.

I kept my eye on Arthur and, although he was less pale, I noticed him holding his head and steadying himself a few times. He never complains, but he worried me. By the way he shuffled his feet and hunched his back, I knew he was exhausted. I took it upon myself to lead us to the parking lot and Arthur chuckled, remarking that I must be ready to go. Abbie and I probably could have stayed the rest of the day, but I wanted him to get home so he could rest and feel better.

It was a short drive from the garden to Arthur's and since we left so early, there was very little traffic. Once we got home, Arthur settled into his recliner and I climbed up on his lap to comfort him.

I was tired from the excitement and running around at the garden and felt myself getting quite sleepy while listening to the soft thump of Arthur's heart. It sounded different than usual, weaker. I was so worried about him and felt something was wrong, but I didn't know what. I only knew Arthur was scared to admit it.

The savory aroma of our meal cooking tickles my nose, but I ignore it and instead reflect on my time with Arthur. I know he trusts Madison and feels such a connection to her. I wish he would just tell her what he's been experiencing. I don't understand why humans don't ask for help. The only things they're better at hiding than physical problems are their emotions. They think so, anyway.

They may be able to fool their friends and family, but they can't fool me. Dogs see what's inside, what's underneath, and we have a keen awareness of how humans are feeling and what's churning inside, deep below the surface. We detect the slightest facial movements that signal disappointment or anger or pain. We can smell fear and anxiety, along with millions of other scents. Certain illnesses, in particular, have a distinct and almost putrid aroma, making it impossible for us to ignore it, even when humans smell nothing.

I know Arthur is concerned and worried, but he's too afraid to divulge what's been happening. With my eyes, I've pleaded with Arthur to tell Sonny. I know his nephew loves him and he wouldn't want anything to happen to Arthur. I'm holding out hope that when we see Madison today, he'll work up the courage to tell her. When she asks him how he's been feeling, I might just have to bark.

Arthur talked to Sonny again this morning and never mentioned how tired he's been. Like all the other weeks, he tells Sonny he's doing well and changes the subject, asking about the weather and telling Sonny about me. I should have barked this morning and then maybe Sonny would have asked more questions.

Arthur's a dignified and quiet man and, although he doesn't divulge much, I know from what little he's said to Madison, he's not a fan of doctors and hospitals. He had his fill of them while taking care of Rosie and wants to avoid them.

I've only just found Arthur and I can't imagine my life without him. Like my mother tried to explain to me when I was still with her, I would find a family who loved me. At the time I couldn't imagine I could love anyone more than my mother, but she told me I would and now that I have Arthur, I understand what she meant. He's my person and this is my family. I would do anything to keep them together.

# CHAPTER 16

## Madison

Saturday is the first day I actually feel great and get up early to take my walk I've missed over the last week. I leave Abbie sleeping and scurry out of the mobile home park, thankful for the scarf I wrapped around my neck on the way out the door. I pluck the gloves from my pocket and slip them over my hands. The air is crisp and smells earthy with a touch of woodsmoke from someone's fire. With it being late September, a few leaves are beginning to turn vibrant autumn colors.

Millbury is quiet this morning with a bit of mist hanging over the creek and I'm alone on the trail. It feels good to be outdoors and active. I've done very little this last week, outside of putting in a few hours at work. Being sick gave me time to think about the upcoming move I planned for December. The more I thought, the more it made me realize I have to come up with a better plan than moving all the time. I can't keep this pace up forever. It's been two years since we left Ohio and I can't imagine finding a better place than this to call home.

Part of my brain tells me it's too risky to stay, but my heart tells me this is where we belong. I keep telling myself I need to be rational and not let my heart override the logic I know is true, which means we'd be safer if we kept to my original plan and moved again.

Abbie even likes school, or at least the music program and her after-school practice for the musical. We hadn't had a drama-free school week since we left Ohio, so this is a welcome change. Her love of music plays a role in her contentment, but I suspect Arthur and Duke are the true reasons for her newfound joy. I know they're the reason for mine.

Had I been laid up like I was last week at any of my other job posts, I'm not sure what I would have done. I didn't know anyone very well and there was certainly nobody I could trust with Abbie. We would have muddled through somehow, but Arthur made it much easier. I feel at ease here, knowing I have someone in my corner.

Arthur's patience and calming presence provide the stability we've been missing. His home is like a refuge, with its gorgeous yard filled with plants and trees that not only provide a wealth of new research material for Abbie, but a quiet and protected space that feeds my soul.

I've been on the run for so long, I've forgotten what it's like to sit and enjoy an evening or a meal with someone and talk about the latest news in the world or in our own little piece of it. While Arthur and I visit, he often tells me about the most recent case law established by the Oregon Supreme Court. He explains both sides of the issue and then renders his own take, sometimes agreeing with the court and other times fearing they made an error.

His mind is sharp and the uptick in his mood is evident when he talks about the law. With his passion for it so strong all these years later, I can only imagine his expertise in his prime. Along with my sense of belonging and feeling like I found something I've been missing, I've seen a transformation in Arthur over these last few months.

The cloud of heavy grief has lifted. When he tells us about Rosie, he smiles more, focused on the happiness they shared instead of only the acute loss of the love of his life. I know Duke was the catalyst that prodded Arthur into action after he lost

Rosie. I'm sure they found each other for a reason, both of them without a family and in need of each other.

When I get back, I have no trouble convincing Abbie to come to the center today. She's intent on practicing a new piece for the musical and happy to use the center's piano. I pack our lunch and include enough for Arthur, knowing he'll be there, as he is every Saturday.

It's a light schedule and Barb is the only one at the center when we arrive. As always, she greets us with a cheerful smile and offers Abbie a hot chocolate. I grab a cup of coffee and head to my office, intent on getting caught up on paperwork.

The notes Abbie plays drift down the hallway and through the open door, comforting me as I plod through charts and corporate messages. I take care of a couple of walk-in patients, who need blood pressure checks and want to chat. When I finish with them, I check my watch and frown.

It's after eleven and Arthur is always here around ten o'clock. I use my desk phone and call the house, but there's no answer. If he's driving, I hate to bother him on his cell phone, and I know he would never break the law and use it while behind the wheel, but I am too worried to care. I get my cell phone from my purse and slide my finger to his name and punch the green button. It rings several times and goes to voicemail.

It's unlike him not to call if he's not coming so I assume he's on his way. Maybe he and Duke decided to walk today, since it's such lovely weather. He could have easily forgotten his cell phone. If they're walking, chances are Duke is stopping to inspect every bush and flower, which could delay their progress. I chuckle as I think perhaps that's why he and Abbie get along so well; they both share a love of plants. Arthur could have run into someone and is busy chatting. That must be it, since even walking, the trip takes no more than twenty minutes. I start sorting through the stack of mail and papers on the corner of my desk, tossing advertisements in the recycle bin, glancing at my watch every few minutes. I scan the parking lot, but don't see his car.

After culling through most of it, I neaten the pile and put the weekly newspapers that I'm behind reading near the top.

I check the time again. I think of that first day I met Arthur, when Bill gave him a ride because he was weak and I imagine him passed out on the sidewalk somewhere between here and home. Worry nags at me. My stomach flips as a horrible feeling creeps through me. Something's wrong.

And that's when I hear it.

A faint noise that shakes me to my core. Something was telling me to worry, an indescribable gut feeling, and though it's soft, I'm sure I can hear the sound of Duke barking.

Duke rarely barks and the sound isn't his usual playful woof; it's more of a high-pitched cry. It sounds desperate, each sound coming closely after the last.

I turn out the lights and put a sign on the door, and as I step outside I see him desperately running toward the center, before circling back closer to the street.

It must be Arthur.

I collect Abbie and our lunch and tell Barb we're going to check on Arthur and to call my cell phone if she needs me. As soon as the door opens, Abbie calls to Duke and he turns at her voice. His eyes are filled with fear. He runs at full speed and she gathers him in her arms, but he wriggles free, barking again.

We load him in the backseat and I speed toward Arthur's house. Duke paces across the seat as I drive like a mad woman. As we turn the corner at Arthur's street, Duke begins whining and moaning. Abbie has been restless in the car, her legs moving and tapping against the door panel, but she's still now. Almost holding her breath.

We pull up and as soon as Abbie opens her door, Duke scuttles over the console and out of the car. How long has he been looking for help?

I sprint around the side of the house, following Duke to the backyard. By the time I get there, Duke has leapt over the garden gate. Abbie's on my heels and when I look through the steel bars on the gate, I see Arthur lying on the grass with Duke already lying next to him, his head resting against Arthur's. Duke's feathery tail is spread across him like a protective arm. His dark ears perk at the clang of the gate opening, but he doesn't move from Arthur. His soulful eyes meet mine and I can see the relief in them, as he rests his head against Arthur and licks his face. Despite Duke's big pink tongue running across his face, Arthur remains still.

# CHAPTER 17

## Duke

When Arthur fell, I tried my best to wake him, but he wouldn't get up. He held his hand to his head like he often does and then collapsed to his knees. I rushed to his side and lent him my back for support and he rested his hands on it, but then toppled over. He and Madison had been teaching me a new trick she called "play dead" where they point at me and I flop over onto my back. I knew Arthur wasn't playing a game, but seeing him keel over reminded me of the trick. It always made him laugh when I did it, but this was far from funny.

I was so scared and barked and barked, running around the yard in a frenzy, eager for someone to notice. Hoping if I barked loud enough Madison would hear me. When I didn't seem to attract the attention of the neighbors, I scrunched down next to Arthur and got as close to him as possible. Licking his face didn't seem to elicit his normal response, but I kept trying. I wanted to make sure he stayed warm, and when I placed my head on his chest, I could hear the slow thumps of his heart. I always listened to it when I snuggled with him for naps in the recliner and it was much quieter than normal.

I only raised my head to bark, holding out hope someone would hear me. My throat was dry and I could have used a drink of water, but I pushed my own needs to the back of my mind; Arthur was my only concern. He's kind and so patient. He's my everything and I knew I couldn't lose him.

I didn't know where the neighbors were, but knew if they were home they'd hear the racket I was making. I eyed the gate and thought about getting a running start to jump over it. I was sure I could do it, but then where would I go?

And that is when I knew I had to go to the center and get Madison. It was my moment. Like those stories my mother told me about dogs that rescue people, I had to be brave and do all I could to save Arthur. I knew there was a risk in leaving him and danger in taking to the streets to find Madison, but he needed help and as much as I had hoped someone would hear me and help us, Arthur couldn't wait any longer.

When I thought, then, of Arthur and all he means to me—we're family and family is always there for each other—I knew I would do anything to protect him, save him, and the love I have for him gave me the courage to act. I would have to break Arthur's rules and leave the yard, off-leash, but I knew he would understand.

I channeled the energy coursing through my veins, focused on Arthur, knowing his life depended on me. I ran toward the arched metal gate and leapt into the air, closing my eyes as I stretched as high as possible and surprised myself when I landed on my feet on the other side. I gazed at Arthur's pale face one more time before I rushed to the end of the street.

I had been to the center dozens of times and knew my way. My mind sharpened as I watched for the dangerous cars on the street and dashed across it, taking shortcuts through yards and vaulting over shrubbery to shave off time. Everything clear now, there was no doubt, no fear, just extreme focus on my goal of getting to the center and finding Madison. When the life of the person you love, your family, hangs in the balance, something transforms inside of you, physically. You can run faster, think clearer, and jump higher than you ever dreamed, because you're doing it for the person you love, the person who is your entire world.

After barreling past the market, I knew I was almost at the center. I didn't have to cross any more streets and bounded over one more hedge and into the parking lot. Now, I just needed to get inside the building. It worried me that Arthur was alone, but I pressed on, determined to get him help, knowing every second counted.

Arthur had been shaky and out of breath all morning, barely able to walk out to the patio without resting. I knew something wasn't right, but didn't know what to do. I nudged him with my nose several times, hoping he'd call Madison and tell her to come and help him.

Today, I wished more than anything I could talk. It's so frustrating to know something is wrong and lack the ability to do anything about it. I hate that I wasn't able to intervene. To convince Arthur that, just this one time, he should ask for help.

# CHAPTER 18

## Madison

It's obvious Duke is trying to wake Arthur as we rush to his side, and a ripple of fear makes me shiver.

"Oh, no. Arthur," Abbie yells as she rushes toward him. I intercept her, grabbing her arm and making her focus on me. Fear fills her dark eyes and the color has drained from her face. I ask her to help by getting Duke's leash and retrieving the throw blanket from Arthur's recliner. I don't want her to see Arthur if the situation is grave and these few minutes will give me time to assess him. She hurries to the back door and I rush to Arthur.

I place two fingers on Arthur's neck to check his pulse, and breathe a sigh of relief when I feel it. I put my ear to his chest and confirm his shallow breathing. That, coupled with his weak pulse, concerns me. I take my phone from my pocket and dial 911 to request an ambulance. I call out Arthur's name and gently shake him. His eyes flutter a few times and then he focuses on me and smiles.

"Madison, what are you doing here?" he says.

"I have a better question. What are you doing on the lawn and when did you come out here?"

He's disoriented and blinks several times. Abbie arrives with the blanket and Duke's leash. The dog can't stop licking Arthur's face and I motion Abbie to attach his leash. I put the blanket over Arthur and tuck it around him and send Abbie to the car for my medical kit.

Arthur begins to raise his head. "I'm fine, no need to worry. I just overdid it this morning."

With a gentle hand to support him, I guide his head back to the grass. "I've already called the ambulance. You're going to need to go to the hospital and have some tests."

Fear flashes in his kind eyes. "No," he whispers. "No hospitals." The dread on Arthur's face worries me. I know how much he hates the thought of going back to where he last saw Rosie, where he spent so many sad days watching her struggle and deteriorate, where he held her hand when she took her last breath, and I understand it is overwhelming. I sympathize with him, but he has to go.

Abbie returns and I use my stethoscope to have a proper listen of his heart. His pulse is still slow and I suspect a valve issue. I grip Arthur's hand. "You need some tests. I can't tell what's wrong without them. I'll be there with you, I promise. I just have to get things organized at work and then I'll come to you."

His eyes water. "Duke," he whispers. "Will you...?"

I hear the wail of sirens. "We'll take care of him, don't worry." I smile and squeeze his hand.

He pulls me closer. "Stay here at the house with him, so he doesn't get scared." The sirens go quiet as the rush of footsteps and equipment pound on the sidewalk.

While the paramedic talks to Arthur, I tell his partner my suspicions and recommend several cardiac tests. He tells me they'll be transporting him to Salem, since the Millbury hospital doesn't have the sophisticated diagnostic equipment Arthur is going to need.

As they get him on the gurney, I spot Abbie, holding on to Duke's leash, her face pale as she paces along the flowerbed. I rest a hand on Arthur's shoulder and tell him not to worry.

"My keys are on the counter. You'll call Sonny for me, will you?"

"I'll call him." I squeeze his shoulder to reassure him. "I'll see you this afternoon and don't worry about Duke, we'll take good care of him. After all, we have him to thank for saving you. He came all the way to the center and got us to follow him here. He's a hero."

As I watch them load Arthur, my legs begin to shake. Despite what I told him, I'm worried. At his age, I know this could be quite serious. I let Abbie continue to pace with Duke, since past experience has taught me it's best not to interrupt her. I know how much she loves Arthur and imagine she's scared, but when she's like this, intent on pacing, that is her sole focus and she won't listen. I have to wait until she calms to explain things to her. Thank God Duke is here.

Instead, I go inside and use my cell phone to let Barb know what's happened. I have no patients scheduled and let her know I won't be back today. Next, I use Arthur's phone and find Sonny's name.

He answers quickly. "Hey, Uncle Arthur."

"Sonny, this is Madison Ward, I'm the nurse practitioner at the Millbury Center."

His cheerful tone is gone, replaced with wariness. "Yes, my uncle speaks of you often. Why are you calling me on his phone?"

"I found him in the backyard this morning. I suspect he fainted. He's on his way to the hospital in Salem; they'll be running some tests. He wanted me to call you."

I'm met with silence and suspect Sonny is in shock. There is no easy way to tell someone news like this on the phone. "Sonny, are you there? Are you okay?"

"I just talked to him this morning and he said he's been feeling fine." Sonny's voice is thick with emotion.

"Does he ever say he isn't fine?" I smile, hoping to come across friendly and reassuring. "He has a habit of downplaying it when he's not feeling well. It's common. Salem has a great cardiac team, so he's in the right place to get this figured out." I can tell he's upset and want him to know Arthur's getting excellent care. He won't be able to be here for several hours and I don't want him spending all of them stressed and worried if I can help it.

"Right, that's good. I just need to check flights and I'll be on the first one I can get."

I want to make sure he's handling this since sometimes when people are in shock, they shut down. "Is there someone I can call to be with you, help you with the arrangements?"

Sonny lets out a heavy sigh. "No, no, I'm fine. My secretary handles my travel and I can get her on it. Just let Uncle Arthur know I'll be there just as soon as possible and please call me if anything changes. Day or night."

"I'll let him know and I promise to call you if anything changes. I'm going to figure out what to do with Duke and my daughter and drive to the hospital this afternoon. I promised him I'd be there and I can help explain anything he doesn't understand." I give Sonny my cell number and tell him to call me when he has his flight information.

I glance out the window and see Abbie, still pacing, but slower, with Duke at her side. I notice my hands are shaking when I fill the kettle with water and put it on the stovetop. I take long, deep breaths as I select a bag of tea from the box on the counter and place it in the oversized Oregon Ducks mug I usually use. I check the fridge and find a pitcher of lemonade and pour it over ice in a tall plastic glass for Abbie. The sugar will help with the shock she has had. The kettle boils and I pour it into my mug, my hands steadier. As my tea brews, I wonder what I have gotten myself into, agreeing to take care of Duke. I love Duke and especially love how he is with Abbie, but how in the world am I going to juggle a sixty-five-pound puppy full of energy with everything else? Leaving him on his own to roam around the house isn't a great option. My head spins as I think of how to care for him and I realize I can't tackle all these problems at once.

I've been trying to figure out how I'm going to let go of Arthur and Duke, the center, actually all of Millbury, and all I'm doing is digging a bigger hole. I can't imagine taking Abbie away from all of this and dragging her to the next place. Instead of distancing us from Arthur and Duke, all I've managed to do is get our lives more entangled. It's going to make it that much harder on Abbie when we leave. That much harder on me, since deep down I don't want to go.

I wander back outside to check on Abbie, and she's sitting on the steps to the patio, stroking Duke's ears. She looks up when she hears me and I hand her the glass of lemonade. "Drink this."

She takes a long swallow. "Is Arthur going to be okay?" Her voice cracks and worry is etched on her young face.

I sit down next to her, steadying my mug with one hand, while I scratch Duke's chin. "I don't know for sure, but I'm going to go and check on him at the hospital. He wants us to stay here and take care of Duke. I promised him I'd go to the hospital, so I just need to think of someone who might be willing to come and stay here while I'm gone."

"I could stay here with Duke. We'll be fine."

"I'm sure you could, but I'm not sure how late I'll be and while I don't mind you staying alone for a few hours, I don't want to leave you for that long."

She looks up at me with wide eyes. "I bet Lisa or Lori from the coffeeshop or Charlotte from the bakery would do it. They're always super sweet to Arthur."

I put my arm around her shoulders. "That's a great idea. I'll call Creekside Coffee right now. We've still got our lunch in the car. Why don't you and Duke go get it and we'll eat while I figure it out?" I collect Arthur's blanket from the patio table and shake off the grass and leaves before placing it on the back of his chair.

Abbie trudges off with Duke in tow and I place the call, my fingers crossed hoping they can help me. By the time Abbie brings the tote with our food inside, I've got things arranged with Lori.

Despite the delicious scent of the stew Arthur put together in the slow cooker, we both pick at our food and I put the leftovers in Arthur's fridge. "Let's run home and get a few things and then we'll be set for the night. Lori will be over in about an hour and can stay until I get back from the hospital."

My phone chimes and I see a text from Sonny letting me know he'll be arriving in Portland just before noon tomorrow.

I make sure the house is locked and Abbie loads Duke into our SUV. We make the quick trip to our trailer and load up our clothes and toiletries. I give Gladys a call on the after-hours number, knowing she'll be concerned if I'm gone and don't let her know. Mindful that Arthur is a private person and wouldn't want everyone in town to know about his situation, I tell Gladys we're housesitting for a friend for a few days.

Lori promised she wouldn't say anything about Arthur to anyone and I trust her to keep his confidence. Gladys has a tendency to overshare, so I don't want to tempt fate.

We carry our suitcases upstairs and take over two of the guest rooms. I scrounge some cleaning supplies from a closet and put Abbie in charge of dusting and sprucing up the rooms while I take a quick inventory to make sure there is plenty of food in the house for the next few days. I make a shopping list and tuck it in my purse. I can stop at a grocery store in Salem while I'm there.

I take the liberty of packing a few things for Arthur from his dresser and bathroom, along with his reading glasses and a book from his nightstand, and scribble down his medications from memory.

Lori knocks on the door and delivers a fancy whipped chocolate drink to Abbie and a latte to me. She comes inside and sniffs at the air. "Something smells incredible."

I nod and say, "Arthur put together dinner this morning, so you and Abbie are set. It's in the slow cooker." I gaze at Abbie and sling my purse over my shoulder.

Lori smiles at me and adds, "Abbie and I will be fine." She points at a pink tote bag on her arm. "I've got games, puzzles, movies, lots of things to keep us occupied."

I find Duke, normally full of cheer and mischief, flopped against the door, his head on the floor with his snout pressed against the doorframe. The normal spark in his eyes is gone and every few minutes he sniffs at the door and whines. I bend down next to him and stroke his ears. "It's okay, sweet boy. I know you miss him. I'm going to go and check on him and you stay here with Abbie. He's going to be okay." I know he's distraught when he shows no interest in the bit of cheese I brought for him.

I'm not entirely sure about my promise that Arthur will be fine, but feel the need to comfort poor Duke. What will Duke do if Arthur isn't able to come home?

# CHAPTER 19

## Duke

Once Madison and Abbie arrived, a calmness came over me. Madison took charge and tended to Arthur and the relief I felt having her there was indescribable.

I thought I'd lost Arthur. I couldn't do much, so watched as Madison gave Abbie instructions and helped Arthur.

When he opened his eyes and spoke to Madison, I wanted to jump into his arms, but Abbie kept me tethered on the leash. I was overjoyed that he was okay, but felt myself grow weak when they loaded Arthur into the ambulance. What was I going to do without him?

Abbie was upset and I knew she needed me, so I focused my attention on her, pacing with her back and forth along the perimeter of the yard, feeling her anxiety dissipate the more we walked. Seeing him hauled off upset me, but as I walked with her, I realized I had to be brave because as much as I would miss him, deep down I understood Arthur needed to go to the hospital. Whatever is going on with him, it can no longer be ignored.

I watched Madison check on Abbie and start to move toward us, but then change her mind and let us continue walking. She was so calm and in control with Arthur, but I noticed her hands shaking when she gathered up the throw she used to cover him. Her worry and fear made me nervous.

Once we went inside, I kept checking the front door and then the back door, hoping Arthur might be back. I couldn't help myself and kept pacing between the two. I knew he wouldn't be there, but I had this overwhelming sense of urgency to check the doors. As I was doing it, I thought of Abbie and her need to pace. It made me understand her anguish even more. Nothing she or Madison said made a difference to me, I just had to keep moving.

It's as if I had way too much energy and couldn't make myself stay still. The constant movement helped distract me and I wondered if it worked the same for Abbie. It made me feel sorry for her, if she lived with such a high level of anxiety that it drove her to this type of frenzied activity. I knew from my own observations and listening to Madison talk about her, that Abbie had calmed since coming here and loved that I was a part of helping her. I wouldn't want to feel like I felt today for an extended period of time and wondered how she coped with it for so long.

Movement. That seems to be a strong theme with the Ward women. Madison doesn't just move her body, but moves the entire household across the country.

Now, I wander to the porch, sniff at Arthur's old straw hat he wears in the garden, letting the scent of dirt and sweat comfort me. Exhausted I settle by the door, waiting for him to come home, trying not to think what I'll do if he doesn't. I will wait as long as I have to, since Arthur is my family, and I'll always be here for him. He knows that and I know he's wishing he was here with me right now. We share a bond like no other, one of unconditional love and support. The love between a dog and his human is the best that life has to offer. This connection and close relationship that has brought me more happiness than I ever imagined also has the capacity to deliver the most miserable blow, the one when Arthur has to leave me.

# CHAPTER 20

## Madison

My mind keeps going through every scenario as I drive. What if Arthur can't come home? What if he's got to be in a care center for an extended time? What will I do with Duke? How will it impact Abbie? There are just too many variables and I will myself to calm down and wait for more information before formulating a plan.

It takes less than thirty minutes to get to the hospital. I check in and learn Arthur has been admitted, but is having some tests done, so he isn't in his room. I take his care package to the fifth floor and find it. He doesn't have a roommate, which I'm sure he'll appreciate.

I put Arthur's cell phone on the table next to his bed and plug it in to charge, and his nurse pokes her head in a few minutes later. I meet her at the door and extend my hand. "I'm Madison Ward, the nurse practitioner in Millbury and Arthur's friend. I have a list of his medications and wanted to make sure you had them in the chart."

"I'm Nancy," she says, as she pulls up his record and keys in the dosages; he was able to provide the names of his medications in the emergency room, but wasn't positive on the dose information. "They should be bringing him back to the room within the next twenty minutes or so. Dr. Ruppert is the cardiothoracic surgeon on call today and he is the best. The guy I'd want doing mine. Dr. Lewis is his cardiologist and she's watching over Arthur and will be the one explaining his test results."

I nod and smile at Nancy. I like her directness and matter-of-fact way. She is sure of herself and it eases my mind a bit to know she'll be here watching over Arthur. "You mentioned the surgeon. Has he been involved yet?" I pause and add, "Arthur is not a real fan of hospitals, so he might need a bit of reassurance."

She nods her head. "Understood. I'll keep a close eye on him. As far as surgeons, Dr. Lewis has conferred with him already." She offers me something to drink and says she'll be back soon before walking through the door on her way to the next patient.

That means Arthur is facing surgery. That could mean a long stay in the hospital and even a stint in a rehab center after that. I'm not sure he would agree to that. Maybe I could manage his rehab care at home. I'd do anything to spare Arthur the distress of it all. I was hoping my suspicions about the valve were wrong and that he wouldn't be confronted with the anxiety of being away from home. He is not going to be happy about that news. Sonny can't get here soon enough.

Over the next thirty minutes, I spend time on my phone researching Dr. Ruppert and Dr. Lewis. I call one of the doctors I've come to know and respect in Salem and ask her opinion of the doctors assigned to Arthur. Her thoughts align with those of Nancy and her words reassure me.

As I'm disconnecting, an orderly wheels Arthur into the room. "Hey, how are you doing?" I ask, standing so he can see me.

His blue eyes brighten amid the paleness of his face. The orderly locks the wheels on the bed and leaves. I reposition the pillows and adjust the bed so Arthur is propped up at a good angle. "It's been a whirlwind of tests since I arrived." Dark circles ring his eyes and he looks much smaller in his hospital gown. He wrinkles his nose. "I hate the smell of this place. It reminds me of…" He turns his head and looks out the window.

I squeeze his hand to reassure him. I know the painful memories of Rosie are flooding his mind. "It's good they're running all those tests today. It will help them figure out what's going on and then come up with a treatment plan." I grip his hand tighter. "I talked to Sonny and he'll be here tomorrow. He lands in Portland just before noon."

Arthur turns toward me and smiles. "That's good news. How are Duke and Abbie getting on?"

"They're fine, but anxious to hear about you. Abbie is practicing her pieces on the piano, so Duke will be entertained. I called Lori and she volunteered to stay and watch over them until I get home tonight."

"Aww, she and her sister are both wonderful. How long do you think I'll have to stay?"

I hesitate to say much as extra stress is not what he needs right now. I don't want to lie to him but I also know he's intelligent enough to realize once they mention surgery, he'll be here longer than just a day or two. He needs to be monitored, so it's not safe for him to go home, but that doesn't take away the anxiety I know he's dealing with just being here. "It's hard to say, but since it's Saturday, I wouldn't count on getting out until next week. Sometimes it takes longer to get things done on the weekends." I glance at the bag on the other chair. "I brought you a few of your things from home." I pull out the book and reading glasses. "Your cell phone is charging. You call me anytime you need to, day or night."

"Thank you, Madison. I don't know what I would have done without you today."

I squeeze his arm. "You've come to my rescue plenty of times; I just returned the favor today."

Nancy walks in with a tray of food. "Doctor said to feed you since you're done with all your tests today. She'll be in soon to discuss them with you." She situates the tray on the narrow table and positions it in front of Arthur. "If you want anything else, just let me know."

I urge him to eat and mention that I plan on buying Duke a special treat to reward him for his bravery.

"I can't believe he jumped the gate and made it all the way to the center. It's remarkable."

I nod as I hand him some juice. "Poor little guy was distraught when we noticed him in the parking lot. He was so determined to get you help. You're lucky he was there."

Tears cloud his eyes. "I know and I can't wait to hold him and tell him how much I love him. I miss him terribly." His phone beeps and I retrieve it for him. He puts on his glasses and checks the screen. "It's a text from Lori. She says it's a video from Duke and Abbie."

He looks at me for instructions. "Just tap it." I look over his shoulder and watch as a short clip of Abbie, playing one of the songs from *Beauty and the Beast* while Duke dozes at her feet, plays on the screen.

Arthur smiles. "That is beautiful and almost makes me feel like I'm there with them. I never thought I'd be thankful for this gadget." He holds up his cell phone and shakes his head.

Keeping him focused on the future and happy events is a great way to divert him from his surroundings. "Abbie's excited about the musical. She has to sell some tickets to it and is going to put up a flyer at the center."

"I want one for sure. How many performances are there?"

"Six, I think. It's the week before Thanksgiving and they start on a Thursday night and then Friday night, plus nightly and matinee performances on the weekend. I'm going to buy tickets to all of them. I'm counting on you to be there on Saturday afternoon, since I'll be working."

"I'll be there. I wouldn't miss it for the world."

A woman with curly auburn hair and a tall man with broad shoulders come through Arthur's door. Both of them are wearing white coats with stethoscopes hanging around their necks. "Arthur," says the woman, with a cheerful smile, "this is Dr. Ruppert and we want to go over your results and tell you what we discovered."

Arthur gestures to me. "Dr. Lewis, this is Madison Ward, my nurse practitioner and my..." He chuckles. "Well, she's like my daughter."

His kind words bring tears to my eyes and I smile at him before extending my hand to Dr. Lewis. Dr. Ruppert shakes Arthur's hand and then mine.

Dr. Lewis explains that they've discovered Arthur has aortic valve stenosis, a narrowing in his aortic valve, which is the reason he fainted this morning. It also accounts for his bouts of dizziness and shortness of breath. "The good news is, we can fix it and Dr. Ruppert is going to explain how."

Dr. Ruppert gives Arthur an overview of how the valve works and explains he can replace it. He tells Arthur there are two methods he could employ; one would be the typical procedure that involves open-heart surgery and the other, which he is recommending, is a minimally invasive procedure known as a transcatheter aortic valve implantation.

He uses the whiteboard on the wall and sketches the heart and shows Arthur how he would access the area through the femoral artery with a small incision in the groin. The catheter would travel through the veins and he would position the self-expanding valve inside the old valve and then expand it. "You don't have to be under a general anesthesia for this procedure and the recovery is quite easy in comparison to the open-heart procedure. We don't have to stop the heart, which means no by-pass machine." He explains that the procedure is performed under monitored anesthesia care along with a local anesthetic at the incision site.

He continues to reassure Arthur by telling him how many hundreds of these he has done since he trained at the Cleveland Clinic in 2008 with the team who perfected this procedure. He and a team of cardiac specialists would be involved and working to make sure the valve is placed correctly and fully functional. "We'd like to do this Monday morning and then we'll monitor you for a few days and send you home."

I know patients who have undergone this procedure and did quite well and the recovery is so much easier than that of an open-heart surgery patient. Also, at Arthur's age, it makes sense to avoid an extensive surgical procedure when there is a viable alternative. But I can see Arthur is overwhelmed.

Dr. Ruppert explains the risks, which, like all surgical procedures, include death. They sound terrifying and I watch Arthur's eyes fill with doubt. He works the edge of the bedsheet between his fingers while he contemplates what the doctors have described.

Arthur studies the sketch and turns to me. "What do you think, Madison?"

"I know it sounds scary, but practically speaking you have only two choices. Doing nothing is not an option. So, we've got this minimally invasive procedure or the open-heart surgery. I think if Dr. Ruppert is recommending the easier one, it makes your decision simpler. If you were my dad, I'd want you to do what he suggests."

While I'm talking, he's fiddling with the tail of the plastic bracelet on his wrist. His watery eyes meet mine and he nods. "You're right. Given those two options, Dr. Ruppert's recommendation sounds best. Let's get it scheduled so I can get out of here." His voice is strong again, as if he's in charge.

Dr. Ruppert nods. "If you think of any questions, just jot them down or ask the nurse and I'll answer them. I'll see you Monday morning. Nice to meet you, Ms. Ward."

Dr. Lewis stays behind and explains the process and that Arthur will go to ICU after the procedure for observation. "If all goes well, you should be home Wednesday or Thursday. You'll have follow-up appointments after, but you should be back to your normal routine in a few weeks."

"His nephew will be here tomorrow, so he may have some questions," I add.

"Not a problem. I'm on call tomorrow, so I'll be around the hospital. Just have the nurse page me." She turns to Arthur and places her hand on his shoulder. "You try to relax and take it easy. I'll stop by and see you tomorrow and then I'll see you after surgery on Monday."

I follow her to the corridor and she slips me her card and adds her cell number to it. "Just call if you need anything. He'll need someone with him for a few days when he goes home. I assume you can help arrange that?"

"Of course. I'll talk to his nephew and between the two of us we'll get it covered. Thank you for your help."

She turns as one of the nurses calls her name. "Gotta run. I'll see you Monday."

I grab a coffee from the café and rejoin Arthur. I tune the television to the classic movie channel I know he watches. "How are you doing, Arthur?" I ask, adjusting his pillows and refilling his water glass.

"I just never expected to be in the hospital today. It's all happening rather quickly. Would you mind calling Sonny and letting him know the latest news?" he asks.

"Sure, I'll call him and give him the details. That way he'll be prepared when he arrives tomorrow."

"You don't need to sit here with me, dear. I'm exhausted and imagine I'll drift off to sleep early tonight."

"I don't mind keeping you company for a bit."

"Not for long, I'd rather you got home before dark."

I place my hand on his. "Now you sound just like my dad."

He smiles and focuses on watching *It Happened One Night*, laughing at the antics and witty banter of Clark Gable and Claudette Colbert. He turns to me and says, "This was one of Rosie's favorites."

I sit by his side until he closes his eyes.

When I get to my car, I call Sonny and explain the test results and what the doctors recommended. "He's very glad you'll be here tomorrow. I'll be at the hospital in the morning, so I'll see you there."

After he thanks me, I disconnect and head back to Millbury, for most of the way praying that Arthur will be okay. I feel such a need to protect Arthur and take care of him. Medically speaking, I know the procedure he's undergoing is the right thing to do, but I can't shake the fear deep inside that something could go wrong. There are real risks, especially at his age. I tried my best to be positive for him, as the last thing he needs to see from me is even a hint of doubt. I've only known him for a few months, but I can't bear the thought of losing him.

# CHAPTER 21

Keeping in mind Arthur's concern that I get home before dark, I wait until I get to Millbury and stop at Village Books & Café for a coffee. The need to clear my head and the beauty of the creek babbling behind the shop beckons me. There's a chill in the air, but not enough to deter me. I don my gloves while I wait for the barista.

I leave my car, take my coffee, and set out along the familiar pathway, resplendent with orange and bronze leaves amid lush bushes, many of which have turned a fiery red. It's my favorite time of year and I delight in the sound of my shoes crunching on a few errant leaves as I cross under the bridge.

Living here, surrounded by the peaceful beauty, calms my mind. This is the first place we've lived since we left Ohio where I've been able to relax. This cozy little town feels like a safe haven and allows me a respite from the constant state of chaos I've been living in for the last two years. I have time to myself, time to think, which is both a blessing and a curse.

When you're busy and running every minute of the day, there's little time for soul-searching. To be honest, I'd structured my life in such a way that I didn't have time to linger with my thoughts. Thinking is too painful. Sometimes the happiest of memories delivers the most misery. If all my energy was focused on our next move and keeping food on the table, I didn't have to think, to remember.

There are certain parts of the past I have relegated to the darkest recesses of my mind, locked away in a cabinet I dare not open. They are too painful, too shameful. Sometimes, when I am feeling brave, I'll let myself open another cabinet, the one that hold all the happy times with my parents, but usually even those joyful memories are too powerful, too strong of a reminder of all that I have lost.

Memories of fall baking, Halloween, and the other holidays that come just around the corner flood my mind. Mom and Dad always went out of their way to make every occasion special for Abbie. Mom made sure they found time to make her famous spice cookies with maple frosting this time of year and she and Dad took Abbie to the pumpkin patch. She made sugar cookies and let Abbie cut out Halloween shapes and decorate them with orange and black sugars and icing. She always made the most delicious Thanksgiving dinner and let Abbie decorate their huge Christmas tree.

Without them, it's just not the same. Abbie and I try, but it's lonely and the looming season, which had always been filled with fun and wonder, now only triggers additional anxiety.

The idea of having Arthur and Duke to spend these moments with this year quiets my unease. They've filled some of the emptiness in my heart and given me recent memories that are safer to cherish. As much as I've told myself I can't get too close, or let Abbie get attached, they've been impossible to resist. Even knowing the risks, the comfort they offer is something I can't imagine leaving behind in just a couple of months. I've never felt grounded like I do here in Millbury and, despite the pull I feel to stay, I know I have to find a new post. A new town. A new run-down apartment. A new place where we aren't known.

When I think about it, though, I get sick to my stomach. How can I take Abbie away from a school she actually likes, a music program that brings her such joy, a sweet dog who understands her more than any human, and a loving man who has welcomed us with love and encouragement, the likes of which I've never experienced except for that of my parents?

Each time we move, Abbie backslides. Her obsessions get worse and she withdraws more. I'm only doing this to protect her, but somehow, I feel like all I'm really doing is adding to her troubles, causing her more pain, and ruining her childhood. She shouldn't have to suffer for what I've done.

Arthur's calming guidance and assurance is what I've been missing and no matter how many times I've told myself to stop relying on him, knowing I won't have him soon, I can't keep from seeking the solace he offers. Now, with him in the hospital and me volunteering to handle Duke, it's only going to make things that much more difficult.

My natural instinct is always to help someone, which is what I enjoy most about my job. Helping patients feel better or getting them connected with the right resources that change their lives in positive ways brings me such satisfaction. It also keeps me from dwelling on my own hardships. Everyone is suffering, everyone has lost loved ones, and spending my time trying to make someone's life a little better helps me realize this.

I wonder if promising Abbie a dog when we move to the next town would help. I kick at a rock in front of my shoe and bounce it back into the dirt alongside the pathway. But the life we can offer isn't fair to a dog. In reality, it isn't a proper life for us either.

I've never hesitated to leave my other posts, but this time I feel like I have two choices. On one hand, there's the risk of staying here. The familiar niggle of fear creeps up my neck. When I even begin to think of what could happen, it stops me cold. Can I risk everything for the warmth and support this small town and Arthur, along with his loyal dog, provide? We could be happy and live here surrounded by a loving community, where Abbie could not just survive, but thrive, finish high school, maybe even get a music scholarship and have the semblance of a family. But we'd be putting these people at risk. Or, we could be safer and hit the road, moving to the next town we've never heard of, where it would take months for Abbie to adjust, if she ever adjusts, and then we do it all again.

Now, with Arthur's medical situation, it's even more complicated. If anything goes wrong and something horrible happens to Arthur, I don't know if I could handle it. Everyone that is meaningful in my life, everyone I love, leaves.

Then there's Abbie. How could I possibly explain another loss to her? She's had far too many in her young life.

Logically, I keep reminding myself, Arthur's prognosis is good. With my background and what I know about the procedure, the odds are in Arthur's favor. I just know things can go wrong, the unexpected happens, and in the blink of an eye life can change.

If things go well, Arthur is still going to need some help and that will require we spend even more time with him, more time with Duke. That means it will be even more difficult to extricate ourselves from Millbury when it's time to leave in December. Visions of driving away as Abbie bawls, waving to Duke and Arthur from the back of the SUV, flash in my mind.

Surprised at the wetness I feel on my cheeks, I use my gloved finger to dry my tears. I hate the idea of moving and have been ignoring the email I received from the HR department about opportunities with January start dates. I have to put in my request by next week and I can't bear the thought of it. I keep hoping for a solution, or at least a sign.

Maybe Arthur needing more of our help is a sign. I just worry with me volunteering to watch Duke and becoming more involved in Arthur's care, what it will do to him if we leave. When we leave. If he starts relying on us too much, it will break his heart. He's already lost Rosie and I don't want to be the cause of another loss in his life.

I reach the reservoir and toss my empty cup in the garbage can next to the bench. The sun is low on the horizon, its brilliant golden light flickering across the water, glinting off the trees lining the shore. The picturesque scene and the quiet wash over me, delivering me the stillness I need. If I am ever going to stop running and try to make a life in a new place, this would be it.

Plenty warm after my walk, I take off my gloves and let the last of the sun warm me. I sit and do nothing, emptying my mind, letting nature work her magic. Several deep breaths later, I feel less stressed. I glance down to check my watch and when I move my wrist a beam of golden light catches the face and flashes from it to the sapphire ring on my right hand. The impact of that tiny spark of light sends chills down my arms.

I've been wearing both the watch and the ring since I picked them up when I took possession of all my parents' things after the accident. They bring me a bit of comfort in that I know the metal that now circles my finger surrounded my mom's for decades, and having the sensation of Dad's band around my wrist makes me feel like he's there with me, holding my hand sometimes. Today, I feel both of them, stronger than I've ever felt them before.

It's as if they're sitting right here next to me, their arms around me, Dad squeezing my shoulder and Mom patting my arm, telling me it's going to be okay. They wouldn't want me wandering the country, dragging Abigail from town to town, living in constant fear and turmoil, and never having a proper home. They'd forgive me anything—even the mess I caused losing all they had left me—but seeing how we're living would distress them.

I know they would admire Arthur and be grateful for the guidance and wisdom he has given me. I also know I can trust him. I need to tell him everything.

I take one more long breath and head back to my car, feeling a bit guilty for the indulgence I've allowed myself when I should have been back at Arthur's. I quicken my pace and am breathing heavily by the time I return to the car.

No longer the least bit chilled, I roll down the window and let the crisp autumn air cool my skin. Someday, I've told myself over and over, I'm going to have to be brave enough to stop running, stay somewhere, make a new life. I think someday is finally here. I just hope I'm not making a huge mistake.

# CHAPTER 22

## Duke

Arthur didn't come home last night.

Abbie told me I could sleep with her in the room she was using upstairs. Arthur never ventured upstairs or used the space and told me I wasn't allowed up there. There was something about the off-limits area that beckoned me, teasing me each time I walked by the staircase.

I'd only disobeyed him once. When he was out running errands one day, I watched out the window and saw his car head toward town and then hurried up the stairs. I explored all the rooms and sniffed in the scents. The most prevalent scent was Rosie's. I recognized it as the same fragrance from the bottle Arthur spritzes his pillows with and the pleasant smell tickled my nose as I wandered through the rooms. One chair, in particular, was saturated with the delightful smell of roses, as were several decorative pillows embroidered with colorful threads. Despite wanting to linger upstairs longer and roll across the carpets to keep the sweet smells with me, I didn't dally and hurried back downstairs to make sure I was where I was supposed to be when Arthur returned.

Now, with permission to roam, I sniffed the bookcase in Abbie's room and let the floral scents from the covers mingle with the rich aroma of dirt from the garden embedded in the pages and waft through my nose. They're the same comforting scents

I detected on the pink gardening gloves and flowered clogs that are by the potting bench on the patio. I took the time to rub up against the chair and roll across the carpets, hoping when Arthur comes home, he'll smell me and be comforted.

I was exhausted last night from the stress of Arthur leaving and not knowing what was happening. After Lori served Arthur's stew and even drizzled a bit of the juice on my kibble, which was delicious, Abbie elected to go to bed early, and I followed her upstairs. She listened to piano music while tears leaked from her eyes. I knew just how she felt and snuggled in next to her, close enough to lick the salt from her cheeks. Without Arthur, a piece of me is missing and I feel that same pain and fear from Abbie.

Madison has been teaching me a new game she calls "clean up." She gives me bites of cheese each time I drop one of my toys in the big box on the porch. It's a fun game that lets me run around the house and gets me my favorite treat and lots of praise when I get the toy in the box. Abbie tried to play it with me last night, but neither of us were in the mood. Without Arthur and Madison, it's just not the same. It's difficult to concentrate on anything but worrying about Arthur.

This morning, I thought for sure Arthur would be home, but while we were sleeping, only Madison returned. I listen as she explains to Abbie about Arthur and his need for surgery. She also tells us that Sonny will be arriving today and staying at the house. With tears in her eyes, Abbie asks her mother if Arthur will be okay, and Madison tries to reassure her, but I notice she doesn't promise anything.

I miss Arthur more than I thought possible. More than I miss my mother. I think about Arthur stuck in a place he doesn't want to be, scared and alone, without me there to comfort him. Sorrow fills my heart and the seriousness of Arthur's condition bears down on me. I'm thankful Madison and Abbie are here to keep me company and distract me from worrying. I just wish I could see him, feel his hand on my head, and know that he is going to be okay.

I wander to the back porch and pick up one of Arthur's shoes, placing my head across it, burrowing my nose inside, sniffing in all the smells that remind me of him—the soil from the garden, his sweat-soaked leather gloves, the rich scent of his pipe tobacco tinged with sweetness, and the salty smell of the pistachios he loves to eat. I think of the man I met that day in the park and how much he has changed.

I know what it's like to feel alone and lost. We are both lost souls.

In our early days, Arthur's smiles were few and far between. He was suffering. I saw it in his eyes when he looked at photos, or touched Rosie's clothes in the closet, or breathed in her perfume. His heart was broken and there was nothing to say to ease his pain. People tried, but Arthur stood tall, thanked them and never let on how devastated he was. I could feel it and I just let him know I was there, allowing him to stroke my head and ears, taking in his sadness, easing his burden.

I know Madison is worried about Arthur, but she's been troubled since the first day we met her. That anguish in her comes and goes, and the more time she spends with Arthur and me, the more it diminishes, but there's more to her story. Something in her past that frightens her. I wish she trusted us enough to tell us.

At times she opens up a bit, but she's holding something back. The way humans do this baffles me. Dogs aren't secretive. I'm not sure we can even hide what we're thinking or feeling. Despite not being able to talk, we communicate how we feel in our body language and our vocalizations. You can see it in our eyes, how we hold our tail, if our ears are up or back, and if our hackles are raised.

When Arthur rests his head against mine, I can feel what he's thinking, his worry, his sadness, and his joy. I let my loving thoughts travel through my forehead to his and transfer all my happy thoughts to him.

Without the ability to use words, we use the tone of our bark or whine to communicate what we're feeling. I often let out a long sigh when I'm on Arthur's lap because I feel content and safe. When I see Abbie or Madison, I sometimes whine or let out a happy bark because I'm so excited. When Arthur fell, my barks weren't friendly or in greeting, they were desperate yells for help and whines filled with fear. If you pay attention, you'll know exactly what we're thinking.

Humans, on the other hand, hide so much from each other. So many secrets, but dogs can tell. We can see through the outside and look inside at the soul. There, we look for kindness and love, like what I saw in Arthur. We're quick to forgive, since nobody is perfect and we don't harbor grudges if we get scolded because we know, deep inside, if a soul is worthy. We always look for the best in humans, and when we find our human, our family, we are loyal forever.

I need Arthur to come home soon.

Abbie has promised me a walk in the park today, and Lori is coming back to stay with us. While Madison is leaving for the hospital and Lori is talking to Abbie, I sneak down the hallway and find myself in Arthur's room. I know he doesn't like me to get on his bed, but I think this one time he'll make an exception. I steel myself and leap onto it, sniffing at the bedspread and burrowing my nose into his pillow. The scent of Arthur is the strongest here and comforts me. I sniff him in, letting the nutty, savory scent of his beloved pistachios, the spicy smell of his tobacco, and the earthy aroma from the garden that follows him everywhere waft through my nose.

If I close my eyes, I can feel Arthur against me and hear his gentle voice soothing me.

# CHAPTER 23

## Madison

Lori offers to stay with Abbie and Duke again on Sunday and I set out for the hospital, promising to be home in the late afternoon, knowing Sonny will be there to sit with Arthur. It's another gorgeous fall day and my ride to Salem is peaceful. After my walk to the reservoir, I spent hours last night researching outcomes for the procedure Arthur will endure, along with checking the hospital statistics, and I feel more confident this morning.

Those of us in the medical profession toss out complex terms and tout studies and statistics and think we're reassuring, but when you're on the receiving end of that conversation, it's frightening. I hope Sonny provides some additional moral support. I'm so relieved Arthur has someone who is willing to race across the country to be there for him. I sensed such concern in his voice when I talked to Sonny and know he has a deep love for Arthur. It makes me realize how alone I truly am. If something happened to me, Arthur is the one who would rush to help. I don't have any siblings, cousins, or lifelong friends, and without my parents, I'm on my own.

I stop at Dutch Bros and pick up a latte on my way to the hospital.

I find Arthur sitting up in bed, reading.

"Good morning," I say. "How are you feeling?"

His eyes light up at my greeting. "Not bad, much better than yesterday. Just finished up breakfast and they tell me I'll need to eat lightly for the rest of the day."

"I talked to Sonny last night and explained everything about the procedure. He's anxious to see you."

"I guess being in the hospital is one way to get him to visit." His normal confident voice is now quiet and sad. Arthur closes the book and shakes his head. "Aww, I didn't mean it the way it sounded. I just wish he'd come out more often, but I know it's not easy."

"It's a long trip and when you're working it can be tough to get away."

Arthur nods. "I woke up early this morning and have been thinking for hours. I realize I'm going to need some help when I get home. I've actually been contemplating this idea for quite some time, but now with this situation, it's brought it to the forefront of my mind. I'm wondering how you would feel about you and Abbie moving in with me? I know you mentioned you receive either the trailer or a housing allowance from your company and I've got that big house, practically empty upstairs. You and Abbie could take over the top floor."

I can't help but think of that little shimmer of light from the sun across the reservoir and Mom and Dad. It's a good thing I took that walk yesterday afternoon. I'm not sure I would have been open to Arthur's idea had I not wrestled with the thought of leaving and searching for a way to stay here.

He clears his throat and continues. "I meant what I said about feeling as if you're the daughter I've always wanted. I can't tell you what it has meant to me to have you and Abbie around. I know it might seem unorthodox, but I've grown quite fond of both of you, not to mention Duke would be thrilled to have you as housemates. From what you've said, I know you like living in

Millbury and I hope you'll consider staying here and making this your home. It would be a wonderful place for Abbie."

I wipe a tear from my cheek and scoot my chair closer to him. "Truth is, I've been fantasizing about the idea of staying in Millbury, Arthur. I love it here. Abbie is thriving and I'm tired and dread the idea of moving again."

He pats my hand. "I sense there's more to the constant travel-ing than just a new job post."

I let out a long breath. Arthur has always been open with me, and I feel like it's time I told him the truth.

"It's a long story, Arthur, and one that embarrasses me." He nods and I feel comforted. "When my parents died, I was a mess. I'd talk to my mom every morning, while we drank our coffee. She always read the paper and would tell me about the latest local news while we chatted. She'd wish Abbie a good day at school and tell me to blow her a kiss from Grandma." I take a swallow from my cup. "My mom and dad were a constant presence in my life. Abbie would often go to their house after school, and many times I'd stay for dinner, visiting with Dad while Mom made dinner and Abbie visited with her. They were just always there. When I lost them, I lost my world."

I swallow hard and continue. "Cody, my long-term boyfriend, took charge when it all happened. He helped me deal with all the legal issues and the estate. I was so grateful for him. I didn't have the mental strength to do it. I was in shock and, honestly, sometimes I still feel like it really didn't happen. I keep hoping I'll wake up one morning and find out it was all just a horrible dream. I let Cody make all the decisions and he handled the sale of their house and property. Once the estate was closed, we opened a joint account and transferred all the proceeds into it."

Arthur frowns and urges me forward with a nod. "We were going to build a house. Cody hired a contractor and bought a piece of land. We picked out a house plan and were set to start on it." I twirl Mom's ring on my finger and reach for another sip of coffee. "I should preface this by saying Mom and Dad never really liked Cody. They were thankful I had help with Abbie, but I know Dad didn't fully trust him. He was always trying to set me up with people he knew. He never came right out and said that he didn't like Cody, but his continual suggestions of where I might find a nice guy were his not so subtle way of telling me he didn't approve. He never warmed to Cody, never suggested they do things together. He tolerated him, but he thought I could do better than Cody." I look out the window and add, "I should have listened."

I've never told anyone this story and the words stick in my throat. "One day, I stopped by the bank to cash a check from a coworker, who was repaying me for something I ordered for her. Anyway, the teller gave me a slip that showed the balances in my accounts. The account with our house money had only a couple of thousand dollars. I asked some questions and the teller gave me a complete printout of the account."

Arthur murmured. "I think I know where this is going."

I nod slowly and study the floor tiles before continuing. "Cody had taken the money. I went home and confronted him and he went ballistic. He kept blaming the bank and I wanted to believe him. Part of me hoped it was true, but the other part of me knew it wasn't. I showed him the evidence from the bank and the withdrawals he had made. It got ugly."

Arthur shakes his head. "I'm so sorry, Madison."

The clatter of a cart coming through Arthur's door interrupts us. I grab a tissue and excuse myself, thankful for a few minutes to compose myself. I make my way to the restroom down the hall, blot at my face and fan a cold paper towel in front of it, hoping the red blotches diminish.

My heart is racing, just like it was that night when Cody grabbed my throat. I thought it had been long enough, I wouldn't have such a visceral reaction to the memory. Telling Arthur just brought it all back, like I was right there again, feeling his hands tighten around my neck, seeing that out of control look in his eyes, knowing there was no easy way to get away from him. My hands are shaking and I try to remind myself I'm far away from him and that Abbie is safe.

I take a few deep, calming breaths, willing myself to relax. Tilting my wrist, I check my watch and brush my fingers over the smooth face, contemplating what my dad would think of Arthur's suggestion. He would love him, no doubt, and be so grateful that I have someone in my life to support me.

Mom's sapphire ring catches the light and sparkles, like it did last night. I choose to think that's her way of telling me staying in Millbury is the right thing to do. The ache that's been wedged between my shoulders has eased a bit. The monster that's been chasing me for the last two years doesn't seem so scary now. Despite Arthur's condition, his strength and confidence bolster my own and the idea of living in Millbury calms me.

I take a coffee to go and head back to Arthur's room. As I get closer, I hear another man's voice and stop. "Uncle Arthur, what are you thinking?"

Moving closer, I can hear more. His tone is urgent and concerned.

"Asking a strange woman and her daughter to move in with you? I can arrange to pay for help if you need it. I don't want you at risk. Are you sure this is wise?"

My heart drops and I know that it's Sonny. I thought he'd be much like Arthur, but it doesn't sound like it.

"Trust me, when you meet her, you'll see," I hear Arthur reply. "Madison's a kind and wonderful woman. She lost her husband when her daughter was very young and both of her parents a few years ago. She's had a bit of a rough go of it. She could use a little support and I need help, so it's the perfect solution for both of us. She and Abbie have already been a huge help to me. Madison is terrific with Duke, and Abbie plays the piano just as beautifully as Aunt Rosie did."

Sonny sighs. "I remember you telling me that and I know she's been kind to you. She sounds very nice and I know how impressed you were with her work to get the grant funding for the transport bus, but I just want to protect you."

"You're not in D.C., Sonny. I know you're cynical based on the work you do and the people you encounter, but I can assure you, Madison is the real thing, salt of the earth. I would trust her with my life. She's been here all morning and she should be back soon. Spend some time with her and get to know her."

"Okay, okay," Sonny chuckles, and he sounds just like Arthur in his laugh at least. "You're obviously as sharp as ever and convinced this is the right decision. I'll meet her with an open mind, I promise."

I wait, listening while they banter back and forth about the merits of a case Sonny must be working on. Something to do with excessive prices for apps purchased via cell phones. I inhale a deep breath, and come through the door. A tall man clad in jeans, his broad shoulders beneath a dark green T-shirt, turns toward me. After listening to Sonny air his doubts about me, I wanted to dislike him, but his thick dark hair and five o'clock shadow soften my opinion.

# CHAPTER 24

Arthur introduces me to his nephew, and Sonny extends his hand. I notice his well-defined muscles and strong forearms. I fumble with my coffee cup as I focus on his whiskey-colored eyes, the warmth in them betraying none of the misgivings I heard in his voice when he quizzed his uncle about me. "Pleasure to meet you, Madison. Thank you for taking such good care of Uncle Arthur."

He doesn't look anything like the lawyer from D.C. I expected to meet. I imagined someone completely different. "I'm so glad you're here. How was your flight?"

"Uneventful. The best kind," he says and laughs. "I do need to grab something to eat, but I don't want to miss the doctor."

"Oh, I'll go chat with the nurse and see if we can get her to page Dr. Lewis. She's Arthur's cardiologist and can explain everything and answer any questions."

I set my coffee and purse on Arthur's bedside table, and he winks at Sonny. "See, I told you she was something else."

I make my way to the nurse's station and find Nancy. She puts in a call, and a few minutes later Dr. Lewis steps off the elevator.

"Hi, Madison. I was just on my way to check on Arthur, so perfect timing."

I follow her to the room, and she introduces herself to Sonny. I make a move to grab my things, and Arthur shakes his head. "You stay here. When she's done, you can take Sonny to find some lunch and keep him company."

Dr. Lewis explains about the problem with the valve in Arthur's heart and the procedure he'll undergo to install a new one. Sonny asks several questions, all of them reasonable and thoughtful. When she's answered everything, she turns her attention to Arthur.

"How are you feeling today?" she asks, listening to his heart and making him take deep breaths as she checks his lungs.

"Wonderful, especially now that Sonny is here." Arthur's smile widens when he looks at his nephew.

"We're all set for tomorrow morning. You're first on the list, so they'll come and get you prepped about six o'clock. The procedure usually takes no more than two hours. You'll be in cardiac intensive care the rest of the day and then probably back in a regular room on Tuesday. We'll keep an eye on you and if all goes as planned, discharge you on Wednesday or Thursday."

"I vote for Wednesday," says Arthur, adding a laugh, but I know he's serious.

She pats his hand and says, "We'll do our very best. I promise." She taps a note in her laptop and wishes us a good afternoon before leaving.

Sonny raises his brows. "She makes it sound easy."

I bob my head. "I wouldn't say it's easy, but it's much easier than the open-heart procedure. I've done quite a bit of research on the procedure, the hospital, and the surgeon. He has the highest outcomes of all the surgeons in the area, even surpassing most of them in Portland. I've checked with another doctor and I'm confident Arthur is in good hands."

Sonny's eyes widen. "I guess Uncle Arthur was right about you. Thank you for going the extra mile for him."

"I'm going to take a nap. Why don't you two kids go find somewhere for Sonny to eat," Arthur says, pulling the blanket up to his chin.

I collect my things and lead the way to the café. Sonny orders and talks me into a piece of pie, so he doesn't have to eat alone.

"How long are you able to stay?" I ask, taking my first bite of the berry pie that, while tasty, doesn't hold a candle to Charlotte's.

"I've got a flight booked for Thursday, but can change it if necessary. I have a case I really need to be home for on Friday. I had planned to hire a caregiver for Arthur, but he tells me he's asked you and your daughter to move in so you can help him. Are you sure you're up for that?" His tone is softer than when he was talking to his uncle and I was eavesdropping.

"I want to talk to my daughter about moving in, but I would be there for Arthur regardless. We've become quite close with him and Duke," I reply. "We have meals together several times a week. I know it may seem odd to you, but I've come to think of him as family, not exactly like my parents, but similar in that we rely on him often and he can count on us to help him with anything he needs. After losing my parents, I've really missed that."

Sonny nods as he dips a fry in ketchup. "I understand. He's like a rock, so steady and reliable. He's been that same force in my life, with my dad dying when I was just a baby. He's always been there for me and my mom, treating me like I was his son. He made sure I went to law school. He and Rosie have been there for every important event in my life." His voice cracks as he finishes the sentence, and I reach across the table for his hand.

"He's strong and he's going to be okay," I reply. "I just know it. I promise I'll keep a close eye on him."

He nods and smiles, turning his hand over to clasp mine. "I know you will." He releases my hand and goes back to his sandwich. "I've been so worried about him since he lost Aunt Rosie. I noticed a change in his mood when he got Duke. He put on like the dog was a bother to him, but I could hear his happiness when he laughed and told me about his antics. When you and Abbie came into his life, his cheerfulness only increased. I can tell in the upbeat tone of his voice when he talks about you."

I smile as I load my fork with another bite. "Yes, Arthur has told me about you and your calls. He thinks the world of you and his love for you is evident." I want to tell him how much Arthur wishes he visited more often, but now is not the time.

He shrugs and a boyish grin fills his face. "I'd love to get out here every couple of months, but it's hard with my work schedule." He finishes the last two fries. "I hate to admit this, especially after seeing you here today and all you've done, but I was worried when Arthur mentioned you. My first thought was some con artist had gotten her claws into him and was going to steal from him or try to get him to sign over his assets. I realize now how ridiculous that was."

His honesty is unexpected. "I can understand how you would think that," I reply. "I've worked with older patients for the last few years and have seen my share of so-called caregivers, who are unscrupulous to say the least. It's sad, but Arthur's demographic is susceptible to scammers. I don't blame you for being suspicious, especially being so far away, but I can assure you I'm not one of them. I detest people who take advantage of others, especially those so vulnerable."

I realize I have to tell Arthur the rest of the story concerning Cody. Now, with Sonny here, it's probably best if he hears it as well. I know Arthur trusts me, and I only hope after I tell him everything else he'll feel the same way. With Sonny already suspicious, I'm not convinced he'll be as understanding.

Done with his sandwich, Sonny reaches for his slice of pie. "Most of my work centers around legislative affairs, but I do quite of bit of pro bono work and love to take on cases where I can help people like those you mentioned get some justice. It makes them feel less like a victim and more like they have some control when they have a voice in the system."

I can feel myself warming to Sonny already. "It's so satisfying to make a real difference in someone's life, isn't it?" I say, warmed by his words. "I enjoy that part of my job the most. Working here at the center is wonderful because I can really get to know my patients and chat with them and be part of their lives, not just the person they see for their medical ailments. It's a wonderful place where they can stay active, get some proper nutrition, exercise, and most importantly socialize and know someone cares about them."

He places his fork down on the empty plate. "It's nice to see you so enthusiastic about your work. Sounds like Arthur was fortunate to meet you."

I laugh, thinking back to the first time I met Arthur. "Actually, Duke introduced us."

"Ah, that's right. Arthur says you're quite the dog trainer."

"I wouldn't go that far. I had dogs growing up, so learned a few things along the way. He's also very motivated by cheese." I finish my pie and slide the plate away from me. "Speaking of that, you'll meet him tonight. Abbie and I have been staying at the house watching Duke, but we can move back to our place while you're here."

He shakes his head and frowns. "No, you don't need to disrupt things. I'm going to spend most of my time here at the hospital. Just need a place to sleep and take a shower." He gestures to the table. "Shall we get back to Arthur?"

I order a coffee to go and wait for it, standing next to our table. "I'm going to pick up some groceries on my way home, so plan to have dinner when you get to Arthur's tonight. You can meet my daughter and Duke. I'm off tomorrow and will be here when Arthur gets out of surgery. I'll just need to get Abbie to school first."

"That's nice of you, but you don't need to cook."

I grimace. "Someone's warned you already, have they?"

He's caught off-guard, unsure how to react to my flippant comment, but grins. "So, I take it you passed up a career in the culinary arts and chose the medical profession instead?"

I laugh. "Right. I'm close to useless in the kitchen. I can make about five things, including toast."

"I love to cook, but rarely have the time and cooking for one is almost pointless."

"I can relate. By the time my day is done, the last thing I want to do is spend time in the kitchen. Arthur and I share responsibility for meals, but my contribution is take-n-bake pizza on Tuesdays. We take turns cooking on Thursday and Friday."

"Rosie was an excellent cook. Arthur never had to do much cooking, so I'm impressed."

"He uses her recipes and they've all been delicious."

"You've probably noticed, he's quite precise, so I'm sure he follows them to the letter. That attention to detail and accuracy, along with a ton of common sense, and a true heart of a servant are what made him such an outstanding jurist."

The barista hands me my coffee, we bus our table, and head back to Arthur's room. "I'm just going to say goodbye and head to the store. Do you want me to pick up anything in particular?"

A crease forms on his forehead. "Hmm, I think I'll treat you to my chicken marsala while I'm here. I'll text you what I'll need."

We take the last few steps to Arthur's door and Sonny turns to me. "I'll be here early tomorrow since I'll still be on east coast time. I'll visit with him before they take him in for the procedure."

"I'm sure that will help calm his nerves. Having someone to talk to will be a good distraction."

We find Arthur having an early dinner and I take the chair next to Arthur's bed, while Sonny leans against the ledge below the windows. After a few minutes, I work up my nerve to finish telling Arthur the story I began this morning.

"Arthur, there's something else I need to tell you. About Cody," I say.

Arthur nods and turns to Sonny. "Cody was Madison's fiancé, who she was just telling me ended up stealing all the money from her parents' estate."

Sympathy tinges Sonny's eyes, and I wince. Arthur speaks so plainly, and the sharpness of it surprises me.

"Arthur was kind enough not to point out I was far too trusting and, having lost my parents, was not handling the grief and depression well. If we're going to be living with you, it's important that you know"—I glance at Sonny—"you both know, the whole story."

Sonny bobs his head. "So, a jerk of a guy takes advantage of you while you're in a fragile state. That's not your fault."

His expression of support spurs me to continue. "I was so hurt, just shattered, really. How could this man I had loved and had been a part of my life, of Abbie's life, betray me like that? For money? I had supported him when he was going to school for computer programming. My credit cards had racked up all the charges that went to helping him start his business with the promise of him paying me back when it started making money. I trusted him." I shake my head. "I was so foolish."

"It happens, dear," Arthur says, reaching for my hand. The night everything escalated is burned in my brain, the memory of it flashes before my mind and I feel like I can't go on. But Arthur's touch is comforting and I know I have to. I've spent so long keeping everything inside.

"He became violent one day. We argued. I shouted. He pinned me up against the wall, choking me. He threatened me and told me if I made trouble for him, he'd make sure Abbie was taken away from me." My eyes start to water and I concentrate on keeping my voice steady. "He said I was a horrible mother and he'd documented the times I had left her on her own when I had to work after I lost my parents." I take some tissues from the box by Arthur's bed and wipe at my eyes. "He was right, I was barely functioning after their accident. Some days I don't even remember and I know I did leave her on her own a few times when I shouldn't have. He told me he'd ruin my life if I tried to report him. I wanted to leave, but he told me not to even think about it and that he'd find me and make sure they took Abbie from me."

Sonny shakes his head with disgust.

Arthur's grip tightens on my hand, and my other one shakes as I balance my coffee cup and take another long sip. "I didn't know what to do. Though he only held me against the wall long enough to make his threat, I knew in my heart he could do something like that again, or worse. For a couple of months, I pretended everything was fine. I didn't let Cody know that I was planning to leave. I told him I trusted him, that I loved him. If I lost my home, my money, my job, I didn't care as long as Abbie was safe. And so, one day, three months later when he was away for his work, I packed Abbie and what I could fit in the car, took the money from our accounts and what little savings I had left and drove away, without a word to anyone."

Arthur slides the box of tissues closer to me. "That's why you told Abbie that Cody is working for the government. That's why you move every six months. You're scared for her." He waits while I wipe a blob of mascara from my face. I nod my head, not trusting my voice.

"Let me assure you, his word against you would be meaning-less in a court of law. His notebook with scribbles of what he deems your lack of parenting skills would have little sway with the system. He's blackmailing you. It sounds like the account he stole from was a joint account, so legally, there's nothing you can do about that. You might have a civil case, but nothing criminal."

Sonny's arms are crossed and his eyes narrow. "Uncle Arthur is right, but I'm more than happy to take a look at your records and see if there is something we could do legally to try and get some recourse for you. There's nothing I hate worse than criminals like him, the kind that prey on the people they're supposed to love."

"I appreciate that, but I was an idiot to let him handle things and to put him on the account with all the money from my parents' estate. I deserve this."

Arthur comforts me, gripping my hand tighter in his. "My dear, grief does horrible things to us. It can rob us of rational thought, of joy, even of ourselves. Cody took advantage of that situation for his own benefit. That's the hallmark of a vile and despicable man and only serves to tell us what kind of person he is, not what kind of mother you are. You may have made a mistake or two. I haven't met a parent yet who hasn't." He smiles and his blue eyes meet mine. "That doesn't mean you're not worthy of being a mother. I would daresay you have a whole town here that will testify to what a fine mother and woman you are and I'd be first in line."

"See why he was such a great judge?" says Sonny. "He's exactly right. Cody's the one in legal jeopardy, not you." Sonny slides a chair up to the other side of Arthur's bed and reaches across to pat my arm.

A sob sticks in my throat. I should have told someone back home what happened. I should have gone to one of my dad's friends. Someone like Arthur, who could have put all of this in perspective. Fear drove my every move at that point. I had been living on adrenaline since that day and rather than fight, I chose flight. It was probably the wrong choice. But I'm scared of Cody.

I regard Arthur's gentle eyes and feel calmer. "It sounds like Cody set you on a path that led you to leave your home behind, all that was familiar, your friends, your support system, everything. That can't have been easy. If I may be so bold, I think you've found a new home, here in our lovely little town. A place where you have support, community, friends." He sandwiches my hand between both of his. "Family, if you want it."

The sob breaks free and I bend my forehead to our linked hands. I can't talk; the blubbering seizes my voice. I try to stifle the burning in my chest and listen to Arthur's soft words. "Don't let Cody rob you of this chance. If he shows up, we'll handle it, together. Realistically, the chances of him finding you here are quite slim, so let go of your worry and rest assured you'll handle it, if it happens. Be kind to yourself, lean on me, lean on Sonny, everyone here. Abbie is so much calmer than the first time we met. You love the center. Give both of you a chance to settle here and absorb all the love our little community can give you. You can't keep going at this pace forever and I can think of no better place to make your new home."

He's right. It's what I told myself last night at the reservoir. I've been struggling to prepare for another move, procrastinating and ignoring it. I keep hoping I can figure out a way to stop running, for Abbie's sake, if not my own. Seeing her smile and her excitement around Duke fills my heart with joy. I don't want to take all of this from her. He came into our lives for a reason. The shuddering subsides and I raise my head.

"You're right, Arthur. I feel like one of those hamsters on a wheel, running and running, but going nowhere. I know something has to change. I've just been too scared to stop. I truly appreciate your offer and it is tempting. I just don't want to take advantage of your kindness or have people think I'm exploiting you."

Arthur chuckles and glances at Sonny, who nods. His steady voice is all business again. "My dear, everyone in Millbury knows me and knows I would not be exploited by anyone, least of all you. You're carrying around all this guilt and shame because of what Cody did. Nobody here knows anything about that. They know you're a kind and competent woman who goes out of her way to help her patients and anyone else she meets. You're the hard-working nurse practitioner who rallied everyone together to get enough funds to get us that JAM bus we've needed for so long. You're a hero, my dear girl." He winks at me. "Part of my offer is selfish. I need some help and with Rosie gone it's quite lonely in the house. You and Abbie brighten my days, and I know Rosie would be thrilled with the idea of having her beautiful upstairs lived in and appreciated. I daresay if she was still here, she'd make the same offer."

Sonny clears his throat. "Like I told you in the café, when Arthur first mentioned you, I was skeptical, but after talking to you and hearing more about you from Arthur, I have no reservations about you living with him." He puts a hand on the thin material of Arthur's gown covering his shoulder. "I'm sorry I doubted you; I should have known better. I was just worried."

Arthur smiles and places his hand over Sonny's. "I know, my dear boy. I know."

As I reach for more tissues, I smile at the kind man who has found a place in my heart. "I don't know what to say, except thank you. From the bottom of my heart, thank you for your kindness and the offer of a real home. I want to talk to Abbie about it, but I'm sure she'll be thrilled with the idea. I insist we come up with some arrangement financially, though. I don't feel right not paying our fair share."

He smiles and nods. "We'll come up with something. For now, just talk to Abbie, and if she agrees, we'll hammer out the details. You can move your things in and get situated while I'm in the hospital. I'll rest easier knowing you'll be there to help when I get home."

"I'll be there for you, no matter what." I stand and reach across and hug Arthur, unable to put into language what he means to me, letting my embrace convey what mere words cannot.

While I pluck more tissues from the box and shudder at the thought of what my face looks like now, the two of them chat about the weather and football, giving me time to pull myself together. The permanent ache in my shoulders has gone. A bit of humiliation still lingers, but sharing the story with Arthur and Sonny and their words of encouragement eased some of my guilt and fear.

I check my watch and it's later than I thought. I interrupt them to give Arthur a quick hug goodbye.

I have wasted these last two years running instead of living. Maybe, just maybe, here in this tiny town, with the help of a kind widower and a sweet pup, I could learn to trust again.

# CHAPTER 25

After I pick up groceries, remembering the ingredients Sonny wants for the night he is cooking this week, I slide behind the wheel. The ride home gives me time to decompress and think about the implications of Arthur's offer. I should really tell Abbie the whole story. She was so fragile after Mom and Dad died and I didn't want her to worry about Cody finding us. It was bad enough she'd miss him and although I welcomed the thought of never seeing him again, I didn't want to burden Abbie with his betrayal.

I tried to keep her memories of Cody positive, for her sake. I felt like such a failure as a mother, and still do. I was too ashamed of how I'd let Cody take advantage of me and how I'd let our financial security slip through my fingers. I couldn't endure the thought of explaining that to my little girl.

I figured I would tell her when she was older and could understand it better. I've not found an opportunity in all the time we've been away and any type of stress exacerbates her behaviors, so it was easy to rationalize keeping it from her. Now, with Arthur and Sonny knowing and the idea of staying here, I really need to tell her.

As I imagine the conversation, my neck tightens. She's finally happy and I can't be the one who ruins that for her. Maybe I can wait until after the musical and after we're settled in at Arthur's.

After thanking Lori and putting the groceries away, I take a cup of tea and sit in Arthur's recliner, letting Duke crawl into my lap. We listen to Abbie practice the upbeat song, "Be Our Guest," for the musical, and I run my hands over his silky ears, feeling the stress of the day lessen. He places his head against my chest, looking up at me, his gentle brown eyes conveying love and understanding. It's as if he knows I'm wrestling with something. We both miss Arthur and are worried about him, but feeling Duke's warmth and his sigh as he relaxes and shuts his eyes, I know I'm providing him the same comfort he's giving me.

We rest together and as I continue to stroke his golden fur and massage the pads on his paws, my mood lifts. I notice the time and leave Duke to keep Abbie company while I tend to dinner. By the time she finishes the last run-through of the song, I have put together a quick lasagna and prepared some garlic bread to heat.

When Abbie comes into the kitchen I offer her some apples and cheese for a snack. As she munches, slipping Duke a bite of cheese, we chat about the musical and I make sure Duke's dinner bowl is filled and add fresh water to his bowl.

While the aroma of my mom's lasagna drifts through the kitchen, I sit down next to Abbie. "Arthur asked a very important question today and I'd like to see what you think." Abbie raises her brows. "He wanted to know if we'd like to move in here to the upstairs instead of the trailer. Not only is he going to need a bit of help when he gets home from the hospital, but he enjoys spending time with us and feels like we've become a family."

Abbie's eyes brighten and she smiles as she nods her head several times. "I love it here and that means I could go out to his yard anytime I want. I could practice piano or play with Duke whenever I feel like it."

I rest my hand on her arm. "What would you think about living in Millbury and not having to move ever again? Do you like it here?"

She springs from the chair and wraps her arms around my neck. "I love Arthur and Duke and my music class. It's the best place we've lived." She slips back into her chair and her smile fades. "Does staying here mean we won't be going back home to Ohio?"

Her question makes my heart ache. If I hadn't been so trusting of Cody, we never would have had to leave. Rather than moving every few months, we could have lived in Mom and Dad's house forever. Instead, it's all gone. Along with the memories of my parents, the only things left for me in the town I had called home for my entire life are embarrassment and shame. My throat burns and tears begin to form in my eyes. I can't tell Abbie all of this, I can't burden her with anything else.

I swallow the lump in my throat and look into my daughter's trusting eyes. "Going back to Ohio isn't an option. It makes me too sad to be there without Grandma and Grandpa. Since we left, I've been hoping we would find a new town we liked and somewhere that felt like home. A place we could stay and make new memories. Millbury seems like the perfect place to me."

Abbie frowns and says, "What about Cody? When he comes back how will he find us?"

She's given me the perfect opening, but I can't make myself tell her. Duke's nose nudges my leg and I glance down to see his soulful eyes urging me forward. I take in a long breath. "I'm not sure Cody is going to come back. I think he likes his new work and it's time for the two of us to make our own life." I feel my pulse thudding in my neck and will her to stop asking about Cody. I don't like lying to her, but I'm not ready to say more, not now. When she doesn't reply, I add, "What do you think about Millbury? Could you be happy living here?"

She smiles and nods. "I like it here and Arthur reminds me of Grandpa. I'm sorry going back home makes you sad. Everything has been a mess without Grandma and Grandpa. I guess I just always thought we'd go back there and things would be like they used to be, when Cody lived with us." She pauses and reaches to pet Duke. "If we aren't going back, then this is the best place we could be. It's where you're happy, Mom."

I can't contain the tears sliding down my cheeks and wipe them away before wrapping my arms around her. "I feel the same way. Seeing you enjoying yourself and knowing we have Arthur and Duke here makes me happy." I move my arms and grip her by the shoulders, looking into her eyes. "Are you sure you're okay moving in here?"

She smiles, gazing around the room. "Why wouldn't I be? It's so much nicer than the trailer." She glances at Duke. "Can Duke sleep in my room again tonight?" The thwack of Duke's tail against my legs and his eager eyes lighten my heart.

And just like that she's moved on. Maybe her anxiety will ease if she knows we're not facing another move and we can try to build a new normal here. "Let's run back to the trailer and pick up some things while the lasagna bakes. Duke can come with us."

On the way, I tell her about Sonny and that he'll be staying at Arthur's while he's in town. It doesn't take long to collect our clothes and personal items. I'll need to talk to the head office and find out if my temporary post at the center could become permanent and then tackle explaining to Gladys that we're moving.

I shove the idea of that conversation to the back of my mind while we drive back to Arthur's and cart our belongings upstairs. I slide the garlic bread in the oven to bake and put together a quick salad.

Abbie sets the table and doesn't bristle when I ask her to get her lunch put together for tomorrow. She snaps the lid shut on a container and puts it in the fridge. "Since I don't have a phone that actually works," she reminds me with a roll of her eyes, "do you think you could call the school and let me know how Arthur is when he gets out of surgery tomorrow? I know I'll be worrying about him all day and don't want to wait until the end of the day or when you get home. Tons of kids get messages from the office during class, so it wouldn't be a big deal."

"Sure, I can do that. I'm going to drive to the hospital as soon as you get off to school, so I should know something before noon."

Duke rushes to the front door and lets out a low bark. I follow, glancing out the window and see Sonny coming up the sidewalk, carrying a bag. I open the door, and Duke bounces out to the porch, wiggling and sniffing at Sonny.

Sonny bends down and ruffles Duke's ears. "He's a lively one, isn't he?" He laughs as he makes his way inside, Duke at his heels.

"Duke," I say, in a firm voice. "Sit." The dog complies, but his eyes drift to Sonny and his tail thumps against the floor while he tries to sit still, but ends up scooting a few inches closer to our visitor.

Sonny is a good sport and after I introduce him to Abbie, he suggests they go outside and play with Duke while I get the lasagna on the table. I hear Abbie laughing and happy yaps from Duke. When the three of them come through the back porch, Sonny and Abbie wash their hands and Duke flops onto the floor, his energy depleted.

Abbie chatters on telling me that Sonny lives three thousand miles away, and I can tell by her enthusiasm for some of the places Sonny describes, Washington, D.C. will be her new research project.

As we finish dinner, Sonny yawns and compliments me on the lasagna. "So, in addition to toast and lasagna, what else can I expect to sample?"

He's got a good sense of humor, something I've been missing lately. "Nobody has died from my scrambled eggs, and I do a pretty good chicken salad and make decent tacos."

He laughs and starts to clear the table, but I tell him to get settled and get some rest, knowing it's quite late for him and tomorrow he's got an early morning with Arthur.

I point up the stairs. "The guest room at the far end of the hallway is unoccupied. Abbie and I are in the first two rooms. I hope that one will work for you?"

Sonny smiles and grabs his bag. "That's the room I've always used, so it's perfect." He gives Duke a scratch under the chin on his way upstairs. "See you ladies in the morning."

Abbie and I get to bed early, with Duke sleeping in Abbie's room. It's been an emotional few days and I'm exhausted and sleep soundly for eight hours.

At six in the morning, I'm wide awake, my mind racing with thoughts about Abbie and Arthur, along with the hope that I can stay on at the center. I check for a reply to the email I sent late last night, knowing full well there is no way the main office would have responded yet. I hear the squeak of Sonny's steps in the hallway and am reminded of something else, actually someone dominating my thoughts.

It's been a long time since I've been charmed by a man, and Sonny has gentle eyes and a warm smile. In reality, I'm more attracted to what's inside—Sonny is a man of character and integrity, like his uncle. Each time I try to close my eyes, I see his handsome face. The spark of interest troubles me. After the disaster with Cody, I convinced myself I was done with relationships and resolved that I'd be alone forever, not willing to trust anyone again. Maybe I was too hasty.

I know I'm not going to get back to sleep, so throw on a hoodie and slippers and make my way downstairs to brew some coffee. I find Sonny dressed, his hair still damp, sitting at the counter lost in his own thoughts.

"Morning," I whisper.

He flinches at my voice and turns. "I hope I didn't wake you."

"No, I fell asleep too early. I tried going back to sleep, but keep thinking about Arthur, living here, all of it." I hit the button on the coffeemaker and lean my elbows on the counter.

A crease forms on Sonny's forehead. "I'm worried about him. I hope this surgery is a success and that he can get back to his old self quickly. Some of my colleagues are dealing with aging parents and it just seems like surgery takes its toll. Some of them have gone downhill after going through what is characterized as a successful procedure." He fiddles with a crumb on the counter as he talks.

I hear the click of Duke's toenails on the floor and watch as he goes to the back porch and returns dragging his leash. My heart breaks for him and I wonder how much he understands about what is happening. "Okay, sweet boy. We'll go for a walk as soon as the coffee is done." That seems to appease him and he carries the leash over to where Sonny is sitting and puts his paw on his knee.

Sonny chuckles and pets his head. Subtlety is not Duke's strong suit. I smile at both of them. "That's his way of telling you he thinks you need to go for a walk with us."

"I could do with a walk. It'll help clear my head."

The scent of rich coffee comforts me and I grab two travel mugs from the cabinet and refocus on Sonny's concerns. "You mentioned the toll of surgery. Anesthesia is hard on the body. Older people take longer to recover from it. The good thing about this procedure is that he won't be under a general anesthesia, so the side effects should be minimal." I pour myself a coffee. "Can I interest you in a cup?"

He nods, and I pour dark liquid into his travel mug and retrieve a carton of cream and the sugar bowl. He adds a healthy splash and several teaspoons of sugar. "I'm thankful for that." His spoon clinks against the sides of the cup as he continues to stir. I add the lids to each of them and attach Duke's leash, scribbling a sticky note to let Abbie know we're at the park. The chance of her waking up early is slim, so we'll have time for a quick walk and can get back in time to roust her.

Sonny slips into his jacket and takes both of our cups while I grab my jacket and usher Duke out the back door. We go through the gate and I take care not to let it slam behind us.

Once we're on the sidewalk, I take my cup from Sonny. "We'll just make a short loop around the park." I can tell he's preoccupied worrying about Arthur. "Arthur's recovery should be relatively easy. Try to stay positive."

He nods and sips from his mug. "I emailed the office to see if I can clear my calendar for the next week or two and come back to help out. I can't miss this Friday case, but my assistant is working on my schedule. I think it's important that I'm here for Arthur and I can do much of my work remotely."

After my experience with Cody, I had sworn off the idea of ever having a man in my life again. I had been blessed once, with Jeremy, who was loving and kind. When he died so unexpectedly, so young, it shattered me and I wasn't sure I could go on, but I had to for Abbie. I'm not sure I would have survived the loss without Mom and Dad.

Jeremy's death, due to an undiagnosed congenital heart defect, was so shocking, but Cody's betrayal gutted me. He destroyed my confidence, making me doubt my judgment. My focus these last two years has been on getting us away from him, keeping Abbie safe, and trying to make enough money to survive and pay off my debts. Coworkers and patients tried to set me up with relatives and friends, but I always refused, using Abbie as an excuse.

Gladys and her attempts to pair me with Jeff were humorous, but the last thing I've needed in my life is a man. Or, so I thought. The genuine love Sonny has for Arthur and his willingness to rearrange his life for him, has stirred something deep inside me. I have met many relatives of patients, but few seem like him. I see why Arthur cares so much for him. And his cute smile only adds to his charm.

I blink, turning to focus on the man next to me, realizing I haven't been listening to him, lost in my own musings and the idea of having a kind and trustworthy guy like Sonny in my life. I shake my head. "Sorry, I guess I'm not fully awake. I'm gonna need more than one of these today." I lift my mug in the air.

He laughs and says, "I was just rambling. I'm not normally nervous, but I'm worried about him. I can't imagine losing him." He offers to take Duke's leash.

I hand it to him and touch his arm. "I know what you mean. I'm confident in the surgeon and the approach they're taking, but I don't think I could handle losing someone else."

Sonny's smile fades and sorrow fills his eyes. "Arthur told me you lost your husband when Abbie was young and losing your parents had to be beyond difficult. I'm very sorry."

I nod and take another sip. "Losing Jeremy, my husband, was horrible, but having my parents softened the blow. He collapsed while exercising and died. I didn't believe it at first. Mom and Dad helped me get through it and I was able to finish school with them there for Abbie. Losing both of them has been something I still haven't overcome. Outside of Abbie, they were my everything. It was like the ground fell out from under me."

Sonny moves his hand with the leash to mine. "I'm sorry, Madison."

I shake my head. "I'm sorry. I need to quit blubbering on about it. It's just Arthur has filled up a big part of the hole in my heart their absence left. I don't feel so alone with him in my life."

Sonny's eyes look sad. "It's a shame he and Rosie never had children. He's an incredible man and would have been a wonderful father and grandfather. In fact, I feel like he's my dad, having no memories of my own father. My dad, Edmund, died in the Vietnam War. I know him only from photos. I have no memories of him, but I'm named after him. When I sign something official, I'm Edmund Arthur Patterson, but have always been called Sonny."

"Abbie doesn't have any memories of Jeremy either." Suddenly cold, I wrap my hands around my warm cup.

"I was lucky enough to have Uncle Arthur and it sounds like Abbie had your dad, at least for her early years."

"Yes, and she tells me Arthur reminds her of Grandpa. That's a high compliment."

We chat as we circle the pathway and watch Duke's happy trot as he walks and sniffs at bushes. As Sonny talks, I learn his mom, Shirley, lives in Florida and remarried almost ten years ago. "I'm glad Mom is happy and Jack is good to her, but I don't have a close relationship with him, not like with Arthur. He's wonderful to Mom and I don't have to worry about her being on her own. They have a full life, a gorgeous home on the water, and lots of friends. I generally spend holidays with them and they're always inviting me down, but I rarely have time to go."

We complete the circle and head back down the street toward Arthur's house.

"I've been trying to figure out how to tell Mom I'm not going to join them for Thanksgiving this year. I want to spend it with Arthur. I know this year will be difficult for him."

His compassion and gentle words only increase his appeal. "I know that would mean the world to him," I say.

Sonny slips Duke's leash back into my hand and opens the gate. "I'm going to get going so I can spend some time with him."

"Give him my love and I suspect I'll be there around nine o'clock. I'll find you. Try to relax and think positive thoughts."

He smiles and moves toward me, giving me a clumsy hug. "Thank you, Madison." He releases me and adds, "I'm beginning to see why Uncle Arthur enjoys your company and is such a fan of yours. I feel better having talked with you."

While I fix Duke his breakfast, Sonny rinses our travel mugs and pours me a fresh cup in the oversized Oregon Ducks mug I've been using. Sensing his angst, I walk with him to the front door, giving him a reassuring smile. I wave goodbye from the porch and watch the taillights on his rental car disappear as he turns the corner. The spicy scent of his aftershave still lingers on my hoodie and I touch my nose to it. His simple little embrace awakened something in me I feared was gone forever.

# CHAPTER 26

Duke doesn't show much interest in his breakfast, even after I add a bit of chicken broth to it. I ruffle the top of his head. "You just miss your buddy, don't you?"

While I tidy the kitchen, I tell Duke that Arthur is going to be fine and will be home in just a couple of days. He tilts his head and looks into my eyes and I swear he smiles. He acts like he knows what I'm saying but his usual happy bounce in his step is absent. I take a seat on the bench by the front door, and Duke rests his head on my knee.

Taking hold of his head in my hands, I tell him Abbie and I are going to be living at the house. "I'm so very grateful that we have you in our life. I've come to love you and Arthur and nothing makes me happier than knowing he'll be home soon and Abbie will enjoy the benefit of having a real family again."

His soft brown eyes meet mine and I see the pure love in them. He wags his tail from side to side and his big tongue slides out of his mouth and slurps my hand. He looks so much happier than he did this weekend and I'm further convinced he understands.

He eats a few bites of kibble while I finish getting ready. I take an extra fifteen minutes before I leave to let Duke sit across my lap, running my hands over his back. I'm sure he senses my worry and I know how much he misses Arthur. Despite setting out to comfort and calm him, he's done just that for me. There's something so utterly soothing about the smoothness of his fur and the thud of his heart against my legs. His weight and warmth, not to mention his gentle all-knowing eyes, ease my worries. A sliver of sunshine filters through the window and illuminates the shimmering gold strands in his fur.

I caress the area behind his ears that I know he likes and smile at his sigh. He lets me rub his soft paw pads and relaxes his toes, while I massage between each one. I love his soft cheeks and the extra skin around them. It's such a contrast to the coarse whiskers that sprout from his muzzle. His pink tongue darts out and licks my hand, and I bend to smell his sweet puppy breath.

Not only is Duke the best therapist for Abbie, spending time focusing on him, letting my hands run over him, brings a sense of relief and respite from the worry about Arthur that has nagged me since the day I found him in the backyard. While I know dogs don't worry like we do, I know he misses Arthur and hope our time together this morning is just as meaningful for him.

After kissing the top of Duke's head and scooching him off my lap, I make sure the dog door is unlocked, fill his water bowl, and do my best to explain to the sweet boy that I'll be out all day and will be home when Abbie returns from school. I tell him Arthur will be home soon, and his ears perk at the name of the man he loves. I'm not sure he understands everything I say, but I know he longs for Arthur and I think he knows I'm going to check on him. I feel bad leaving him and suspect he'll be lonely since it will be the first time he's been on his own for the day.

I make it to the hospital a few minutes early and, after checking with the nurse's station, find Sonny in the waiting room. Relief fills his face when he sees me. "Any word yet?" I ask, taking the chair next to him.

He shakes his head. "They got a bit of a late start and came out to tell me so I wouldn't worry."

"It's hard not to worry. There's not much else to do when you're sitting here." The television is tuned to morning game shows and we're the only ones in the room.

As I'm trying to think of a good topic to distract Sonny, Dr. Lewis comes through the door. Sonny jumps to his feet with an expectant look, and she smiles at him.

"We just finished up with Arthur and everything went well. He's doing fine and will be transferred up to the ICU in a couple of hours. I suspect he'll be with us until Thursday, as Dr. Ruppert has him on blood thinners, so we'll need to monitor him."

Sonny lets out a breath and his shoulders drop, releasing the tension they've been holding. She gives him a reassuring smile. "You two should go get some breakfast and when you get back, it should be close to the time they'll let you visit him for a few minutes."

Sonny turns to me and wraps his arms around me. "I'm so relieved. Thank you for being here and for all you've done for Arthur."

When he releases me, I notice his eyes are wet and grip his hand in mine. "It's my absolute pleasure. Arthur is a special man and I care about him more than you know. Let's go find somewhere to get a bite to eat."

We walk a few blocks in the crisp morning air and settle in at a booth in a diner. I remember my promise to Abbie and call the school asking them to deliver a message that Arthur's surgery was a success and he's fine.

Over hearty omelets, we chat and decompress, with the stress of the procedure behind us. His cell phone purrs and he checks the screen. He smiles and taps in a reply. He slips the phone back into his pocket and says, "That was my assistant and she shifted things around so I can fly back here on Sunday and stay for another two weeks."

"That's terrific. Having you here will be such a comfort to Arthur."

"Are you able to stay with him this week, when they discharge him?"

I swallow the last of my coffee and nod. "Yes, that should work. I have a bunch of vacation time and can use a few days this week. I'm off Sundays and Mondays."

"I really appreciate you doing that. I feel horrible that you're using your vacation."

I laugh and say, "No need. I haven't taken a vacation in two years, so I have plenty of time on the books. I'm happy to do it, honestly. Arthur has helped me more than I can ever repay. It's the least I can do."

"I'm cooking dinner tonight and you can plan on me cooking while I'm staying at Arthur's. That's the least I can do for you."

"Deal," I say, returning his kind smile and reaching for the check the waitress delivered with our two coffees to go.

He grabs it before I even touch it. "My treat, I insist," he says, pulling a credit card from his wallet.

With time to spare, we stroll through the gardens connected to the hospital. The leaves haven't yet reached their peak, but the colors are still gorgeous. He stops at a bench and gestures for me to join him. "It's beautiful here," he says. "I never have time to enjoy a leisurely breakfast or a walk through the park back home. I'm always rushing, and despite all the access to beautiful areas nearby, I don't seem to find time to enjoy them." He stares at a raised planter of colorful mums in deep autumn hues. "It's pathetic really, that it takes something like this, the possibility of losing the most important man in my life, to make me stop and slow down."

"Life gets busy. I think we're all guilty of powering through our days, with the best of intentions, but sometimes without the gift of extra time. I'm always on the run and, in fact, living here in Millbury is the first time I've felt at peace in a long time. Work and Abbie are my priorities, but having Mondays off, I actually have a bit of time for myself. It's a foreign concept and I still feel guilty when I while away an hour or two strolling through town, sipping a latte, or browsing at the bookstore, but I'm getting better at enjoying it."

"I don't even have a girlfriend." Sonny laughs, looking off into the distance. "I can't imagine what it's like as a single parent, trying to do it all. I couldn't do it."

I smile, noting his comment about not having a girlfriend. "Thing is, when you have a child, you don't have a choice. You just have to keep going. Abbie is challenging. She's had her struggles and doesn't fit in or make friends easily, so it can be exhausting. She actually likes it here and is involved in the musical program at school, which she loves. This is the first time since my parents died that I've begun to relax and worry about her less. Arthur and Duke are a big part of that."

"Well he's clearly delighted that you've decided to make Millbury your home. I loved coming here to visit Arthur and Rosie when I was growing up. I always marveled at how everyone in town knew them. It's always felt like home here."

"I feel the same way. Everyone has been kind and welcoming."

He takes another swallow from his cup. "I wish I could say the same about my work. I was so excited to work in D.C. and looking back I realize I was too idealistic. I had all these hopes of making a difference and changing the world, but in reality, the system is just too big and there are too many people that don't want it to change. Now, I slog through my days and my only real satisfaction comes from the pro bono work I do." He checks his watch and adds, "We should probably get back."

We make our way to the cardiac unit and they let us both in to see Arthur, but limit our visit to fifteen minutes.

Arthur is hooked up to monitors and I scan the numbers, relieved to see his pulse, oxygen levels, and blood pressure are in the healthy range. His color is good, and when Sonny says his name, his eyes pop open and a smile fills his face.

"How are you feeling?" Sonny asks.

"Not bad, just a little drowsy. They tell me everything went well."

I nod and take his hand in mine. "Yes, Dr. Lewis came and told us. I'm so glad."

He turns his eyes toward me. "How's Duke?"

"He's been sleeping in Abbie's room, I explained he'd be on his own today, but I'm not sure he understood. I'm sure he'll adjust, but I'll try to squeeze in another walk after I pick Abbie up from practice. He'll need some exercise."

Arthur closes his eyes and nods. Sonny squeezes Arthur's hand and says, "We'll let you get some rest and come back in a few hours."

We make our way back to another waiting area, where Sonny puts in a call to his office and I use the time to check my phone. Knowing Sonny has to fly home on Thursday, I submitted a request for vacation last night and it has been approved. I scroll further and see the head office has replied to my inquiry about a permanent position. I read through the reply and my heart fills with joy. Meredith, the woman in charge of placement, has replied that Mr. Cox had sent her a letter just a week ago requesting that I fill the job on a permanent basis, citing my skills, dedication to my patients, and love for the community. Coupled with my request, she says she is happy to approve it and the job would be permanent as of the first of the year. She outlines the salary and benefits package associated with the permanent position. I will lose my housing allowance, but my salary and benefits would increase, more than making up for it.

Things are coming together. I almost don't believe it. I tap out a short message to the housing department and request the change in my housing status. I suspect I may have to wait until

November to make the change, since I'm sure the mobile park requires at least a thirty-day notice period, but that will give me two months of rent to put into my savings account.

I do some quick math in my head, as I want to make sure I pay our share of the household expenses at Arthur's. The benefit of living in a house supplied by Regency Health is that I never had to worry about utilities or other upkeep expenses. Even paying half of Arthur's household expenses, I estimate I'll have more money to put toward my debt once my raise comes through in January.

With Arthur doing well and resting and knowing he will most likely sleep the rest of the day, I decide to leave early and go into the office for a few hours to catch up and try to rearrange my patients and see them all on Tuesday and Wednesday, since I'll be taking off the rest of the week. I let Sonny know my plan and tell him I'll see him at Arthur's tonight.

"That sounds great. I'm going to take off here early and try to be home around five, so I can make you and Abbie dinner. I'll see you at the house."

When I get to Millbury, I drive straight to the center to get caught up on work. The dermatologist is still seeing patients in the exam room, so I scoot into my office and shut the door.

It takes me most of the afternoon to reschedule patients and it means I'll skip lunch and work late both days, but I'm able to shift them around and clear out the rest of the week. I look at the stack of mail on my desk that has grown a bit since Saturday and elect to leave it for another day.

I decide to make a stop at the trailer and pick up the rest of our belongings just in case Gladys is able to rent the trailer in October. After loading my car with the remaining items, I wipe down the kitchen and bathrooms and trek across the street to see Gladys in the office.

Despite not saying anything about Arthur, everyone at the center knew about his trip to Salem and asked me to pass on their well wishes. I'd be surprised if Gladys doesn't already know about his situation, but I owe her the courtesy of letting her know I'm moving out of the park, which will lead to telling her about Arthur.

As I step through the door, she greets me with a warm welcome. "Oh, Madison, I'm so glad you stopped by. I wanted to see how Arthur is doing." She flicks her hands across her chest and I notice her nails are decorated with copper-colored glitter and tiny leaves.

"He's doing well. The procedure was a success and I expect he'll be home Thursday."

"What a relief. He's such a gentleman. I heard you saved his life, dear."

"Oh, I wouldn't go that far. I just checked on him and called the ambulance."

"You're too modest." She picks up the ringing phone and after a brief conversation turns her eyes back toward me. "What can I help you with?"

I pass my keys across the counter. "I'm moving out and wanted to get you the keys back and let you know. I'm not sure if you'll be able to rent the trailer, but wanted you to have them just in case. Regency Health will be getting in touch with you, I'm sure."

Her smile disappears. "Oh, don't tell me you're leaving Millbury?"

"Quite the contrary. I'm going to stay in Millbury. My position at the center will be permanent in January. Arthur has asked Abbie and me to move into his place. He's going to need some help for a bit and we rely on Arthur, so it makes sense to be together. We've really come to think of each other as family."

Her brightly colored lips curve into a full smile. "That's wonderful news. I'm so glad you'll be staying. I do hate to see you and Abbie go, but moving in with Arthur is perfect. It's been hard for him losing Rosie and he's such a fine man. It's an excellent solution for all of you."

She insists on hugging me and promises to stop by the center to visit with me soon. I wave goodbye, relieved with that task over. I steer the car to the high school and park, waiting for Abbie to emerge. I reach for my purse and realize in my haste to get to the mobile home park, I left it in my desk drawer at the center.

Abbie tosses her backpack in the rear seat and says, "How is Arthur?"

"He's drowsy, but doing well. Did you get my message?"

She beams with pride. "Yes, I was in English when they delivered the note."

"I need to run by the center and grab my purse and then we'll head to Arthur's. Sonny's cooking dinner and you can take Duke in the yard and let him run around for a bit."

She frowns. "I need to finish my paper for tomorrow. Could you just take me to Arthur's so I can get started on it? I don't want to be up all night working on it."

I let out a sigh, trying to focus on the positive aspect of Abbie making homework a priority. I pull to the curb at Arthur's and let her out, noticing Sonny's rental car isn't parked in front of the house. "I'll be right back," I say, as she hurries to the front door, unlocking it with the key I gave her.

I make a U-turn and head toward the center. There are only a couple of cars in the parking lot, as it's a few minutes after five o'clock and the center is closing. I dash inside, wave to Barb at the reception counter, and hurry to my office. My purse is right where I left it. Barb and I walk out together, chatting about the cooler weather expected in the next few days and I hop in the car.

I pull up in front of Arthur's, parking behind a rental car. I retrieve my bag and notice Abbie's backpack in the rear seat. I shake my head, wondering how she meant to do her paper without it.

As I juggle my tote and the heavy pack, I hear footfalls behind me. I turn and my breath catches when I look into the wild eyes of the man I have been running from these last two years. The man I once loved and trusted, but now despise and fear. Cody sneers at me, chuckling at the panic I can't hide.

# CHAPTER 27

"You're not an easy woman to find, Maddy. In fact, I'd almost given up. Seems the good people at the *Millbury Gazette* can't resist singing your praises. Some kind of a bus for old people. They even pointed out where you worked, so it made it easy to follow you."

My mind is racing as I stare at him. The dark eyes I used to get lost in spark a ripple of fear in me. His thick black hair is matted and messy, and his T-shirt stinks of sweat. Despite him being under six feet tall, he's strong and I know I'm no match for his muscular arms gripping mine. I know those same arms I used to think would protect me are about to imprison me. I need to get him to leave before Abbie notices. He gestures to the house.

"I'm not sure how you scored a sweet place like this one, but it's time you and Abbie come home. With your little disappearing act, you've only made things worse."

The hair on the back of my neck stands on end and I shiver. I remember Arthur's calm voice and summon all my strength to keep my own from shaking. "I did not steal anything and I'm not going anywhere with you."

He smirks at me. "Abbie's in there right now, packing her suitcase. She was so thrilled to see me. Asked me about my top-secret job. Not sure what she's talking about, but probably just another one of her crazy delusions."

My blood runs cold. He's talked to Abbie? Everything I've done these last two years flashes before me. The story I made up to protect Abbie and keep her from living with the fear that plagued me now puts her in jeopardy. The constant moving, the loneliness, all of it has been for nothing. I should have told Abbie the truth instead of creating a tale that put Cody in a good light. She still trusts him and that's my fault.

Everything I did to protect us has exposed us to danger. I can't let him take her, but how am I going to stop him? I don't have a weapon. Everything sharp is in my medical case, in the car. My keys are the only thing that could possibly inflict harm and they're in my bag.

Fear ripples through me. I've got to convince Abbie that Cody is a threat and not the man she thinks he is. I should have told her everything the other night. It was the perfect time and I've blown it.

I don't know what I'm going to do now that Cody has found us. We can't stay here. I became complacent and got too comfortable. Too happy. I was a fool to think I could start over here. Now what am I going to do?

My cell phone is in my bag, which is resting at my feet on the sidewalk, where I dropped it. I need to distract Cody, so I can get it and call for help, but finding it and calling will take too much time. I'll never be able to get away from him. Instead, I elect to do the only thing I can think of and shout as loud as I possibly can. "Abbie, call the police. Don't come out of the house. Help, someone help."

I don't have a loud voice and normally do everything possible to avoid attention, but tonight I use every ounce of the adrenaline coursing through my blood and yell with everything I have. Someone, I'm convinced, will hear me. I'll keep screaming until someone does. My throat hurts from the strain, but I let out another loud yell, roaring as I imagine a mother bear does to protect her cub. That's what is at stake here, my precious daughter.

I don't care what he does to me and reason that if Abbie sees me in distress, she'll realize something is wrong, despite all the sweet stories I've told her about Cody. I can't let her be the one who pays for my mistakes. As long as I'm breathing, I will make sure she stays in the house and locks the door. I inhale and scream again, trusting a neighbor has to have heard the commotion by now.

"Shut up, Maddy. I'll make sure they take your defective kid away from you if you don't," Cody says, as he reaches out and grabs me around the upper arms, hard enough to make me squeal, and begins pulling me toward the street. I go limp, for once glad I haven't lost the weight I've been trying to lose, dragging my shoes along the sidewalk, making things as difficult as possible.

Then I hear a low growling behind me and everything goes dark.

# CHAPTER 28

## Duke

The moment I hear her scream is something I'll never forget.

That guttural almost-growl that comes from Madison signals distress and fear. It is the same type of sound I heard as a young pup at the farm. All mammals are designed with instincts and that urge a mother gets to protect her young supersedes her own innate impulse to preserve her own life. She will gladly sacrifice herself to save her children. That maternal drive to protect overrides all logic. I learned about it firsthand when a coyote wandered into the farm one night when we were all puppies. My mother stood tall and ferocious. I'd never heard a growl like hers, and she created enough of a ruckus that people came out of the house to investigate and scared the mangy predator away. Hearing that jarring shriek, I know Madison needs help.

I hurry from Abbie's room, where she is gathering her clothes, muttering about how excited she is that Cody has found them and is going to take them home. None of this makes any sense to me, and I can't imagine Abbie and Madison leaving, especially with Arthur in the hospital.

My first whiff of Cody told me he is not a dog lover, and I assure you, the feeling is mutual. When he came to the door earlier, the hackles on my back stood on end. That piloerection is my body's way of alerting me to danger. Dogs are gifted with superb instincts and the ability to sense danger, both by observations of facial expressions and our keen sense of smell. My body reacted to him before I'd even processed what he was doing and I knew I was not going to ignore what every cell in my body was telling me. I had no intention of letting Abbie go anywhere with him.

When I hear Madison's cries for help, I rush down the stairs and through the front door that Abbie didn't quite close. I leap from the porch steps, not sure exactly what I plan to do, but the drive to protect Madison and Abbie overrides all else. I'm still a puppy, but no longer a runt, and I can hurl my sixty-seven pounds at this man threatening them. The instinct to protect is strong and I don't hesitate to do all that I can to keep my family safe. Nobody is going to hurt them while I'm here.

I make a slight miscalculation and in the process of ramming myself into Cody, I also topple Madison over and she goes down, but I can't stop to help her and concentrate on my mission—to make this man leave my family alone.

From the look in Cody's eyes and the fast pace of his pulse, I know I've startled him and I begin to growl.

The caustic odor I smelled when he first came to the door is stronger, more pungent. He's slick with a foul-smelling sweat, laced with anger and violence, reminding me of the man who abandoned me here.

I hear Abbie screaming at the front door, but block her out of my mind, continuing to bark as loud as I can, keeping my mouth next to Cody's face, noticing the fear in his eyes.

Moments later, the squeal of tires at the curb and rushing footsteps overshadow Abbie's yelling. I hear Sonny's voice calling for the police, but nothing else.

Goldens, by nature, are not aggressive and our friendly nature makes us ill-equipped for guard dog duty, but when our family, those precious humans we love more than life itself, are at risk, we will do everything to protect them. In the commotion of people arriving, I know Cody is no longer a threat, and I go to find Madison.

As I get into the house her hands tremble as she struggles to flick the lock on the door. She steadies herself against the heavy oak slab and looks through the window.

Tears leak from Madison's eyes, and I turn from the window to see Abbie crumple to the floor. Blue and red flashing lights reflect off the windows, turning Arthur's quiet street into a spectacle.

Madison hurries to Abbie and gathers her in her arms, rocking her back and forth. She closes her eyes and hums her grandma's favorite song—the one she said she always sang to Abbie when she was a baby. The familiar melody does little to calm either of them, and Madison opens her eyes, staring at the door. I move away from the window and position myself alongside them, resting my head against Abbie.

I smell the fear and stress coming from both of them and know they need my calming influence to help their bodies relax. Dogs are built to spring into action when needed. We can fend off an attack or act aggressively to protect our family from a threat, but when the job is done, we're able to relax. I think it's because we focus only on the present, the moment we're in right now. When the danger is eliminated, our mind doesn't relive it, doesn't play it back frame by frame. As quickly as we're able to leap into motion to protect ourselves or our family, we're able to recover.

That's what Abbie and Madison need right now. I scrunch between the two of them, sniffing at the heavy scent of adrenaline coursing through their blood. I feel both of their hands on my back and soak up their anxiety, letting it drift from their fingertips into me. It doesn't impact me and I can let it float right through me, helping them to calm. With my head between them, I hear the pounding of their hearts and know they're reliving the frightening experience we just endured. As they move their hands over me, their breathing slows, some of the tension evaporates in Abbie's body and I feel her slacken against me.

A few minutes later, she raises her head off Madison's shoulder.

"I thought Cody loved us," she says, her voice shaking.

I put my head in her lap and look into her sad eyes, hoping she understands that I love her and would never betray her. That's what makes dogs so special to humans. I crawl across her and position my whole body in her lap. That makes her smile and she bends her head toward mine. With our heads touching, I focus my thoughts on her and what I want her to know. Dogs don't care who you are. The only thing we care about is making you happy, easing your burdens, bringing you joy, and spending as much time with you as we can.

Abbie needs to know this. I want to blanket her with goodness and kindness. She lifts her head and when I look into her eyes I see a spark of what was there before today. I burrow closer to them both, reminding them I'm here and that they're not alone and that everything is going to be okay.

# CHAPTER 29

## Madison

I hear the front door unlock and Sonny walk through it, followed by Bill. With my eyes, I gesture toward Abbie.

Sonny nods and suggests Abbie help him make some hot chocolate in the kitchen. She is calmer and a hint of a smile forms at his idea. She untangles herself and follows him, asking if she can have whipped cream on hers.

What would I have done without Duke? I've never felt so scared in my life, but as he leapt into the air and came to help me, I knew Abbie would be okay.

But though I heard Sonny say Cody was trespassing, that he assaulted me, I know Cody. What if he can get himself out of this?

I meet Bill's kind eyes. "So, I'm not in any trouble?"

Bill smiles and shakes his head. "Sonny told me everything. I'm so sorry for what you've been through, Madison. You haven't done anything wrong. Don't let this guy steal any more of your happiness. Arthur's lucky to have you and so are we. Sonny told me you intend to stay, and I'll do everything I can to make sure you do."

I smile, relieved, even if just for a moment.

He opens his notebook. "I just need to clarify a couple of points with you," he says, and I tell him what I remember and he scribbles a few notes. "Did Cody speak to or touch Abbie?" he asks.

I shake my head. "Initially, when he got here, but no, not while I was here. She was in the house the whole time."

"Sonny said Cody grabbed you. Let's take a look at your arms. I'd like to get a photo of them if that's okay?"

I sigh, feeling a bit humiliated, but roll up my sleeves, exposing the harsh red outline of handprints around both arms. Surprised at the bright redness, I gasp and look away while Bill examines them. I forgot just how strong Cody could be.

Bill takes a few photos on his cell phone and then closes the cover on his black notebook, slipping the pen back into his shirt pocket. "I'm so sorry this happened to you, Madison. You won't have to worry about Cody any longer. We're going to take him in and I'll just need you to sign a statement with everything you told me. The guys tell me he's actually got an outstanding warrant for financial crimes and a failure to appear out of Ohio, so I imagine they'll be extraditing him."

As I watch Bill walk to his patrol vehicle, I steal another glance out the window. Cody is now sitting in the back of a patrol car, not looking nearly as confident as he had an hour ago.

I turn around and lean against the heavy door, taking in several deep breaths before making my way to the kitchen.

I arrive in time to watch Sonny take a glass measuring cup from the microwave and pour melted chocolate into the saucepan of milk. Abbie is staring at him, mesmerized by the process. He uses a whisk and blends the chocolate with the hot milk. After pouring the mixture into three mugs he adds a dollop of fresh whipped cream to each and sprinkles a bit of cinnamon on top.

He presents each of us a mug and joins us at the large granite counter. "Aunt Rosie always made this for me and it's the best hot chocolate you'll ever taste. Guaranteed to lift your spirits." He brings his mug to his mouth and takes a sip. "Mmm, I haven't had this since the last time she made it for me."

I take my first taste and watch Abbie's eyebrows arch as a smile fills her face. "That's so yummy. The best hot chocolate I've ever had. Can you teach me how to make it?"

Sonny laughs and says, "Sure, it's easy because Aunt Rosie always kept a jar of chopped bittersweet chocolate in the cupboard. That's the secret. You just heat up milk with a little sugar until tiny bubbles start to form and then add in the melted chocolate. So simple, but so delicious, right?"

I take another sip, letting the warm liquid coat my throat. "I agree. It's the best I've ever tasted. The whipped cream and cinnamon make it all the better."

"Are you ladies getting hungry?" asks Sonny. "I haven't started dinner yet, but was about to when, uh, well anyway, it won't take long."

"Dinner sounds great." I flinch at a soft knock on the door and remember Bill will have something for me to sign. I raise my brows at Sonny. "I'll be right back. Abbie, you can work on your homework and watch Sonny make dinner. He claims to be quite the chef." I wink and reassure her with a smile. I retrieve Abbie's backpack from the bench by the front door and sit it next to her, giving her a quick kiss on the top of the head. I don't want her to have to relive all of this and the normalcy of homework might distract her from the chaos.

Duke and I meet Bill on the front porch, and I gesture to the comfortable chairs with the fluffy pillows. I use his metal clipboard to write out a statement and sign it, my hands steadier than they were.

He scans the sheet and signs it as a witness. "Okay, Madison. That should do it. If we need anything else, I'll be in touch. You have a good night. Things will look better in the morning, I promise. Give Arthur my best and tell him I'll swing by for a visit when he gets home."

He gives Duke a quick scratch. "You saved the day, Duke." He waves as he gets in his SUV.

I turn and look at the gentle eyes of my golden protector. "I'm thankful Arthur wasn't here for all of the stress of the evening, but he would be so proud of you." Dogs are simply extraordinary. Their instincts are nothing short of miraculous. People joke about the fact that if their dog doesn't like you, it's a sure sign they shouldn't like you either, but I think it's true. Somehow, Duke knew that Cody wasn't a good person. He heard my cries for help or sensed the danger and didn't hesitate to put himself between us. After Abbie and I were safe, he never left us, making sure he was nearby to lend his support and comfort.

It was like when he jumped the fence and made his way to the center to find me when Arthur collapsed. He just knew what to do. He was willing to do whatever it took to protect us. Dogs are the most selfless creatures.

We make our way back inside and find Sonny hovering over Abbie, who is cutting up mushrooms, a happy smile on her face. Neither of them notices us and I step back and wait around the corner, listening and sneaking an occasional peek.

Sonny supervises her slicing, warning her to leave any bits of the mushroom that are too small, so she doesn't risk cutting herself. He explains he's frying the chicken fillets and will add the mushrooms and butter to the pan once he removes them.

Once she's done slicing, he asks her to add water to a pot for the pasta. They chatter back and forth and she tells him about the musical she's in at school. He asks her more about the show and tells her he saw it on Broadway in New York before it closed and that it was one of the longest-running musicals there. I'm glad to see her able to be distracted so quickly.

"You and your mom will have to make a trip to Portland and watch one of the off-Broadway performances. I'm sure Arthur would enjoy it. He and Rosie used to go to several productions. You can look at the upcoming calendar online."

The fragrant aroma of butter, garlic, and mushrooms fills the air. Abbie gasps and says, "You know I can't drink wine, right?"

Sonny chuckles and says, "The alcohol will burn off as it cooks, leaving behind the flavor. It's Marsala wine, that's where the dish gets its name."

She accepts the reasoning with a crinkled forehead. "I can play you one of my songs while you finish. I need to practice anyway."

"Terrific idea," Sonny says, as I take the opportunity to step from around the corner.

Abbie darts across the room to the piano and I go to the kitchen.

"Thanks for being so kind and patient with her." I look over Sonny's shoulder into the pan as he adds the cream and the crispy chicken fillets back into the golden sauce. "That looks delicious."

He puts a gentle hand on my shoulder and raises his brows. "Are you okay?"

I nod and gesture toward the living room, where Abbie is playing.

"Could you dump the pasta into the boiling water?" he asks, gesturing to the package on the counter.

I do so and then keep busy setting the table while he adds the finishing touches and puts the pasta and the chicken in serving dishes. Abbie concludes her repertoire and joins us at the table. "Did you finish your homework?"

She shrugs as she tears off a piece of bread. "Sonny quizzed me on my spelling."

"She only missed one and we tackled it." He passes me the pasta.

"Thank you for helping her." As we eat, Abbie quizzes Sonny about the memorials and monuments in Washington, D.C. while I take a second helping of pasta and pass the bowl to Abbie.

Abbie is staring at her plate. "Why did Cody come here today and why did he say such mean things about me?"

The hurt in her voice makes my heart break. I take a long drink of water, choosing my words, before turning to Abbie. "I need to apologize to you, Abbie. I haven't told you the entire truth about Cody. I didn't want you to worry and I was trying to protect you. Cody did some bad things and that's the reason we left Ohio. He's a bad person. He didn't have a top-secret job with the government. I just told you that so you wouldn't wonder about him or think badly of him."

I glance at Sonny before turning back to Abbie. "Cody lied to me and took all the money from Grandma and Grandpa's estate. Remember, we were talking about building a new house for the three of us?" Abbie's wide eyes reveal her surprise. She frowns and nods her head.

Sonny shifts in his seat, his eyes wide, and he's biting his lip.

She glances at me. "Dr. Ernst says bullies usually aren't confident and mask their fear with anger and aggression. He's a bully, isn't he?"

I nod and smile at her, amazed and thankful. "That's exactly it, sweetie. Bullies have to put others down or make fun of them to make up for their own shortcomings. Sometimes bad people disguise themselves as good ones and they get really good at deceiving people, especially those who are kind and loving toward them. That's what happened to us."

I let that sink in before continuing. "You know how you started your walks after we left Ohio?" Her eyes narrow and she nods. "I think that's my fault. Taking you away from home and then moving all the time has created so much anxiety and stress for you and I'm so very sorry. I was only trying to keep you safe and get us away from Cody, but I feel so horrible that it's caused you such distress. That constant movement when you pace, does it help you feel calmer?"

Tears pool in Abbie's eyes and she bobs her head. "Deep inside, I knew something wasn't right," she says, and her honesty surprises me. I've never asked her why she paces, and hearing her explain it, it makes so much sense. "You were upset and I didn't know exactly why. Pacing helps. I can't stop it. I've tried, but I have to keep moving until the feeling goes away. It's like I'm so nervous I can't think, I can't sit still."

I reach for her hand. "I know, that's what I thought. I'm so very sorry. I was sort of stuck and didn't have many options. The only thing I knew was that we had to get away from Cody and my only solution was to keep running, keep moving."

Abbie chews on her lower lip. "I miss Ohio and everything there. I don't like moving to new places." She glances down at Duke, who is pressed against her leg and grins at him. "This is the first place we've lived that I like. It almost feels like home. I don't want to leave Duke and Arthur."

"I feel the same way." I squeeze her hand in mine. "I think there's a way for us to stay here, so let me work on that."

The knots in my shoulders relax as I watch the worry in her eyes fade, replaced with a gleam of excitement. I hate that Abbie had to witness what happened today with Cody, but if nothing else, it's forced me to tell her a few things. Things I should have had the courage to tell her before and maybe the anxiety she's been under wouldn't have been so hard for her to bear.

We finish the meal and I suggest Abbie go upstairs, finish her homework and practice her spelling, before getting ready for bed. Once she's upstairs, I gather the dishes and take them to the sink, while Sonny spoons leftovers into containers.

I place a hand on his shoulder. "Thank you for being so kind to Abbie, to me. I didn't want to say anything in front of her, but Bill told me there is an active warrant for Cody from Ohio and that they will most likely extradite him. It sounds horrible, but I'm glad. All I could think of when I was waiting inside and the police were outside was that all my plans to stay in Millbury were ruined. I'm so tired of running and I hope that means I can stay here and not worry about him coming back."

"I'll stop by the police station tomorrow and see what I can find out. Regardless, after what happened here, I don't think you'll need to worry about him returning."

"I just feel so inadequate, so stupid. What I've put Abbie through, all the chaos..."

Sonny clears his throat. "I know this is none of my business, but you need to understand you weren't stupid. This is not about what you did or didn't do, this is about a man who probably did care about you in the beginning, but something changed in Cody. Cody made a decision to value money over all else. He somehow justified his actions in his mind and made up the lies to trick you. I'm sure you feel like you should have spotted the trouble, you should have avoided what happened, but like you told Abbie, people do bad things. People like Cody become masters at manipulating people, especially loving and trusting ones, like you. It's like an addict, in that his quest for money colored all his other actions. You need to quit blaming yourself and concentrate on what makes you happy. Start living again, Madison."

Tears threaten to spill from my eyes. "That's kind of you to say. Part of me is so relieved it's out in the open so Abbie understands." I finish loading the dishwasher. "I'm just glad Arthur wasn't here to witness all of this." I lean against the counter and face Sonny. "Having his support and encouragement to stay in Millbury made me realize I could quit running. I kept thinking of him today when I was out there with Cody. I'm not sure how he does it, but just having him around inspires confidence."

Sonny chuckles as he wipes the counter and the stovetop. "That sounds just like Uncle Arthur. He's right, you don't need to worry about anything. If you need any legal help, I'm happy to handle it for you, but I think Cody's threat will evaporate when he's facing the extradition and what I suspect are stalking and assault charges for what he did here. If it makes you feel better, we can petition the court for a restraining order against him."

"That might be a good idea, just so it's on the record and he knows I'm not going to tolerate his threats." I add detergent and push the button to start the dishwasher before loading Duke's bowl with kibble, adding bits of leftover chicken on top.

Abbie patters down the stairs and stands on the landing. "I'm done and ready for bed, Mom."

The urge to touch her makes me climb the stairs and grip her in a tight hug. "Terrific. I'll make your lunch for you and leave it in the fridge. I don't have time for any delays in the morning, so make sure you set your alarm. I've got to work late tomorrow and Wednesday, so I'll be at the center all day until I pick you up from practice."

She gives me the okay sign and turns to go upstairs. I clear my throat and arch my brows. "What do you say to Sonny for dinner?"

Abbie stops and bends her head over the banister. "Thanks for dinner, Sonny. It was better than anything Mom ever made." She hurries up the stairs and a few minutes later her door clicks shut.

I retrieve my cell phone and begin tapping keys, raising my eyes to meet Sonny's. "Telling Abbie about Cody makes me realize this could set her back. I'm just hoping we can start over from a place of truth this time. Arthur connected me with a therapist Abbie likes and I don't want to forget to call her tomorrow. Dr. Ernst has been seeing her every other week, but I suspect this will trigger a need to increase it back to a weekly schedule."

"That's a good idea. I don't know much about kids, except they are more resilient than adults. It's probably a relief for you to have everything out in the open. After what he did, that can't have been easy trying to keep her memories of Cody positive."

I shrug. "It's all I could think to do at the time. It wasn't for his benefit, believe me. I only cared about keeping her from more heartache."

"That's what makes you a good mom," he says, smiling.

Duke wolfs down his dinner, eating all the chicken first, as the tea kettle Sonny put on whistles and he adds water to two mugs. He gestures to a chair at the counter and we settle in next to each other. He places a jar of honey between us. "I've been thinking, I really don't feel right leaving you on your own with all of this. I'm going to figure out a way around my Friday case and just stay here for the duration. Until the situation with Cody is resolved, I don't want you here alone."

"Oh, no, don't mess up your schedule and your tickets. I'm sure I can manage and chances are he'll be in jail, right?"

His brows arch. "He should be, but I'd feel better knowing he's on his way to Ohio for a nice long stay. I'll know more this week after I talk to the police or the district attorney."

"I feel horrible to be the cause of all this uproar."

He reaches for my hand. I savor the warmth of his hand surrounding mine and the flutter in my chest, unsure of how to respond.

"Believe me, two cross-country flights back-to-back are not appealing. I'd much rather stay here with you. And Arthur, of course."

# CHAPTER 30

## Duke

After the commotion with Cody, things have settled down. These last few days, I've noticed a change in Madison. That nervousness and anxiety that lingered just below the surface, the uneasiness she thought she hid from everyone, has diminished. She and Sonny both reassure me that Arthur is doing well and he'll be home this week.

I can't wait to see him, but am enjoying watching Madison and Sonny together. There's a spark of something special between them. I smell the chemistry and magnetism when they look at each other or their hands touch.

I wasn't sure about Sonny, just listening to him chat with Arthur on the phone and hearing the doubt in his voice when he questioned his uncle's friendship with Madison, but when I met him, that all changed. Immediately, I knew Sonny was full of kindness and love and took in his scent. His love for and devotion to Arthur were apparent in the way he smiled at him and cared for him.

He did the same for Madison, but there was something more. They shared secret glances and I sensed Madison's heart rate increase whenever he leaned close to her. The scent of attraction hung heavy in the air the more time they spent together and the closer they sat to one another. The fog of anxiety that had surrounded her had disappeared and I knew Sonny was part of the reason.

Not only was he responsible for the new flicker of joy in Madison's eyes, but he has also had a hand in easing Abbie's burdens. With Madison being more relaxed, that constant hum of electricity coursing through Abbie has disappeared, and Sonny has brought a smile to her face. He has an easy way about him, laughing and teasing with her as he prepares meals, involving her in the process and giving her homework tips.

He's fun-loving and always up for an adventure. He raked a few leaves and didn't even get upset when I bounded into the pile and made a mess out of them. Instead, he laughed and we played together. He has a way of bringing out the best in everyone.

He shares Arthur's appreciation for music, and Abbie is blossoming as she plays special songs for him, and he promises to return for her performances in the upcoming musical. His sincere interest in the short time he's been here has boosted her confidence.

After she goes to bed in the evenings, Madison and Sonny sit close together on the couch, watching television or just visiting. They've been letting me snuggle next to them and I love being close to them. It's the first time I've heard Madison giggle and laugh with abandon since I've known her. I can tell she feels safe with Sonny, like she does with Arthur, but even more.

When Sonny slips his arm around her shoulders and she leans her head against him, it fills my heart with joy. I wish these moments could last forever.

The only time she shows any signs of distress is when the conversation turns to him leaving and going back home. As much as she cares for Sonny, I can tell she's holding back, afraid to get too close, only to have another person disappear from her life.

# CHAPTER 31

## Madison

Wednesday evening is the first chance I've had to put my feet up and sit for a few minutes. Tonight, Sonny is staying late at the hospital and I picked up a pizza. After a quick dinner, Abbie exercised Duke and then went to her room to do her homework and study for a test. Duke is now sprawled in my lap.

Sonny took the time to call me today to let me know he had things organized at work and didn't have to fly home on Friday, but could stay for a couple of weeks, to help with Arthur. He also talked with the district attorney handling the case against Cody. After he explained the legalese, the bottom line is that Cody will be in court tomorrow, where his public defender has convinced him to waive his extradition hearing and he'll be transported back to Ohio to face the multiple charges he's wanted for in connection with financial crimes and identity theft. He'll most likely be in prison for several years in Ohio. In return, he'll get a suspended sentence for the assault on me, but if he comes back to Oregon and makes trouble, he'll go straight to jail.

The relief I felt after Sonny's call this afternoon is something I never imagined I'd feel again. I didn't see an end to my constant running and hated even thinking about it. Now, I can finally relax and plan the life I want to have, the life Abbie deserves. When I looked into Cody's eyes and faced my worst nightmare, I never envisioned him finding me would turn out to be the solution to my dilemma.

That news, coupled with Arthur coming home tomorrow, has made this one of the happiest days of my life. Having welcomed him into my life not long ago, the thought of losing him, or having him end up in a care center, had me worried. I spoke with Nancy today and along with reassuring me about Arthur's medical condition, she went over his restrictions, medications, and follow-up labs and appointments to make the discharge process quicker. When I disconnected, I felt confident he was ready to come home and with a bit of rest and care will make a full recovery.

I run my hand across Duke's silky back and rub his soft ears between my fingers. I don't know what I would have done if something had gone wrong and Arthur wasn't here any longer. I had pushed those thoughts to the back of my mind, focusing on the positive, but late at night those chilling notions would plague me. I just didn't have the physical or mental energy to deal with what it would mean for us, for Duke, for Sonny.

For the first time since losing my parents, I finally feel like I'm going to make it. I just might survive all of this and make a new life. Be happy. Build a new family, however unconventional it may be, with Arthur and Duke. My mom always said people come into your life for a reason and things are meant to be. I'll never understand why Mom and Dad had to leave, but I'm so grateful I found this little piece of Oregon. Despite all the bad things that have happened in the past two years, I'm pleased my crazy journey brought me here, where I feel like I'm home.

As I let my hands travel over Duke, massaging his ears, he sighs and I know exactly how he feels. Safe and secure, surrounded by love—it's what we all desire and I wasn't sure I'd ever have it again, until now.

"Arthur will be home soon," I say, stroking his ears. "I know you're going to be so excited to see him, but you have to be gentle and slow around him. He's going to need time to regain his strength and can't be lifting you up or having you pounce on him. Do you think you can be calm?"

He leaves his head on my thigh and moves his eyes upward. His look implies his undying love for Arthur and his promise that he will try to contain himself, but I have my doubts. Puppies don't have the best impulse control.

I close my eyes and let it all sink in. To have a job I truly love, a comfortable home, the company of a gentle and wise man and his puppy, both of whom I've come to adore, and the joy of watching Abbie blossom and thrive amid the acceptance and unconditional love she's received from Duke and Arthur, brings tears to my eyes. When we arrived in Millbury, I assumed we'd move on to the next stop on the map, with no end in sight, since I couldn't bear the thought of thinking that far ahead. I only knew I had to keep moving to keep us safe.

Looking back, I let my guard down. I got too comfortable surrounded by the good people of this lovely town. Unlike the other places we had been, I became part of the community and that's how Cody was able to find us. I was careless and it almost cost us dearly. If Duke hadn't made such a commotion, surprising Cody, and Sonny hadn't arrived home, I hate to think how things might have gone. I shudder at the memory and focus on the warmth of the dog in my lap.

He seems to always be there, reminding us we're not alone and we're loved, whenever we need it most. The way he's helped Abbie grow over these few months is nothing short of miraculous. She's so much more confident and her pacing has reduced, only appearing at times of great anxiety, like when Arthur collapsed. Without the daily stress, her behavior has improved and she has an interest in outside activities and isn't so lonely.

I bend my neck and touch my forehead to Duke's. He's still and lets me hold his soft ears between my hands, looking into my eyes, as if he knows what I'm thinking. "Thank you, sweet boy," I whisper. He'll never know what a blessing he's been in our lives. I have him to thank for bringing all of us together and for being such a loyal friend to Abbie.

Sonny has been the biggest surprise. His kindness and intelligence remind me of Arthur, and I can see why Sonny chose to practice law. Arthur's influence must have been profound on a young man who looked upon him as a father figure. Arthur is his happiest when he's reliving memories with him or discussing the nuances of current legal cases.

He's going to miss Sonny when he goes back to D.C.

We're all going to miss him. I'm already counting the days until he returns for the Thanksgiving holiday.

Headlights glance across the front of the house and I jump to my feet, with Duke at my heels. The altercation with Cody still has me on edge. I let out a sigh when I realize it's Sonny's rental car, taking time to study it, since I mistook Cody's rental car for Sonny's before. I unlock the front door and retrieve my almost empty mug of tea.

Sonny comes through the door toting grocery bags and a couple of shopping bags from a clothing store I recognize. He greets me with a smile and dumps the groceries on the kitchen island.

"How's Arthur doing?" I ask, getting up to help stock the fridge and pantry.

"He's ready to come home and told me Rosie's Greek chicken soup sounded good, so I stopped by the market."

"There's some leftover pizza and salad," I offer, pointing to the fridge.

"Oh, I grabbed dinner at the hospital, but could go for a cup of hot chocolate."

"Sounds good. I'll get it started." I pour milk into the saucepan and scoop out some of the chocolate to melt.

After taking care of the groceries, he takes the whisk from me and incorporates the melted chocolate into the bubbling milk, adding a dash of vanilla. Topping each mug with whipped cream and a sprinkle of cinnamon, he hands me mine. Duke follows us into the great room, poking his nose into my leg and tugging on Sonny's jeans, practically herding us to the sofa, where he jumps onto the cushion and burrows in between us.

"I'm so glad you don't have to fly back tomorrow and can stay, but feel guilty knowing Cody will be gone, which was the reason you rearranged your schedule."

He swallows another sip from his mug. "Not only am I glad not to have to deal with the flights, but I enjoy being here. Making sure you and Abbie were safe was just part of the reason."

Behind the kindness in his eyes there's a slight hint of boyish mischief.

"Well, I'm grateful you're here. I've been rattled since that day Cody showed up here. Not to mention having to tell Abbie the whole story and the embarrassment of you knowing all the horrible details."

He frowns and says, "Madison, you don't have anything to be embarrassed about. I admire your strength and determination to keep Abbie safe. Not only did you have to deal with the stress of losing all your money and your home, but you provided for your daughter and made up a story to protect her. That tells me the kind of woman you are and, in a word, I'd say you're exceptional, one-in-a-million."

Tears sting my eyes as I stroke Duke's head. How can I feel such affection for a man I barely know? It must be something with the Patterson men, since I was drawn to Arthur almost immediately upon meeting him. I'm probably overreacting to his kindness. I admit it feels rather nice, almost special, to have a man like Sonny, charming, handsome, smart, and kind, in my corner for a change. I've been going it alone for so long, I've forgotten what it's like to have a bit of help.

It's too bad I didn't meet Sonny years ago. Maybe I could have saved myself all the heartache I went through with Cody. As I take in his scruffy chin and cheeks and the sincerity in his warm eyes, I imagine what my life could be like with someone like him.

"That's nice of you to say, but I've only felt exceptionally foolish these last years. I've beat myself up for taking Abbie on the road. She's always had her quirks, but the compulsiveness ramped up as soon as we left home. This job, this town, Arthur, and the people here, they've given me new hope, a second chance. I want to believe what you say is true about Cody going back and leaving me alone. I'm just not sure I'll trust it until it happens."

"You know what I think?" Sonny's eyes meet mine. "I think you need a break from the stress you've been under. You need to let someone help you for a change. I'm definitely up to the task, and while I'm here, you can relax. Maybe even do something fun. I can manage Arthur and we can both help out with Abbie. It will give you a little freedom to do something you enjoy. I think that's the least you deserve."

A delicious aroma wakes me Thursday morning. It's still an hour before my alarm is set to sound, but I slide my feet into my slippers and tiptoe down the stairs. Sonny is at the stove, hovering over the source of the enticing scent. As he moves the spoon around the stockpot, he's listening to a podcast on his phone. I don't want to interrupt him, so crouch down and sit on a stair.

My mind wanders to last night and how enjoyable it was to have him here, to have someone to laugh with, someone to fix me a hot drink and tell me everything was going to be okay. That's what I love about spending time with Arthur, but with Sonny it's different. There's a definite spark between us, something I hadn't anticipated, but is a welcome surprise. It reminds me of when I first met Jeremy, with all those wonderful and exciting feelings bubbling to the surface.

I hated saying goodnight to Sonny and would have loved to stay up all night talking. He has an easy confidence about him and a great sense of humor. His gorgeous smile that reaches all the way to his eyes and makes the corners crinkle when he laughs only adds to his appeal.

I feel like a high school girl with a crush and the idea of Sonny around for the next few weeks has me figuring out how I can spend more time with him. When Arthur talked about him, I hadn't expected to like him much and overhearing him talking to Arthur in the hospital only solidified my early opinion of him. I knew I wouldn't like him, but that all changed when I understood how much he cared for his uncle. That kind of deep love and devotion is something I miss, something I admire.

A single guy who would rush across the country and rearrange his busy life and career to stay in Millbury is someone special. All to help nurse his elderly uncle back to health while serving as a bodyguard to a tired, single mom with a difficult teenager. He doesn't draw attention to Abbie's obsessiveness and makes a point of talking about her interests. Last night he asked me how she was doing and if the counselor was helping her deal with Cody's appearance, and it's been so long since someone else knew as much about Abbie as I do. The sound sleep I've enjoyed these last couple of nights is all because of Sonny. He has that same manner about him as Arthur; his kindness and assuring nature bring the calmness I need. I strive to be independent and think I can handle most things on my own, but it's comforting to know someone I can trust is there for me and watching over us.

If I had been on my own when Cody pulled his latest stunt, it would have been a very different story. If we'd managed to escape him, there's no way I could have functioned and we'd probably already be in another town, another state.

I stand from my perch and take a few steps. "Morning," I whisper, hoping not to startle him.

He turns, wearing Arthur's apron, and smiles. "I hope I didn't wake you with all my clattering around down here. I tried to be quiet."

"No, I didn't hear a thing, just smelled something delicious."

He pours me a cup of coffee and bends over the stockpot. "It's Rosie's soup. I'm still not adjusted to the time, so thought I'd use these extra hours and whip up a big batch."

I move to the fridge. "I need to make Abbie's lunch while I'm thinking about it."

"I thought we could just have soup for dinner tonight. Will that work?"

"Sure, I'll pick up a loaf of bread from the bakery to go with it and maybe a celebratory pie for Arthur. I've just got a few errands to do and get Abbie off to school before we head for the hospital."

He puts the lid on the pot and joins me at the counter. "No point in getting there too early. They said he'd be ready to go home around noon, so I figure we could leave here by eleven o'clock and still be plenty early. Maybe we could hit Village Books & Café for breakfast on our way?"

"Sounds perfect." I drink the rest of my coffee and before I can get up for more, Sonny's there with the pot, pouring me another cup. "Thank you. I was going to get a load of laundry going and make sure all of Arthur's clothes are clean and ready. Do you need anything washed?"

"Yeah, I've got a few things. I didn't pack much, hence the shopping extravaganza on my way home last night. It'll be great not to have to wear a suit for the next couple of weeks. I just picked up some jeans and shirts and can leave them here for when I come back for the holidays."

"I'm getting used to having you around. It's going to be hard to let you go . . . I mean Arthur is going to be sad to see you leave."

With a playful glimmer in his eye, he flashes me a grin. "I'm already dreading leaving."

That flutter of attraction I never imagined I'd feel again rises in my chest. "I guess we'd better make the most of it. While you're here, I mean." I take my coffee and head to the laundry room, wondering what in the world I just said. You'd think by the time I was thirty-eight I'd have figured out how to communicate with an attractive man instead of rambling like a silly adolescent.

I get Abbie off to school and finish the laundry, before we leave for breakfast. After the meal and lingering over coffee, where I learn Sonny hasn't had a serious girlfriend in years and his arduous work schedule leaves little time for dating, we head to Salem.

That little flicker of interest I felt earlier intensifies while I listen to Sonny as he navigates the road. "I'm going to try to talk Uncle Arthur into one of those medical alert buttons. I hate to think what would have happened to him if you hadn't come to check on him." His voice breaks and there's a glint of tears in his eyes.

I reach across and cover his hand with mine. He turns his over and weaves his fingers between mine. "I'll help you convince him. I've got some brochures with a discount offer at my office. I'll bring one home."

As I start to move my hand, he grasps it tighter and smiles at me. We pass the twenty-minute ride linked together, chatting mostly about Arthur. I let him do most of the talking as my muddled mind concentrates on Sonny's strong and firm hand and the gentle brush of his thumb against my finger. Before I know it, we're pulling into the parking lot. We agree to tell Arthur about Cody's appearance, so he has time to process it and ask questions without Abbie within earshot.

Nancy is on duty again today and greets us with a smile when we get off the elevator. "We're just waiting for one more signature and then he's all yours. He's anxious to get out of here."

We find Arthur sitting in the chair next to his bed, dressed in the sweatpants we had a hard time convincing him to wear. A packed plastic bag full of Arthur's belongings sits atop the bed. "I'm glad to see the two of you," he says. "Are we ready to go?"

I explain it will just be a few minutes while we wait for Nancy and his instructions. I check through the closet and drawers to make sure they're empty. "You have your cell phone?"

He smiles and pats his jacket pocket. "Right here, dear."

Sonny distracts him by telling him he made the soup Arthur requested. He follows up with the good news that he is staying and doesn't have to fly back for work. Arthur beams at him. "That's terrific. I hated you making that long trip back-to-back."

I raise my brows at Sonny, and he nods. "I also have some news. This started out as bad news, but trust me, it ends well." I recap the situation with Cody finding me and following me to Arthur's, along with the arrival of the police and subsequent information about the warrant in Ohio.

Arthur nods and turns his eyes to Sonny. "Did he waive his extradition hearing?"

"Even better," Sonny says and tells Arthur about his discussion with the district attorney and the suspended sentence, along with the charges from Ohio.

"How's Abbie?" Arthur asks, reaching for my hand.

"Cody was horrible and she was understandably upset that night. I told her the whole story and explained why I had felt the need to hide what Cody had done from her. I got her in to see Dr. Ernst for some extra sessions and"—I glance at Sonny—"this guy was a big help in getting us through the ordeal. He's great with Abbie."

Arthur smiles and reaches for Sonny with his other hand. "He's a fine man and I'm not surprised Abbie has taken to him. He told me about her interest in the monuments and memorials." He winks at me. "He has no idea what he's getting into."

Nancy knocks on the door and holds up a handful of papers. "Anybody in here ready to go home? I just need a signature and you're free," she says, showing Arthur where to sign.

Much to Arthur's dismay, Nancy wheels him into the elevator and out to the curb where Sonny meets us with the rental car.

I help Arthur into the front seat and once he's settled, climb into the backseat. Arthur spends the short ride to Millbury commenting on the changing fall colors and how nice it is to be outside. He asks about Abbie's musical and if we were able to get settled in the house. He nods with approval when I tell him which bedrooms we took.

"I'm looking forward to taking Duke for a walk in the park," he says, seeing a woman tethering the leash of her two dogs.

"One of us has to go with you just to make sure Duke doesn't tug too hard on the leash," says Sonny, glancing at me in the rearview mirror.

I slip my hand around the headrest and place it on Arthur's shoulder. "You just have to be cautious while you're on blood thinners to make sure you don't fall or hurt yourself." I give his shoulder a squeeze and add, "I told Duke he has to be extra gentle with you."

Arthur chuckles. "I can't believe how much I've missed that rascal." He reaches across the console and grasps Sonny's arm. "Almost as much as the two of you."

When Sonny pulls into the driveway, Arthur points to the house across the cul-de-sac with the sold sign planted in the lawn. "Looks like Mrs. McIntyre's kids finally got her house cleaned out. I can't believe it already sold."

Arthur sighs as he continues to gaze at the house. "I guess it's inevitable, like it was for Rosie, but I hate to think of ever leaving this street, our home."

Sonny doesn't say anything, but slips his hand across the console and grips his uncle's hand.

With a Friday off, I'm up later than usual and in between getting Abbie to school and making sure Arthur has a shower and gets in a short walk, I enjoy a leisurely walk to the reservoir with Duke. After admiring the golden reflection of the sun with a sweet golden dog at my feet, I guide us along the creek and stop at the coffee shop. In addition to treating everyone to homemade pancakes this morning, Sonny volunteered to make dinner. I don't know a woman alive who would refuse a handsome man doing the cooking. It could be an act of self-preservation on his part, but I'll never pass up an opportunity to let him handle the cooking.

All I have to do is pick up Abbie from school after practice, which leaves me the entire day to myself. It's been a day of complete freedom and although I feel a bit guilty for letting Sonny handle Arthur most of the day, I enjoy my latte, while I savor the crisp air and the splendor of the early fall colors.

When Abbie and I make it home, we're greeted with the most delicious aromas wafting from the kitchen. Arthur is in his recliner, with Duke nestled against it and Sonny has the dining room table set, complete with flowers and votive candles.

"Dinner's about ready," he hollers from the kitchen. Abbie hurries to the powder room, and I help Arthur get to the table. Sonny is serving us his homemade turkey chili and baked potatoes with all the toppings imaginable.

Sonny carries the slow cooker to the table and ladles the chili into bowls. Arthur regards the festive table and the rich autumn colors in the flowers and puts a hand on Sonny's shoulder. "This reminds me of the spreads your aunt used to make for us."

Sonny leans his head into Arthur. "Those were the best times." He makes sure Arthur has what he wants on his chili and potato and pours waters and iced teas for everyone and then stands and clears his throat.

"It's a beautiful fall evening and not only did I want to pay tribute to Aunt Rosie by having dinner like she enjoyed for so many years, but I wanted you all here to tell you something."

Arthur looks at me and I shrug, giving him a questioning look. He returns my shrug and looks at Abbie. She lifts her shoulders and says, "I don't know what he's talking about." We all chuckle, looking expectantly at Sonny.

He takes a deep breath and says, "I know I promised to be back here the weekend before Thanksgiving, but that's not going to happen."

The happiness I've felt all day begins to fade, and I see Abbie's lip protrude as she crosses her arms.

I whisper, "Abbie, mind your manners. I'm sure Sonny has a good reason."

"That I do," he says, moving to rest a hand on Arthur's shoulder. "I'm going to start a new job the second week of November."

My pulse thuds in my neck. "Well, that is exciting news." Confusion clouds my thoughts.

"There's more," says Sonny. "I bought Mrs. McIntyre's house."

The crease of worry in Arthur's forehead dissolves as a grin fills his face.

Sonny nods at Arthur. "I've taken a job I've been offered in Salem and I'm going to move back here, right across the cul-de-sac. Someday, I'd really like to open my own practice right here in Millbury, but for the time being, I'll be working at the Oregon State Legislature."

I jump to my feet and wrap my arms around Sonny's neck. Abbie rushes from her side of the table and engulfs both of us in a hug. Even Duke gets involved and sprints toward us, running around in a circle. My cheeks are wet with tears, this time happy ones.

Arthur is beaming and rises from his chair, maneuvering between Sonny and me, an arm around each of our shoulders. "This is the best surprise I've ever received and all I could have hoped for."

After more hugging and squealing, we all sit down and dig into the meal. Sonny radiates happiness as he explains he connected with a colleague from the Office of Legislative Counsel at the Oregon State Legislature. When he mentioned he was thinking about a job change, the director jumped at the chance to hire him. Sonny sent the law firm a letter of resignation and will be going back to D.C. to take care of a few current cases and arrange to have his things moved to Oregon.

"When I saw Mrs. McIntyre's house for sale, it prompted the idea of moving here, to the place I've always thought of as home, next door to the man I admire most and who I think of as my father."

Tears fill Arthur's eyes as he gazes at the man who I know means the world to him. I have to use my napkin to dab at my eyes.

Sonny smiles at his uncle. "I'm looking forward to being close to you. Spending time with you. Being a family." Sonny shifts his gaze to me. "And close to you." He flicks his eyes across the table to Abbie. "And most of all, to you."

Abbie's smile melts my heart. "That means you'll be able to come to all the performances of *Beauty and the Beast*, not just the weekend."

That makes all of us roar with laughter. "That's right, Abbie. I'll be at every one of them." Sonny reaches for her hand.

We finish dinner, chattering back and forth about how wonderful it will be to have Sonny next door, how we can have dinner together, go on outings to the garden, hikes to the waterfalls outside of town, cut down a Christmas tree, and decorate both houses for the holidays. Arthur laughs and adds, "Not to mention he'll be around to clean my gutters and mow my lawn."

Sonny tops off the meal with his famous hot chocolate and a decadent-looking carrot cake with thick cream cheese frosting. He gestures to his uncle. "I know you're not supposed to indulge in sweets, but carrot cake counts as a vegetable, right, Madison?"

I nod and laugh, noticing the gleam in Arthur's eyes. "Tonight, yes."

After dessert, Arthur volunteers to supervise Abbie while she cleans up the dishes. Sonny grabs our jackets from the coat hooks and gestures for me to follow him outside. He leads me to the gate, where we have a view of his soon-to-be new house and slips his arm around my shoulders.

"I wanted to tell you, but thought surprising all of you at once was better. I know this is the right decision for me. I've never felt this happy, like I'm finally home."

I lean my head against his and whisper, "I know exactly how you feel." His arm tightens around me and I know I'll never feel alone again.

# CHAPTER 32

## Duke

When I think about all those months ago when I was unhappy, I knew the man I was living with was not my family. No matter how much I tried, I wasn't in the right place, with the right people. Despite the fear I felt being left at the gas station that day, it was the best day of my life. It was the day I met Arthur and found the family I'd spend the rest of my days with. I knew it the moment I met him. I could tell he had kind eyes and a gentle soul. Even more, I knew he needed me. His heart was broken and I could mend it.

Those same feelings flooded through me when I saw Madison that first day at the center. I sensed she needed someone in her life, someone special, like Arthur. They were both sad and suffering, and living with fear as a constant companion. I knew they would benefit from helping each other and their friendship would fill the void in their lives left by such profound loss.

Everything Madison went through with Cody reminded me of my early life, hiding in the barn, trying not to catch the wrath of the man who owned me. He was always angry and not just with me. His wife cowered each time he was nearby.

At first, I was unhappy about being relegated to the barn, without all the love my mother had told me I would find. As I learned more about the man and listened to how he treated his wife and the horses and goats, I realized I was fortunate to have my tiny corner in the barn. I entertained the thought of running away several times, but was too scared to be on my own. I knew it was not the life my mother dreamed for me. I kept hoping for a way out, a path that would lead me in the right direction.

I admire Madison for having the courage to leave and get away from Cody. I know she thinks she is weak and doubts herself, but with Sonny's help she is beginning to understand she is a good mother and worthy of happiness.

When I met Abbie out in front of the center, I could tell she needed a friend. She reeked of the bitterness and sourness of anxiety and unease. Pacing calmed her and when she played the piano her anxiety disappeared. When she saw me, her serious expression evaporated and a smile filled her face. I snuggled into her, letting her know I would never leave.

These last weeks with Sonny here and Arthur home, Abbie has been the happiest. It's as if the day I found Arthur in the park set off a chain of events and Arthur ended up rescuing not just me, but Madison and Abbie, too. Actually, all four of us were lost and when we found each other, that's when the magic happened.

I wish my mother could see me now, but she seemed to know all along that I was destined for important work. That I would make a difference in someone's life. She'd be so pleased to see how happy I've made this family. I may not be a certified service dog, but I know my humans would struggle without my comfort and support and that's what being of service means. Some dogs retrieve items from the refrigerator, getting their master's slippers, and helping their masters walk, steadying them when they're tired. Some dogs help their owners understand loyalty, some help them see the light within a dark day. Some dogs help their owners forget their loss. But every dog has a role to play. It could be as simple as sharing a smile or helping console their tears, or as risky as tackling a dangerous man threatening their family. Whether it's merely snuggling close to them to remind them they're not alone, guarding and herding sheep on a ranch, or befriending a shy child who needs a buddy, our duty is to our family. My mother was right. I have an important purpose, and that is to serve my family, which I'll gladly do, until my last breath.

Vest or no vest, I'll never leave Arthur's side and will always be there for him. He needs me, as do Madison and Abbie. They're my whole world.

I settle in at their feet while Sonny and Madison sit next to each other on the porch swing.

The sun is setting and the sky has turned a brilliant orange with bands of gold slicing between the clouds. The colors make the perfect backdrop for the rich fall hues of the mums, asters, and black-eyed Susans that line the walkway and burst from the pots on the porch.

As they glide back and forth, Sonny slips his arm around Madison and her head rests on his shoulder.

I close my eyes, content that the world is giving all of us a second chance. A chance at a family, a chance at love, a chance at happiness. And the best part is we'll all be together. We're family now.

# A LETTER FROM CASEY

I want to say a huge thank you for choosing to read *A Dog's Chance*. If you did enjoy it, and want to keep up to date with all my latest releases, just sign up at the following link. Your email address will never be shared and you can unsubscribe at any time.

*https://www.tammylgrace.com*

As with my previous book, *A Dog's Hope*, I was fortunate to find inspiration in my own golden retriever. This time, a new puppy named Izzy. It's been some years since I've had a puppy and she is full of energy, fun, and mischief. She is becoming my new writing buddy, and even as I write this, her head is resting in my lap.

The grief of losing my first golden was so profound I wasn't sure I could endure getting another one, but Izzy helped heal my heart and filled it, like only a dog can, with love. Spending my days with her and practicing with her to improve her skills and behavior helped bring to life some of Duke's training, and like Duke, I know she is destined for greatness.

I hope you loved *A Dog's Chance* and if you did I would be very grateful if you could write a review. I'd love to hear what you think, and it makes such a difference helping new readers to discover one of my books for the first time.

I love hearing from my readers—you can get in touch on my Facebook page, through Twitter, Goodreads, or my website.

Thanks,
Casey

f CaseyWilsonAuthor

🐦 CaseyWilsonAuth

# ACKNOWLEDGMENTS

I love writing and spending time with the characters I create, but even more, I'm grateful for the talented team at Bookouture, who share in the excitement of creating such a book as *A Dog's Chance*. My editor, Jennifer Hunt, and my publicist, Noelle Holten, are both fellow dog lovers and have championed this book and the previous one, with great enthusiasm and care. Just as they fell in love with Buddy from *A Dog's Hope*, they've embraced Duke and are just as excited as I am to introduce him to readers everywhere.

I'm both humbled and honored to have the continued support and encouragement of my family, my friends, and all my loyal readers. My career wouldn't be where it is today without their incredible help.

# READING GROUP GUIDE

## *DISCUSSION QUESTIONS*

1. *A Dog's Chance* is told from the perspective of both Duke and Madison, but Arthur plays an important role in the story. How did Arthur change as the story progressed?
2. From the first glimpse into Madison's life, it's clear she's avoiding or running from something. She chose work in small towns rather than a large city. Do you think that was wise or would it have been easier to hide in a larger city, and why do you think so?
3. Although not a character, the small town of Millbury plays a part in the story. It's the first place Madison feels could be a home for her and Abbie. What do you think made her feel that way? Have you ever visited a new place and felt such a connection and sense of community? And if you have, what do you attribute it to?
4. Arthur's nephew Sonny is immediately suspicious of Madison and her intentions. Putting yourself in his shoes, being thousands of miles away, how would you have reacted to the news that your uncle is letting someone new move in with him and what would you have done?
5. When Duke discovers Arthur in the park, they are both at a very low point. That first meeting changed Arthur's life in so many ways. Without Duke, what do you think would have happened to Arthur?

6. Along with impacting Arthur's life, Duke has quite an impact on Abbie. Despite his not being able to talk to Abbie, he was able to offer her something she was missing. What is the greatest lesson or gift Duke was able to give her?

7. Madison's life is harried, and she has little time or interest in making connections with anyone. That changes when she meets Arthur. What do you think it was about him that made her relax and risk a relationship?

8. Madison was set on leaving Millbury after her six-month contract. What factor had the greatest influence on her decision?

9. Arthur, Duke, Abbie, and Madison all changed throughout the story. Which of them do you think changed the most and how?

10. If Madison hadn't become so involved in the fundraiser, do you think she could have stayed hidden from Cody forever?

11. What do you think the future holds for the characters? What would you like to happen?

# Q&A WITH CASEY WILSON

**Q.** *Duke is the reason Madison, Abbie, and Arthur meet. Have you ever seen an animal bring people together who may have not connected otherwise in real life?*

**A.** I haven't witnessed a connection as profound as the one between the characters in *A Dog's Chance*, but I have seen animals forge friendships between people who would have never met, except for their common love of animals. For instance, we met several people through our dog trainer working with a group of her clients and have become friends while walking and letting our dogs play together. I've also witnessed the change in people, especially seniors, who are living a lonely life and then they get a dog and their entire outlook transforms. The dog not only enriches their lives, but it provides a bridge to allow others to interact, expanding their world and bringing smiles to their faces.

**Q.** *There's a charming sense of community in the town where Madison and Abbie move to at the start of the book. Were you inspired by a real place?*

**A.** I live in a small town and have been lucky enough to experience that sense of community throughout my life, so some of it is ingrained in me and it's what I enjoy most about writing in small town settings. The inspiration for the location came from a trip I took with my mom when we went to a tulip farm in Oregon a few years ago. We spent some time exploring the nearby town of Silverton, and I borrowed several of the elements of it for the fictional setting in *A Dog's Chance*. Arthur's house, in particular, was inspired by a walk we took through a neighborhood near a park.

*Q. Duke is a naughty puppy that needs some serious training! What has been your experience raising golden retrievers?*

**A.** Our current dog, Izzy, is our second golden retriever, so we are not the most experienced dog owners. I do think goldens are one of the easier breeds to train, as they are natural pleasers. Our first golden was so well behaved and rarely did anything wrong, but our new dog is a little different. She's much braver, assertive, and more confident. Consistency has been key and also making sure she gets to exercise, both physically and mentally, so she uses her never-ending energy for good things.

*Q. Arthur, like so many people these days, is lonely. Why is Duke exactly what he needed to come out of his shell?*

**A.** Arthur was grieving the loss of his beloved Rose and Duke gave Arthur a purpose and a friend, wrapped up in a cute furry package. Arthur wasn't the type of man who would complain or admit to being lost or lonely, but Duke was able to fill that void in his life, while allowing Arthur to maintain his dignity. Duke captured Arthur's heart and provided him a place to share his compassion and love. Duke also needed a family, and the two of them together were a perfect match at the perfect time in their lives.

*Q. Madison's shocking past and Abbie's anxiety are the central focus of the book. Did you do any special research into domestic violence and anxiety disorders to help you get into their mindsets?*

**A.** I did delve into elements of a few types of disorders and how they manifest in children. I worked in a school district long ago and have many friends who are teachers, so drew upon my own experiences and reached out to a few who encounter children with those types of disorders when I was crafting Abbie, especially. I also did some research related to the use of therapy dogs to help assist children and although Duke wasn't a certified therapy dog, he was able to provide support to Abbie and was a huge part of the reason she improved. Duke gave Abbie a much-needed friend and his presence calmed her and boosted her confidence.

**Q.** *Why do you think dogs, or animals in general, are such amazing parts of our lives and can help us get through tough times?*

**A.** I think it comes down to their unconditional love and loyalty. You can bare your soul to a dog and they will love and support you, no matter what you've done. They don't judge and don't base their affection on what we look like, where we live, or how much money we have. Dogs have a way of lifting our spirits when we've had a bad day and sensing when we need them near us. They are a comfort when we're down and a loyal friend to those who are lonely. They are nothing short of miraculous when it comes to being trained to assist humans with physical and emotional needs. Like most dog lovers, and Duke, I believe all dogs are therapy dogs for their owners.

Dogs are happy to just to be with us and love nothing more than our attention, whether that's playing fetch, taking them for a walk, or just snuggling next to them. We truly are the most important thing in their world and I believe they make us better humans, just by being in our life.

**Q.** *Is there a special dog in your life that helped inspire Duke's personality?*

**A.** My furry soulmate was my previous golden retriever, Zoe. She inspired all the dogs in my books, and I drew on her again for this book. Much of the inspiration for the puppy antics and goofiness of Duke came from my new golden retriever puppy, Izzy. It had been a long time since we had a puppy, but Izzy was new to our home when I was writing this book, and like Duke, she wanted to behave, but sometimes her wild personality just wiggled right out of her and had her doing bad things like digging holes in our yard. Like Duke, she knows it's wrong and hangs her head in shame when she does it, but the drive to do it is overwhelming. Like Duke, she blames squirrels for most of her problems.

**Q.** *Do you have any advice for new dog owners?*

**A.** While writing *A Dog's Chance*, we brought our new puppy home. It had been ten years since we had a puppy, and we had forgotten how time consuming they can be. She stretched my patience, so I would say brace yourself and organize your time so that you have ample amounts to dedicate to training. We ended up finding a great dog trainer that worked with us, and I highly recommend doing that if you find yourself struggling with getting your puppy to obey and behave. The key about making her focus on me and look to me for her guidance was life-changing. She likes having a job and we still do drills with her, which gives her an opportunity to stretch her mental muscles.

**Q.** *How do you start a book? Is it your characters that come alive first? Do you come up with the storyline and then create characters around it? Or do you just go with the flow and see where it takes you?*

**A.** Most of the time characters and setting come to me first. There is always a whisper of a story idea, the "what if" type of question that gets an author thinking about a plot, but I am definitely character driven. I tend to delve deep into characters first and get to know them before I do much with plotting. Once I know the characters, they often lead me down a path I may not have even considered. It sounds strange, but when I'm writing, I often feel like I am the character and find myself taking action based on the character's thoughts or motivations. That can only happen if I've fleshed out the characters before starting to write and I employ an extensive type of character interview to craft them as fully as possible.

# ESSAY FROM CASEY WILSON

I'll admit, I'm biased when it comes to dogs. I think they are selfless and pure of heart, with their greatest desire being to love us and bring us joy. Most are, as Duke thought in *A Dog's Chance*, destined for greatness. Even though all dogs may not be official service animals, they make a huge difference in the life of and are of great service to their person.

We have such a strong bond with our dogs, and although we know they aren't human, I believe they have a soul. My own golden retriever was the inspiration for all the dogs in my books (almost twenty at this point). She was my heart dog—my furry soulmate, and I'm not sure I'll ever be lucky enough to have another dog like her. Sadly, I lost her just before I wrote *A Dog's Hope*, and I think the emotion of that profound loss came through in that book. Coincidentally, our new golden puppy arrived as I was writing Duke in *A Dog's Chance*. She helped provide some of the puppy antics that make Duke so lovable.

I mentioned the bond between us and our dogs, but I believe there is even a more special bond between dogs and seniors, like Arthur, who are alone. When I was working on the book, I drew from my experience volunteering at our local senior center for years and watching the joy dogs brought to our members. The unconditional love and companionship those who spend their days alone crave is delivered in a cute, furry package, that brings a smile to their faces and fills a void in their hearts. Many of our seniors are forgotten but have so much love to give and are often left in circumstances without close friends or family. So the addition of a dog in their lives gives them the opportunity to both give and receive affection.

Dogs boost their confidence and provide an incentive for them to get outside and interact with people, much like they do for special needs children, who may not be vocal or able to articulate their feelings. Dogs have an innate ability to sense their emotions and know exactly what is needed. They offer the warmth of a friend and don't judge us by our looks, financial status, or popularity. They only care about our hearts.

I've seen the difference dogs make in the lives of seniors who were fading and depressed, until the love of a dog helped them realize they didn't have to be alone. Along with their companionship, they offer a purpose for many who spend hours sitting alone, interacting with very few people, and rarely leaving their house. Seniors who have a dog have a reason to go outside, are forced to get a bit of exercise and fresh air, and enjoy happier and more fulfilling days with their furry friend at their side.

It's a bond that is unbreakable, until the sad day comes when they can no longer care for themselves or their dog. If they are forced to go into care, usually their first concern is for their beloved dog. I wish there was a way for facilities to allow seniors to keep their dogs with them. It is truly heartbreaking to witness the sadness that comes when a senior must relinquish their treasured companion to move into an assisted living facility. Oftentimes, it's the beginning of a long period of decline in their physical and mental health.

In *A Dog's Chance*, Abbie is like so many children who suffer from behavioral issues or illnesses and the addition of a dog is life changing for them. Like Abbie, children who are different often have very few friends and feel isolated. Having a dog by their side, children with disabilities or emotional challenges suddenly have a bridge to a larger social circle. Their peers may be reluctant or scared to approach them because they are different, but will interact with a sweet dog who will connect them with each other.

Dogs, especially those specifically trained by professionals, support children by helping them with physical obstacles, alerting others to medical problems like seizures, and perhaps most importantly, provide the comfort and companionship they need.

I'm working on a new book in a series and have included a dog being trained as a companion for a hearing-impaired man. In researching for the book, I've learned more about organizations that train and support service dogs, like Canine Companions for Independence. Hearing dogs, as they are known, help their humans by alerting them to a variety of sounds like microwaves, doorbells, fire alarms, and telephones. But, more than just that, they develop a deep bond built on love and trust and provide the confidence needed for their human to be independent and walk the streets alone knowing their dog will be there to help them. They open a world that would otherwise be closed or quite small, to their humans.

Even dogs that aren't professionally trained provide many of the same benefits to us. We never take our dog for a walk without meeting a new friend. Her happy smile and swish of her tail invite everyone she meets to greet her. In turn, they visit with us and leave smiling. We recently took her to a big home improvement store, and an older gentleman asked if he could pet her, got down on his knees, tears in his eyes, as he ran his hands over her head and ears, telling us how much he missed his dog.

It's hard to stay angry or sad when you're near a dog. They have an exuberance for life and can quickly turn a bad day into a happier one. They're always in the mood to play and can lift our spirits with a game of fetch or sometimes just snuggling next to us.

It's truly a bond like no other. Scientists have studied it in a quest to discover how dogs became man's best friend. Theories abound about the domestication of wolves, the breeding that took place to enhance the sociability humans desired, and the introduction of them into our lives. Recent genetic research has offered theories as to why dogs seek human interaction and attention.

Regardless of the science, I believe it can be boiled down in simpler terms to love and loyalty. They offer us unconditional love, companionship, and loyalty until their last breath. They are always happy to see us, they don't hold grudges, they keep our secrets, they offer protection, and they make the most of every moment. They comfort us when we're sad and remind us to live in the present, where every treat is the tastiest, every walk is the best, and every game of fetch is the most fun.

Filling our lives with love and joy, comforting us and providing a sense of calm when we need it, listening to our problems like a patient therapist, and reminding us what it truly means to be a loyal friend. In short, they make us better people. They do all of this, and ask nothing from us in return.

There are some things in life that only a dog can teach you.

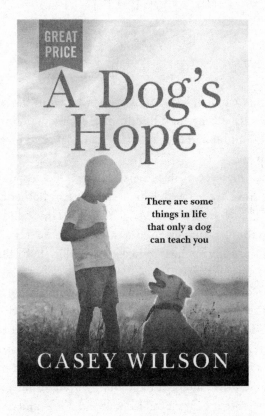

Please turn the page for a preview.

AVAILABLE NOW.

# CHAPTER 1

## Now

With a gentle touch, Karen runs her hand over my back, sluicing the rainwater off my fur. "Buddy, please come home with me." She sighs and blows her nose. "It's getting late and it's too cold. I need to go."

I move my eyes to meet hers, but my chin remains on the cold flat stone etched with letters. Rain doesn't bother me. Cold weather doesn't bother me. My golden fur is thick and protects me from the elements. Even snow can't penetrate it. I can roll in it for hours, using my nose to make a tunnel in fresh fallen snow. It makes me sneeze, but it's *so* worth it.

I notice Karen's pleading look. She has to realize I can't leave. I'm waiting for Toby. As long as it takes. I beg her to see this with my eyes. Toby always understands me; we've never needed words.

Karen shivers as she dabs at her cheeks, but kneels down in her dress on the wet grass. She steadies the umbrella over both of us as she places a tender hand on my head, using her thumb to pet the corner of my ear. "I know you don't understand, but he's gone. Our boy isn't coming home."

Karen has always had a gentle voice, but it breaks as she murmurs to me. I detect her scent—lavender. She always smells of it. Soft and calm. I lick her hand and she rewards me with a caress of my graying muzzle. Tears drop from her eyes and land on my paw.

Karen says we have to say goodbye to Toby today, but it doesn't make sense to me. I nose closer to the worn baseball mitt resting atop the stone, the familiar smells of leather, oil, and dirt mingling with my favorite scent—Toby.

How many times have I rested my chin in the palm of that glove and looked at Toby's face? I shut my eyes and let the scent take me back to the field on our way home. Toby and I cross the skinny ribbon of water that runs alongside of it and have the whole green pasture to ourselves. Mounds of dirt dot the sturdy grass, but I don't let the enticing scent distract me. My sole focus is my boy and our game.

I wonder how Toby came up with such a clever way for us to spend time together, but I'll be forever grateful for it. It's more than a simple game. It's our connection. I hear the thwack of the ball in his hand as he prepares to throw it, and in his eyes when they meet mine, I can see we're alone in the world, just the two of us. There's a glimmer when he's about to release the ball, but I keep my eye on the white sphere and I know it's coming. As soon as he lets it fly, I rush to snag it before it hits the ground.

I detect all of Toby's scents on the ball. Pencil lead, paper, the burrito he had for lunch, the sweat on his palms, the citrus aroma of his hair gel—all of them combined together smell like my boy. I make a beeline for him. My eyes focus only on him and his smile urges me forward. There's no time to think when you're staring into your best friend's eyes, waiting for the next ball.

Karen's sobs interrupt my memories. Her sorrow surrounds her like a mist of dark fog. I watch her weep as she moves her hands from me and traces the letters carved in the stone. It makes me want to go home with her and comfort her, but I can't. I whine in sympathy, but don't shift from my position. Toby needs me more. I've always waited for him, ever since we met. I'll wait for him now.

I remember listening to the men in their pristine uniforms and shiny buttons who had arrived at the house. They told Karen how sorry they were that Toby's body still hadn't been recovered; they had lost hope and in turn so did she. If they couldn't find his body, how could they return his remains? I watched her crumple to the floor, her sobs uncontrollable, heart-wrenching, and my licks did little to console her.

At first, she was like me—she refused to believe. Since the day the men came, she hasn't been able to work. Instead, I comfort her as she sits on the bench in the backyard overlooking her beloved flowers. She strokes my back for hours on end as she struggles to accept the news. She sips cup after cup of tea, and I make sure I'm close to her, so she knows she isn't alone. Unlike me, it's too painful for her to hope, so I'll bear the burden. I'll be the one to wait for Toby. All of her days, recently, have been filled with tears, but today has been her saddest day.

The man who prayed and stood by the stone drove away hours ago. He held Karen's hand and stayed with her long after the men in uniforms had come and gone. My ears still hurt from the sad tones that came from the music one of them had played.

The flag Karen holds crackles as she clutches it against her chest and gets to her feet. Startled by the noise, I raise myself into a sitting position, but make no attempt to stand. She shakes her head and gives me a look I don't see often. Her frustration with me is clear. She thrusts the handle of the umbrella into the wet grass and positions it over me.

It has been a long day. I'm weary with the weight of all of my twelve years bearing down on my tired bones. My eyes grow heavy as I stare at the stone in the midst of the grassy expanse. A breeze tickles my nose and I sniff the air again, but Toby isn't here.

Karen walks away, through the wet grass, and I shut my eyes.

The crunch of her footsteps on the asphalt pathway wake me, and I have no idea how long she's been gone. She's concealed under a bright yellow raincoat, trudging across the grass, carrying an armful of stuff from her car: a bowl of food and one for water.

"You need to eat, Buddy. Please." Tears dot her cheeks. "I can't lose you too." She puts a piece of my favorite pumpkin cookie treat next to my mouth and I remember the first one Toby ever bought me. I recognize the thick bone-shaped confection, drizzled with yogurt glaze. They're crunchy on the outside, softer on the inside, and have a spicy flavor that always makes me drool. My nose draws in the comforting scent of cinnamon, nutty flour, and egg; the mellow aroma of pumpkin softens the savory peanut butter scent. My nose twitches; my body's urge to leap for a bite is overwhelming and I can't help the drool forming in my mouth. Natural instincts are hard to control; our instincts are so deep, we cannot resist them.

Since Toby's been gone, Karen's taken to baking me treats. I love licking the bowl after she's scooped out all the batter. Pre-washing—that's my job. Each night after dinner I take up my appointed position in front of the dishwasher. Karen gives some of the plates a cursory rinse, but I handle the rest. I run my tongue over all the silverware and get any stray food from between the tines of the forks. My favorite nights are the ones when she uses the outdoor grill. She never rinses the platter and I relish the juice and bits of meat that are always leftover.

She looks so sad; I take the treat from the ground and that, at least, makes her smile, just for a moment.

She tugs on my collar. "Can you get up, Buddy?"

I'm too tired to comply. She walks back to her car and returns with one of my old beds. The rain has stopped and she removes her hood while she puts down a ratty towel on the grass and positions my bed. "Get on the bed, Buddy. Come on, be a good boy."

I recognize the worry she's feeling. She reeks of sorrow and despair and I don't want to cause her any more grief than she has already endured. I struggle to raise myself. She bends and helps me, placing her soft hands—the hands that always smell like flowers—under me, and heaves to help me stand. I shake and release a cascade of water to splatter over her.

She squeals, but grins. "Good boy, Buddy. I understand you want to stay here. I just want you protected. Toby would want you safe. He would never forgive me if something happened to you."

I follow her gesture and ease back down on the bed. She uses another towel to dry my fur and I let her continue, even though I know my thick coat will endure the water. I know it makes her feel better, so I indulge her. The massage she's giving me is soothing; it warms my muscles and relaxes them. The pressure of her hands on my back feels wonderful and I sense her touch lighten when she gets to my hips. My eyes are getting heavy as she continues to dry my belly, so I let them close and pretend it's Toby drying me off after a bath. He'd let me wallow on the grass to dry my fur and then use a towel to finish off. I'd let him almost complete the task and then lunge and grab the towel in my teeth. He'd tug on it and we'd go back and forth. There's nothing like the satisfying sound of a towel splitting between my teeth—the fibers as they strain, desperate to keep together, and the sudden break sending us both across the lawn. Plus, it was an easy way to identify which towels were mine.

She makes another pass over me and presses too hard on my hip, sending a jolt of pain through me. I flinch and lift my head. It only hurts if I stay in one place too long and I haven't moved much today. I should walk more, but I can't. "I'm sorry, Buddy." She rests her cheek against my back and pets my ears. The pain subsides.

She moves Toby's glove so it's near my head. "There you go. Now you'll be off of the wet grass tonight. The rain is over so you won't get wet." She covers me with a blanket I recognize from the back of her car.

"One night, Buddy. I'll be back in the morning and we'll go home, okay? I have to go to work this week and I don't want to worry about you."

I don't commit. I'll come home when Toby does. Karen leans over and kisses the top of my head before she makes her way to her car.

The old bed makes a far more comfortable spot than the ground. Since Toby left last year, it has been getting harder for me to stand. I have a difficult time finding a comfortable position and have to move often. Karen added soft rugs to the hardwood floors where I like to rest, making it easier for me to gain a foothold.

When Toby was home, we exercised and played each day, so maybe I didn't notice my hip much. Now, Karen takes me for walks near our house, but my heart isn't in it. It's not the same as when Toby and I play together. My favorite person, my purpose, is missing.

It's quiet here, except for the soft rustle of the trees in the breeze and the scuttle of squirrels in search of food. I watch them dart close to my food bowl and then scamper away in distress. The squirrels are wary, but have nothing to fear. I'm in no shape to chase them.

I pretend I'm asleep and let them get closer. There are two of them, less than a foot away from me, rummaging through my bowl, gathering bites of my kibble. With a swift motion, I raise my head and watch them scurry away, cheeks full. A dog has to have a little fun. Even an old dog.

The view from the grassy hill I'm on is idyllic. The valley below is dotted with the farms and orchards Toby and I walked by each day. With a slight turn of my head I take in the shimmering water of the lake in the center of town. I love walking along the path by the lake with Toby. When he comes back, he'll take me there again.

I know Toby wouldn't leave me. He told me he'd be back and he keeps his promises.

I gaze across the grass, admiring the huge trees. It's quiet and peaceful. I've never been here during the time I've lived with Toby and Karen.

The breeze carries the scent of apples. Along with the crunch of a few leaves falling from the trees, this delicious sweet aroma announces the arrival of fall in Riverside. It's my favorite time of year and the perfect weather for a golden retriever with a heavy coat like mine. Toby and I liked to watch apples fall from the trees along our walk to and from school. He would always scoop one of them up as it rested on the ground, shimmering red among the grass, and bite chunks off for me on our way home from practice or games.

Toby and I missed baseball season again this year. I reposition his glove with my snout and place my head on the rubbed and scarred leather. As I sniff his scent embedded in the laces and webbing, I let my mind wander to Toby's games. I never knew much about the sport until I met Toby and spent so much time watching him practice and play, listening as the coach gave directions. I learned it's much more than just a game.

Baseball teaches humans to be more like dogs, to live in the moment. I learned that quickly, but Toby took a little longer to understand. "It ain't over till it's over," Coach used to say.

I know it's not over for Toby. Baseball teaches you not to give up and I'm not giving up on Toby. I'm hoping for one more inning.

I reposition myself and exhale a long breath. I have to admit, this old bed isn't bad. I would always try to stay on the rug beside Toby's bed, but from the first night he let me snuggle under the covers with him.

Toby's my everything.

# CHAPTER 2

## Then

Mom's heavy sigh when I put the gearshift in park makes me turn my head. "Really? I'm not that bad of a driver, am I?" I resist the urge to roll my eyes.

She chuckles and shakes her head. "No, you did a fine job, especially for someone who's not been driving for very long. I'm just tired." She heaves her purse from the floor and retrieves the keys to our new house, looking still, for a moment, as she surveys the front. I stare at the rather plain-looking tan exterior trimmed in white. It's smaller than our old house, single-story instead of the two-story house we left, with nothing but vacant land and a few rolling hills behind it. The house is on a large plot of land, at least a quarter of an acre. A new wooden fence surrounds the property, with a gate to the backyard. The front yard is planted with grass, but it's dormant and brown, with just a couple of evergreen bushes decorating the bare flowerbeds. The house next door has a Realtor sign in front of it and I can see that the lot on the other side of us is empty.

I can't imagine cramming all of our stuff from our old house into this space. In the car, Mom chattered on about the house being brand new and how nice it would be not to have to worry about maintenance, but I know she sees more than this: peace and quiet, serenity. The first house she's ever owned on her own.

"I'll unlock the doors. Could you move the van and back it up to the garage door to make it easier to unload?" she says, brushing a hand against my shoulder.

My jaw tenses but I stop myself asking Mom why she couldn't have told me that before I parked. I'm tired and I know she is too from staying up late and packing last night. I'm not in the mood to listen to any more lectures about turning over a new leaf or keeping on the right path. Sometimes I think she forgets I'm not one of her students. I reposition the old silver vehicle she has driven for years and I get out to start unloading boxes as she steps inside the garage.

"The movers have all the furniture placed. At least the heavy stuff is done," she says, poking her head from under the garage door as it rises, and I survey the stacks of boxes left by the movers that cover almost the whole floor of the space barely big enough for a single car. Our old house had an oversized garage that housed two cars and still had room left over for storage.

"Do you want all these moved into the house?" I ask.

"No, let's work on the stuff we brought in the van first." She gives me directions based on the labels attached to each box and leads the way into the house. "You can pick from the two bedrooms. I thought you'd probably want the bigger one. It will get less morning sun," she says. It may be her house but of course she doesn't come first. Mom has always been like this, leading the way, unselfishly sacrificing her needs for mine: serving my food before her own, making sure the tears in my jeans are sewn before she moves on to her dresses with her battered wooden sewing box.

When we left Seattle this morning, it was overcast and drizzling. It's chilly here, but the sun is shining and I feel the warmth on my back as I collect the boxes and bring them inside. Mom said we would get less rain in this part of the state, along with more snow in the winter and heat in the summer, explaining it as if it mattered much to me. I had no choice in moving here. I follow her inside to check out the house.

It's super clean and smells new, with that slight chemical odor that accompanies new carpet and new cars. I step through the tiled utility room off the garage and notice the cheap, imitation wood flooring. It's an open design with a large space in the middle of the house that serves as the living, kitchen, and small dining area. Mom leads me on a tour and shows me the spare bedroom choices, on either side of a bathroom. The bedrooms aren't carpeted, but I take the bigger one, like she suggested. There's no point in arguing with her today.

Mom's master bedroom is a little larger than mine but nothing special, and her bathroom is a definite downgrade from her old one with double sinks and a walk-in shower. I wander back to the main area, taking in our old battered furniture that has been put in place, and look out of the sliding glass doors to the patio and yard in the back of the house. There's nothing behind us, just a view of the hills and some open space. Nothing like the city, where there were houses in every direction, people watching us from all sides, thousands of neighbors to avoid getting to know.

I start unpacking my stuff while Mom works in the kitchen, opening the flimsy-looking blinds to let more light into the room, giving me a view into the backyard. I unload dusty books I've never read and framed photos of me as a little kid with Mom and Dad. We're all smiling in the photos, but that was a long time ago. There are no recent photos of our happy family in the house, no other trips to the zoo or drives down to the ocean. I'm not sure you can include someone in your family if they're never around.

# ABOUT THE AUTHOR

**CASEY WILSON** is the author of *A Dog's Hope* and *A Dog's Chance*. Born and raised in Nevada, she is the owner of a gorgeous golden retriever, who may or may not have inspired the dogs in her novels.